**Catherine Ryan Howard** is the author of *56 Days*, which was an overall No. 1 bestseller in Ireland and a Kindle top-ten bestseller, as well as winning Crime Fiction Book of the Year at the Irish Book Awards 2021, and *The Nothing Man*, which shot straight to the top of the Irish bestseller charts on publication, was a Kindle No. 1 bestseller in the UK and was shortlisted for the Ian Fleming Steel Dagger. Her work has been shortlisted for the CWA John Creasey/New Blood Dagger and the Mystery Writers of America Edgar Award for Best Novel, and she is currently longlisted for the Dublin Literary Award 2023. She lives in Dublin.

# THE TRAP

## Catherine Ryan Howard

PENGUIN BOOKS

TRANSWORLD PUBLISHERS
Penguin Random House, One Embassy Gardens,
8 Viaduct Gardens, London SW11 7BW
www.penguin.co.uk

Transworld is part of the Penguin Random House group of companies
whose addresses can be found at global.penguinrandomhouse.com

Penguin
Random House
UK

First published in Great Britain in 2023 by Bantam
an imprint of Transworld Publishers
Penguin paperback edition published 2024

A CIP catalogue record for this book
is available from the British Library.

ISBN
9781804991169

Typeset in 11.25/15.25pt Sabon LT Pro by Jouve (UK), Milton Keynes
Printed and bound in Great Britain by Clays Ltd, Elcograf S.p.A.

The authorized representative in the EEA is Penguin Random House Ireland,
Morrison Chambers, 32 Nassau Street, Dublin D02 YH68.

Penguin Random House is committed to a sustainable future
for our business, our readers and our planet. This book is made
from Forest Stewardship Council® certified paper.

MIX
Paper | Supporting
responsible forestry
FSC® C018179

*Praise for*
**THE TRAP**

'~~Everything a thriller should be: clever, page-tearing,~~
devastating. Catherine Ryan Howard makes you feel
for her characters so much, whether you love them or
absolutely loathe them. It's impossible to stop reading – or
to stop thinking about *The Trap*, long after you're done'
**Abigail Dean**

'*The Trap* will lure you in and keep you captive
until the very last page. Catherine Ryan Howard is
the Queen of the Unguessable Twist'
**C. L. Taylor**

'*The Trap* is everything you want in a book – breathless
pace, clever plot, addictive characters, and very pertinent
social commentary on how victims are judged'
**Andrea Mara**

'Topical, twisty, and with a real heart stopper of a moment
halfway in that'll make you turn the lights back on'
**Gillian McAllister**

'Dark and witty and clever. An original and highly
gripping read, I couldn't turn the pages fast enough.
Catherine Ryan Howard has a deliciously dark
imagination and always tells a good tale'
**Alice Feeney**

'As brain-teasing as it is gripping . . . [a] psychologically
dazzling novel'
***Sunday Times* Thriller of the Month**

www.penguin.co.uk

# THE TRAP

She'd been *out*-out, and town had been busy. Stumbled out of the club to discover that there wasn't a taxi to be had. Spent an hour trying to flag one down with one hand while trying to hail one via an app with the other until, resigned, she'd pushed her way on to a packed night bus headed not far enough in sort of the right direction. Her plan was to call someone at its terminus, apologize for waking them and ask them to come get her, but by the time she got there – to a tiny country village that was sleepy by day and empty by night – her phone had died. She'd been the last passenger and the bus had driven off before she could think to ask the driver if she could perhaps borrow *his* phone. It was four in the morning and beginning to drizzle, so she'd started walking. Because, really, what other choice did she have?

This is the story she tells herself as she leaves the village and crosses into the dark its streetlights had been holding back.

All around her, the night seems to thrum with disapproval.

*Silly girl. This is exactly the kind of thing your mother told you not to do. There has to be some kind of personal responsibility, doesn't there?*

An ex-boyfriend had once told her that his favourite part of a night out was the walk home. Just him and his thoughts on deserted streets, the evening's fun still warm in his chest. He had no tense wait for a taxi. He didn't need to walk to the front door with his keys squeezed between his fingers, ready to scratch, to disable. He had never texted a thumbs-up emoji to anyone before he went to sleep so that they could go to sleep as well.

The part of the night he loved was the part *she* had to survive.

When she'd told him this, he'd pulled her close and kissed her face and whispered, 'I'm so sorry that you think that's the world you live in,' in so patronizing a tone that, for a brief moment, she'd considered using her keys on his scrotum.

The drizzle gives way to a driving rain. When the footpath runs out, her high heels make her stumble on the crumbling surface of the road. The balls of her feet burn and the ankle strap on the right one is rubbing her skin away.

For a while, there's a watery moonlight inviting forms to take on a shape and step out of the night – a telephone pole, a hedgerow, a pothole – but then the road twists into a tunnel of overhanging trees and the dark solidifies. She can't see her own legs below the hem of her dress now. Her body is literally disappearing into the night.

And then, through the roar of the rain—

A mechanical whine.

Getting louder.

She thinks *engine* and turns just in time to be blinded by a pair of sweeping high-beams. Twin orbs are still floating in her vision when the car jerks to a stop alongside her. Silver, some make of saloon. She stops too. The passenger window descends in a smooth, electronic motion and a voice says, 'You all right there?'

She dips her head so she can see inside.

There's a pair of legs in the driver's seat, lit by the blue glow of the dashboard display, wearing jeans.

'Ah . . . Yeah.' She bends lower again to align her face with the open window just as the driver switches on the ceiling light. He is a man in his thirties, with short red hair and a splotchy pink face of irritated skin. His T-shirt is on inside out; she can see the seams and, at the back of his neck, the tag. There are various discarded items in the passenger-side footwell: fast-food wrappers, a tabloid newspaper, a single muddy hiking boot. In the back, there's a baby seat with a little stuffed green thing belted into it. 'I got off the night bus back in the village, and I was going to ring for a lift but—'

'Sorry.' The man taps a forefinger to a spot just behind his left ear, a move which makes her think of her late mother applying a perfume she seemed to fear

3

was too expensive to ever actually spritz. 'My hearing isn't great.'

'I got off the night bus,' she says, louder this time.

He leans towards her, frowning. 'Say again?'

The passenger-side window isn't all the way down. An inch or so of glass digs into the palm of her hand when she puts it on the door and leans her head and shoulders into the opening, far enough for the roar of the rain to fall away into the background, for the sickly-sweet smell of a pine air-freshener to reach her nostrils and – it occurs to her – for the balance of her body weight to be inside the car.

If he suddenly drove off, he'd take her with him.

'I got off the night bus in the village,' she says. 'I was going to ring home for a lift, but my phone died.'

She pulls the device from her pocket, a dead black mirror, and shows it to him.

'Ah, feck,' he says. 'And I came out without mine. Although maybe . . .' He starts rooting around, checking the cubbyholes in the driver's door, the cup holders between the front seats, inside the glovebox. There seems to be a lot of stuff in the car, but not whatever he's looking for. 'I thought I might have a charger, but no. Sorry.'

'It's OK,' she says automatically.

'Look, I'm only going as far as the Circle K, but they're open twenty-four hours and they have that little seating area at the back. Maybe you could borrow a charger off someone there. Or they might even let you use their phone. It'd be a better place to wait, at least?'

'Yeah.' She pulls back, out of the window, and looks down the road into the empty black. 'Is it far?'

'Five-minute drive.' He's already reaching to push open the passenger door and she steps back to make room for the swing of its arc. 'Hop in.'

Somehow, the last moment in which she could've decided not to do this has passed her by. Because if she steps back now, pushes the passenger door closed and says, 'Thanks, but I think I'll walk,' she may as well say, 'Thanks for your kindness, but I think you might be a monster so please leave me alone.'

And if he *is* a monster, then he won't have to pretend not to be any more, and she won't be able to outrun him, not out here, not in these shoes – and where is there to run to?

And if he *isn't* a monster, well, then . . .

It's perfectly safe to get in the car.

She gets in the car.

She pulls the passenger door closed. *Clunk*. The ceiling light switches off, leaving only the dashboard's eerie glow and whatever's managed to reach them from this wrong end of the headlights. Her window is ascending. Then, as the engine revs and he pulls off, she hears another sound.

*Click*.

The central locking system.

'So,' he starts. 'Was it a good night, at least?'

Now the seatbelt sensor sounds and she fumbles in the shadows, first for the belt itself and then for its buckle, both of which feel vaguely sticky.

'It was all right,' she says. 'If I'd known how much trouble I'd have getting home, I might have just stayed there. How about you?'

*Why are you out driving around at four in the morning?*

'I was fast asleep,' he says, 'when I got an elbow to the ribs. I'm on a Rennies run. My wife is expecting our first, and she can't eat a thing now without getting heartburn. You got kids?'

She says, '*God* no,' before she can think to be a bit less aghast at the idea of doing the thing this man and his wife have already done.

He laughs. 'There's plenty of time for all that.'

In front of them, the surface of the road is dashing beneath the wheels. The wipers slash furiously across the windscreen, back and forth, back and forth. There are no lights visible in the distance.

They don't pass any other cars.

He asks her where she's living and she provides the name of the townland, purposefully avoiding specifics.

A sideways glance. 'You there by yourself, or . . . ?'

She wants to say no and leave it at that, but saying that risks coming across as unfriendly, mistrustful, suspicious. But telling him she lives with her boyfriend is telling him that she *has* a boyfriend, and that could

sound pointed, like she's trying to stop him from getting any ideas, which would also be accusing him of
*having* ideas, and offending him might anger him, this
man she doesn't know who's driving the locked car
she's in. But then, saying yes would be telling him that
the young woman with the dead phone he just plucked
off a country road has no one waiting up for her, no
one wondering where she is, and if she doesn't come
home tonight it could be hours or even days before
anyone realizes—

'I live with my sister,' she lies.

'That's who'll come and get you?'

'If I can find a way to call her, yeah.'

'They're a curse, those bloody phones. Always dead
when you need them.'

And yet, he's come out without his.

*Would you, with a pregnant wife at home?*

*Maybe you would*, she concedes, *if you're only on a
quick run to the shop.*

'You know, you look really familiar to me,' he says,
and then he turns his head to look at her some more,
for a fraction longer than she'd like on this road at this
speed and in these conditions. 'Have we met before?'

'Don't think so.' She's sure she's never seen this man
before in her life.

'Where do you work?'

She tells him that she works for a foreign bank, in an
office block near the airport, and he makes a *hmm*
noise.

Twenty, thirty seconds go by in silence. She breaks it by asking, 'Is it much further?' Because all that is out there in the night ahead of them is more night.

Still no cars. Still no lights.

No sign of anything except more road and dark and rain.

'No.' He jerks the gearstick with more force than he has before and, as he does, she feels his warm fingers graze the cold, damp skin of her bare knee. The touch is right on the line between an accidental graze and an intentional stroke. His eyes don't leave the road. 'Nearly there.'

'Great,' she says absently.

She doesn't know what to do. If it *was* an accident, wouldn't he apologize? Or is he not apologizing because there's nothing to apologize for, because he hasn't even realized he did it, because he didn't *do* anything at all?

The rain is heavier now, a steady roar on the roof.

'Awful night,' he says. 'And you're not exactly dressed for it, are you?'

Then he turns and openly appraises her, and there can be absolutely no mistake about this. His gaze crawls across her lap, combing over the thin cotton of her dress which, wet, is clinging to the outline of her thighs.

It feels like some slinking predator, cold and oily, slithering across her skin.

She moves her hands to her knees in an attempt to cover up and waits for his eyes to return to the road while a cold dread swirls in the pit of her stomach.

But then, she *isn't* dressed for this weather. That's a statement of fact.

*Jesus Christ, you really can't say* anything *these days, can you?*

'Yeah, well,' she says, with a brief smile she hopes won't encourage him *or* antagonize him. 'I thought I'd be able to hop in a cab.'

'They really need to do something about the taxi shortage.'

'Yeah, the—'

'Especially considering the missing women.' He glances at her. 'How many is it now? Three? Four?'

The temperature of her cold dread has dropped a few degrees to an icy, nauseating fear.

But then, what if it were a woman behind the wheel? She wouldn't think anything of this. They'd just be making conversation. They'd just be talking about what everyone was talking about, discussing what was in the news.

Now he's pointing towards the mess at her feet.

'Did you see the latest?' he says. 'It's on the front of the paper, there.'

The safest option feels like reaching for the folded tabloid. As she picks it up, it obligingly unfurls to reveal its front-page headline, screaming at her in all caps. MISSING WOMEN: SEARCH CONTINUES IN WICKLOW MOUNTAINS. There are two pictures underneath it: a large one showing people in white coveralls picking through a wild landscape, and a smaller one of a young, smiling brunette holding a dog in her arms.

She is familiar to anyone who follows the news. Not just the woman herself, but this specific picture of her.

'That's not that far away from here, you know,' he says. He jerks his chin to indicate the road ahead. 'If you drove for fifteen minutes up into the hills, you'd probably be able to see the floodlights.' A pause. 'They're always at that, though, aren't they? Conducting searches. Everyone gets all excited, but they never find anything. Thing is, people just don't understand how much space we got up here, you know? My old fella was always giving out about that, back when the first lot went missing. The ones from the nineties. There was always some reporter or relative or whatever saying, "Oh, she's up in the Wicklow Mountains, we just need to search." They'd think if you just looked everywhere, you'd find them. But you *can't* look everywhere, you see. Not around here. There's just too much ground to cover.' Another pause, this one a shade longer. 'So they probably *are* out here somewhere, but no one's ever going to fucking find them.'

There's a pinching pain in her chest now. She forces a breath down into her lungs in an attempt to alleviate it, but it feels like the oxygen can't get past her throat.

'You know,' he says, turning towards her, 'you have the look of one of them.'

She lets the paper drop.

She thinks about the *clunk* sound the passenger door

made when she pulled it closed. How a few minutes ago, it might have represented rescue. A portal to the warm and the dry, to lights and transport, to other people, ready to save her from the dark abyss of this endless night.

But what if every threat that dark had posed had climbed into the car with her?

What if she was trapped in here now, with them?

With *him*?

'Is it much further?' she asks again.

He doesn't answer.

This was a mistake, she can see that now. She's been foolish, full of bad ideas. She's not cut out for this.

Keeping her eyes forward, she puts her left hand down below her left thigh and starts surreptitiously exploring the door panel with her fingertips. Nothing feels like a button that will reverse the lock. And even if she gets the door open, what then? She's strapped in and releasing her seatbelt will trip the alarm, alerting him. She's wearing a small cross-body bag. It has a strap. She could take it off and loop the strap around his head, but it's a cheap, fast-fashion item; it could snap, and even if it doesn't, what's her plan exactly? To choke him, she'd really have to be behind him, but once she makes a move there won't be time to climb into the back seat of the car. And he's driving. If she does anything, the car will crash. She has a flash of his face inches above hers, his skin even redder, his features strained, one rough hand around her neck and the other fumbling in her underwear as he prepares to force the burn of his body into the delicate depths of hers, and she thinks that maybe dying in a car crash is the better option. She could suddenly reach over and yank on the steering wheel, forcing them off the road, or pull on the handbrake, which she thinks would lock up the wheels and send them skidding.

But what if there's no need?

What if she's overreacting? What has he *done*, really?

What if she crashes this car and he turns out to be just a man and not a monster?

But what if he just *wants* her to think like that, so she does nothing until it's too late to do anything at all?

'My sister will be freaking out,' she manages to say, the words feeling dry and dusty on her tongue, sounding limp and untrue even to her.

'At this time of night?' In her peripheral vision, she sees his shrug. 'Nah. She's probably dead to the world.'

*Dead to the world.*

The car is a depressurized airlock whose hatch has just been blown out into space by those words. There's no air left in it at all. The pinching in her chest flares up, igniting, and now every attempt at a breath feels like a searing burn. Her chest won't move, won't expand, and it feels like it's getting smaller, clenching like a fist, and her throat is closing, and she—

Lights.

Up ahead. Lots of them.

So close she thinks they must be a mirage.

The headlights have punched a hole in the night big enough for an entire service station to get through. It's the one he promised, the Circle K. She can see a flood-lit forecourt. A canopy in colours she recognizes, a familiar logo illuminated by a spotlight. A glowing square of white fluorescents – the shop – with bundles of peat briquettes stacked outside its glass façade and handwritten signs advertising special offers. There are even other people: a man leaning against a Jeep parked at one of the pumps and a woman walking out of the store's automatic doors, twirling her car keys around her finger.

When he pulls in and parks by the shop's entrance, it's so bright it feels like daytime. After she releases her seatbelt, she has no trouble finding the handle that will open her door, but it doesn't work.

It's still locked.

'Oh,' he says. 'Hang on one sec—'

*Click.*

She presses down on the handle again and this time, it opens easily.

A tidal wave of relief vaporizes all the adrenaline in her system, leaving her cold and clammy. Something lurches in her stomach and her mouth fills with a sour, acrid taste she can't seem to swallow away, and she realizes that she's about to be sick. She pushes the door back and climbs out of the car, unsteady on jelly legs.

There's a sign at the corner of the shop, TOILETS,

and an arrow directing people who want to use them around the side.

'I'm just . . .' She points at the sign by way of explanation. 'Thank you . . . Thanks for the lift.'

If he says anything in response, she doesn't hear it.

The bathroom is lit only by a flickering fluorescent strip with a large moth trapped inside, its panicked wings thrumming loudly against the ridged plastic casing. There are two stalls, two sinks and no windows. The air is warm and stale and smells of fetid things. Puddles of water have pooled on the floor and the vanity area is festooned with clumps of wet toilet tissue.

She pushes herself into the nearest cubicle, slamming its door back against the partition wall, and throws her face over the toilet bowl.

Her insides retch and spasm, but it's only dry-heaving; nothing but saliva comes up. Tears mix with make-up, making her eyes sting and water more. An acid burn starts to push its way up her oesophagus and into her chest.

Chasing it is a crushing weight of disappointment.

Because he *was* a man, not a monster.

And so, not the man she's been desperately trying to find.

There have been many nights like this. She turns off her phone and walks aimlessly along country roads, dressed for a night in the city, pretending to be a girl who hasn't managed to make it home, hoping a monster stops to pick her up.

*The* monster.

The one who took her sister.

And the other women.

She straightens up and turns to go to the paper-towel dispenser on the wall. She pulls and yanks and tugs until all the napkins inside it have come out, until she's holding a bundle just about big enough to muffle the sound she makes when she presses her face into it and screams.

Tonight's failure feels different because, for a moment there, she was sure her searching had come to an end.

A Samaritan who just happened to be on a lonely road at an ungodly hour, dispatched to the shop by his pregnant wife. Without his phone, conveniently, and with a reassuring baby seat in the back. He'd talked about the missing women.

And there's another, bigger reason to be disappointed. When she felt that she'd found him, she'd also felt fear. She'd panicked. She'd started plotting her escape.

So if, one night, she *does* find him, well . . .

Now she can't even trust herself to carry out the plan.

He'd even said her sister was *dead to the world* – which she is. Missing, presumed dead by everyone whose job it is to find her. The Gardaí, the only people who have the necessary resources. The media, who play favourites with the missing women and whose favourite has always been someone else. Anyone among the general public who might have, back at the start, been praying and hoping alongside her and Chris, but who has now given up, moved on, resumed their normal life.

And there weren't that many of those people to begin with, given the circumstances.

Most days, it's impossible to say which is worse: the grief, waiting patiently on the sidelines for some kind of confirmation, or the torment that just never ever lets up.

*Where is she? What happened to her? Will we ever know?*

*Is there any possibility that this* isn't *my fault?*

The only certainty that she has is the answer to that last one.

Sometimes she accidentally catches snippets of things on TV, where someone is describing the moment they learned that a loved one had met an unexpected and violent end. The knock on the door. A phone ringing in the dead of night. A welfare check that turned into a gruesome discovery, a scene that will remain etched on the back of their eyelids for the rest of their natural life.

And she'll find herself feeling jealous.

She *has* to know what happened to her sister, no matter what the cost. And until she's finished searching, it seems crazy to start grieving.

It's far too soon to give up yet.

Isn't it?

There's a splintered version of her in the cracked mirror above one of the sinks. She watches herself power up her phone and use it to summon a taxi. There's no problem securing one, although it'll take a while to get all the way out here.

The mirror that should be over the other sink is missing, the rectangle of paler paint its ghostly mark.

# Wake Turbulence

When Lucy opened her eyes, she enjoyed one glorious heartbeat of not remembering, of just *being*, before, in the next, the questions came rushing in.

*What happened to Nicki? Where is my sister? Is she waking up somewhere this morning or has she never woken up since I saw her last?*

For the four hundred and fortieth day in a row, there were no answers.

But there was blue sky. And a thick, dry heat. And when she moved, a shooting pain in the side of her neck.

'You all right in there?' a muffled voice asked.

A man she didn't recognize was looming over her, frowning. When she didn't answer his question, he rapped his knuckles on the glass between them.

For the second time, she realized now.

The first was what had woken her.

The last, lingering tendrils of sleepy fog dissipated and Lucy was finally able to put it all together: she'd fallen asleep in her car. Which she'd parked outside the local SuperValu. The man standing outside was wearing a high-vis vest over his T-shirt that said SECURITY on the chest and, judging by the blinding sun, the number of people pushing trolleys across her field of vision and how utterly shite she felt, she'd been here for far longer than she'd planned to stay.

'Yeah,' she said. She lowered the window and said, 'Yeah,' again. 'Everything's fine. Just, you know . . . Long drive.' She smiled; he didn't. 'I thought I was going to fall asleep at the wheel so I pulled in for a power nap.'

'You were here when I got in,' he said flatly. 'That was two hours ago.'

'Two . . . ?' The clock on the dash only came on with the engine and she didn't know where she'd put her phone. 'What time is it?'

'Just gone nine.'

Which meant she'd been here for at least *three* hours. She was only five minutes from home, but she'd been so late – or early – getting back, she hadn't wanted to risk going straight there. If Chris had heard her pulling in at five o'clock in the morning, he'd have known exactly where she'd been and what she'd been doing there.

And she'd promised him she'd stop doing this.

Told him she *had* stopped, already.

'Shit,' she said. 'Really?'

The security guard was stony-faced, his lack of sympathy betraying the fact that he didn't recognize her – which she didn't mind at all. Lucy would take anonymity over pity any day of the week.

'Go in and get yourself a cup of coffee,' he said, jerking his chin towards the store, 'and then get going.'

'I will. Thank you. Sorry.'

But she had absolutely no intention of going inside. She hadn't darkened the door of the SuperValu in months – or any other local businesses, for that matter. She did her best to avoid her neighbours.

She did her best to avoid people in general.

The world, she'd discovered, just wasn't designed for people with open wounds. Instead, it seemed packed with the privileged and their petty problems, their shitty attitudes, their blatant ungratefulness. Pressing on their car horns because the lights had gone green one whole second ago and the car in front hadn't seen it yet. Asking to speak to a manager because the food they'd ordered from a location half an hour away from their home had arrived not-quite-steaming hot. Relentlessly offering uninformed opinions no one asked for all over social media, and then taking offence whenever anyone more informed disagreed with them.

Ever since Nicki had disappeared, Lucy felt as though she was constantly trying to swallow back a silent scream, to stop it from coming to a ferocious boil in her throat.

*Don't you realize how bloody* lucky *you are?!*

What she wouldn't give for one single moment of peace, one in which Nicki was not gone, or even just one in which Lucy knew where she'd gone (and how, and why), and here were all these people with nothing but those moments, and they were squandering them. She wanted to grab them and pinch them and make them realize how good they had it.

And then she wanted to go back in time, to the Lucy that had existed before Nicki disappeared, and do the same thing to her past self.

The security guard turned to walk away.

'Sorry,' Lucy said again, to his retreating back.

She pulled on the rear-view mirror, angling it towards her until it showed a bleary-eyed, puffy-faced woman whose smudged mascara was only accentuating the dark circles under her eyes. Her hair was frizzy and one cheek was bright red from where she'd slept with it pressed against the window.

She couldn't go home looking like this. She may as well walk in the front door carrying a neon sign flashing LIAR.

There was a bathroom inside the store. And a beauty aisle. She could buy some make-up wipes, toothbrush and -paste, and something to tie her hair back with. Splash some water on her face and make herself look like she'd got a night's sleep. Or any sleep. And then, on the way out, grab a bucket of coffee to drink until she started to feel like she had.

But the last thing she wanted to do was go in there.

It had been disconcerting to discover that, even when your life had a person-sized hole in it, you still occasionally had to pop to the supermarket. You had to eat, even if you'd no appetite for it. And no matter what else was happening in your life, you were going to need things like toilet paper and rubbish bags.

Lucy had never fully appreciated how many mundane items were needed to keep the complete and utter breakdown of civilized life from the door.

But she always made sure to go to a supermarket far away, late at night, to minimize the sting of stares, the not-very-whispered whispers behind her, the curiosity disguised as concern. This one, on the other hand, was small, and more of the local area's central meeting place than a grocery store. And here she was at just gone nine o'clock in the morning the week the schools were starting back; she'd have to run the gauntlet of chattering Sweaty Betties seeking out their post-school-run skinny flat whites.

But the only thing worse would be having yet another argument with Chris over her late-night excursions.

She didn't have the energy for it and, anyway, it was pointless now. Because she had made a decision after last night's misadventure: she was going to stop. She was going to accept that Nicki wasn't coming home. She was going to move on with her life.

Starting today.

Starting *now*.

And this time, she meant it.

Lucy grabbed her wallet and got out of the car, her limbs stiff from sleeping for three hours sitting upright behind the wheel.

The early-morning air felt cool and fresh in the wake of last night's rain showers, but the ground was already dry and the strength of the sun promised it was going to be another scorcher of a day. It had been a long summer of unexpectedly summery weather, the kind Ireland prided itself on not being used to or built for. There wasn't a fan to be had, the outdoor dining hastily installed to get around lockdown rules had come into its own and the news was full of gorse fires and drownings.

Lucy thought the bathrooms were just inside the entrance, but they either had never been or weren't any more, and as she stood by the fresh flowers searching for them, she felt a sudden, vice-like grip on her arm.

She turned to see Mrs Daly, her octogenarian neighbour, peering up at her.

'Lucy,' the woman said gravely. 'How *are* you, dear?'

'Fine, thanks. You?'

Mrs Daly had lived opposite since the estate was built back in the nineties and had, she claimed, been friendly with Lucy and Nicki's late mother, although neither of them could remember seeing any evidence of this when their mother was alive. The reality was probably more that, even then, a single mother attracted the likes of Mrs Daly, prospecting for gossip she could share with her equally disapproving peers. Since Nicki's disappearance, the woman seemed permanently stationed at her gate, usually in conversation with one or more of the other neighbours. They'd stand there chatting for hours, tugging absently on the small gold crosses around their necks, with their eyes on Lucy's house, relishing her misfortune like a premium-channel spectator sport.

Chris called them the Grey Gossips.

'"Fine"?'

When Mrs Daly repeated it, it sounded like an accusation.

'Managing,' Lucy corrected.

The other woman relaxed, nodding approvingly at this far more acceptable answer. In the outside world, you always had to be the exact right amount of devastated. Look like you're on the verge of falling apart, but not let it actually happen. Be grateful that people were enquiring as to how you were, but thank them by never burdening them with the raw, horrible truth. Be OK, but not *too* OK.

A Goldilocks of grief.

'Would you happen to know where the bath—?' Lucy started.

'I hope you're looking after yourself, love. Are you sleeping?'

Translation: *You look terrible.*

'Yes,' Lucy said. 'I am, thanks.'

Even though she couldn't remember the last time she'd met the morning feeling in any way rested.

'And I see the FOR SALE sign is up again?' Mrs Daly said.

Translation: *Didn't your mother leave that house to both of you? Are you trying to run off with your missing sister's inheritance?*

Lucy nodded. 'It is.'

Although every time the estate agent rang to say he wanted to set up a viewing, she fobbed him off.

'And how's Chris doing?'

Translation: *Are you still living with her boyfriend, just the two of you, in the house where he used to live with her?*

'He's fine.'

Mrs Daly raised her barely-there eyebrows.

'Managing,' Lucy corrected.

'We're all praying for you this morning.' Mrs Daly's hand was still tight on her arm, holding her in place. Lucy could smell something eggy on the other woman's breath, and the cloying sweetness of some magnolia-scented powder or perfume. 'What are the guards saying? Have they any news on Nicki?'

There was never any news on Nicki, but there was also nothing but.

Since her disappearance had, six months after the fact, been linked to two other vanishings, the 'Missing Women' – the country had many more, but it was specifically those three people meant when they said that – had dominated the national headlines, social-media discussions, podcast charts, talk-radio shows . . .

Lucy had even heard that someone was already writing a book.

But no one ever had any new information, and the vast majority of the coverage was focused on Jennifer Gold, the most recent disappearance of the three and, at only seventeen, by far the youngest.

'No updates, no,' Lucy said, deploying her stock answer.

There *were* new searches going on in the Wicklow Mountains, but Lucy had learned not to get her hopes up. There were always searches. The first time it had happened, she'd stayed awake for two days with her phone in her hand, convinced that if they were going to the trouble of assembling dozens of Gardaí and earth-moving equipment on a hillside, it was because they had a good reason. Now, operations like that barely registered.

And then Lucy realized what Mrs Daly had actually said. *We're all praying for you this morning.*

Why specify this morning?

It was like someone turning down the volume dial on a stereo. All the sounds of the supermarket – customers chatting, tills beeping, trolley wheels squeaking on the linoleum floor, Mrs Daly saying something about *bring all those poor girls home* – slowly receded into the background until they plunged off its edge and into silence, until there was only the sound of Lucy's own heart thumping in her ears.

And she knew.

Something had happened.

She yanked her arm free of Mrs Daly's grasp and felt for her phone before remembering that it was in the car somewhere, that she hadn't checked it after she'd woken up, that it could be on silent or even dead and if people were trying to contact her—

Lucy turned back towards the doors, intending to start for them.

That's when she saw the headlines, screaming at her from the newspaper rack.

*Gardaí: 'Major Break' in Vanishings Investigation*
*Shock Twist in Missing Women Case?*
*Garda Source Claims Missing Women May Be Alive*

Chris must have heard her pull up, because he opened the front door just as she went to put her key in it.

'Something's happened,' she said to him at the exact same time he told her, 'Denise is here.'

They desperately searched each other's faces for more information.

'I don't know what it is,' Chris said. 'She just got here.'

He was already holding her hand and now he used it to pull her into the house and towards the kitchen. This kind of unconscious physical contact often occurred. Lucy would realize she was leaning against him, or had curled into him on the couch, or had her knees against his under a table. She wouldn't be able to remember how it had happened, much less determine who had initiated it.

Neither of them had ever brought it up.

At the end of the hall, he turned back to her. 'Where were you? We've been calling.'

Lucy had found her phone in the bottom of her bag, accidentally on silent. There were so many notifications on the screen that she'd put it back there without checking any of them and just concentrated on getting home.

'I was at the cafe,' she said.

'You were at the cafe,' Chris echoed, in a tone that would've also worked if she'd just told him she'd come from the moon. He seemed to notice her appearance for the first time. 'Did you sleep there too?'

'You really want to do this now?'

'Luce, you promised—'

She pushed past him and opened the door. Denise, their Family Liaison Officer, was already in the kitchen, standing by the table.

She was tall and lithe, like a ballet dancer, and always wore her hair pulled back into a smooth, tight chignon, which made Lucy wonder if she'd actually been a ballerina at some point. She was a detective so she wasn't uniformed, but seemed to stick to her own unofficial version: dark jeans, starchy white shirt, dark-blue blazer that fitted perfectly except for the little bulk on her right hip. She seemed like a woman who ought to be effortlessly running a corporation from the top floor of a glass tower somewhere, wearing a blinking Bluetooth earpiece and sipping a dainty espresso, not standing at Lucy's scratched kitchen table with sagging packing boxes piled up behind her, preparing to say—

'I don't have any news on Nicki. I'm sorry.'

Some version of this was always the first thing out of Denise's mouth. Not because she didn't have a heart, but because she did have one.

'But,' she continued, 'I *do* need to talk to you about something.'

She suggested they all sit down.

The kitchen smelled of coffee – the pot on the drip machine by the sink was full and steaming – but Denise had a glass of water in front of her, which she took a small, quick sip from now.

Lucy was convinced the water was some sort of FLO strategy, a tip they gave them in training. Even when something horrible had happened to your family, the societal norms of Irish hospitality were hardwired into the brain, so you felt obligated to serve all visitors *something*: a cup of coffee, a plate of fanned-out digestive biscuits, an off-brand chocolate bar. But no matter what you offered Denise, she'd say, 'A glass of tap water would be great, thank you.' It was a stroke of genius. Accepting something meant the strain of incessant offering could be brought to a swift and decisive stop, and the thing being water only required the traumatized to find a clean glass and a tap.

There was a bundle of what must have been this morning's post sitting in the middle of the table. All the usual suspects: past-due bills, cards from the crazies, letters that began *Despite numerous attempts to contact you* ... The item on top was a thick business envelope with something red stamped above its window and a barcode sticker showing it had been sent by registered post.

That was a first, and it couldn't be good.

Lucy swept the lot off the table and on to the seat of one of the empty chairs, feeling two sets of eyes on her as she did it.

A beat passed.

'Perhaps you've seen or read something already this morning,' Denise started. 'But I wanted to come here to make sure you've got the facts. The stories in the media ... They're all just speculation at this point. And they will be for the foreseeable, so I'd avoid them if you can. Trust me as your source of information.'

'What stories?' Chris asked.

Lucy leaned forward. 'Is it Roland Kearns? Has he been arrested?'

The ex-husband of the first woman to have gone missing, Tana Meehan, had never officially been declared a suspect in her disappearance or any of the others, but he'd also been the only person across all three cases brought in for questioning, and several women had gone to the media to share pictures of skin he'd split open with his fists.

'Luce,' Chris said reproachfully.

'No,' Denise said. 'It's not about Roland.' She paused.

'Does the name Lena Paczkowski mean anything to you?'

They both shook their heads.

'Lena was reported missing by her parents two weeks ago,' Denise explained. 'She'd been out in May-nooth on a Saturday night, socializing in a pub with friends. Her boyfriend was expecting her to walk to his house afterwards, about fifteen minutes away, but she never arrived. He presumed she'd changed her mind and gone off with friends, but the following day, on his walk into work, he found her phone lying on a grassy verge not far from his door.'

Under the table, Lucy felt Chris's hand reach for hers.

Each of the three missing women's phones had been found close to their last known locations. The last positive sighting of the first woman, Tana, had been at a bus stop in the middle of Kildare town; her phone had been handed in to a coffee shop on Market Square by a woman who'd found it lying in a gutter. Nicki's had been in a city-centre laneway, its screen smashed to smithereens, around the corner from the pub that CCTV had captured her leaving, alone. The third and last woman, Jennifer Gold, had been abducted as she walked her dog along a road near her home. Her phone had been found in a hedgerow.

'Lena wasn't linked at first to the others,' Denise went on. 'The consensus was that she'd left of her own volition. She was arguing with her parents about want-ing to move out of the family home and into student accommodation. They felt that this was a private matter, and turning it into headline news would only make it difficult for her to return. I'm sure I've said this to you before, but when it comes to missing person cases, we very much have to follow the family's lead.'

'OK,' Chris said with a twinge of impatience.

'There's a road called Red Lane to the south-east of the Great Sugarloaf. There's a car park there with a distinctive cement archway over the entrance. Very busy at the weekends with hillwalkers and what have you.' Denise looked from one of them to the other. 'Do you know it?'

Lucy didn't, but she knew that the Sugarloaf was in the Wicklow Mountains, an area otherwise known as everyone's first guess in a game of Where Are They Now?: Missing Women Edition.

All three had disappeared from places within an hour's drive of what was arguably the best place to hide a body in the entire country.

Chris squeezed Lucy's hand. It felt more like tension than comfort.

'We're talking about a rural area,' Denise continued, 'even though it's only a few minutes off the N11. A narrow road winding through countryside. Stretches of it don't even have a dividing line.' She paused. 'Late last night, there was a road traffic accident near the car park's entrance. An American tourist driving a rental hit a pedestrian who suddenly ran into the middle of the road. The pedestrian was conscious when the paramedics arrived and was able to say a few words to them, but she was severely injured and is now in a medically induced coma. The prognosis is very much wait-and-see. It was Lena.'

Chris shook his head. 'I don't understand.'

But Lucy was terrified that she did.

'In an ideal world,' Denise said, 'I wouldn't be telling you any of this. It's just happened, we have a lot to process and we're still trying to establish the basic facts. But the driver' – the briefest of eye-rolls – 'posted about it online, and then one of the tabloids got wind of it, and we expect that it'll be all over the news by lunchtime. The front pages are already' – air-quotes – '*reporting* that something big is coming down the line, even though they've no actual information. They can't have, because we don't either. Not in terms of hard facts. But what Lena said to the paramedics—'

Lucy felt dizzy and sick. All she wanted was answers, but now, faced with the possibility of actually getting them, she wasn't sure she was ready for them.

'—is of significant interest to our investigation into Nicki's disappearance and the others. *If* it's true. And that's what we're working to establish. For all we know, Lena could've panicked about being in trouble and made it up.'

*What did she say?!* Lucy screamed in her head.

'What did she say?' Chris asked.

Denise put her elbows on the table. 'Lena told paramedics that on the night she disappeared, she was actually abducted by a man who bundled her into his car and brought her to a house where she was held captive for the last fortnight. Somehow, she managed to escape and took off running, and eventually ran into the path of the car that hit her. And she said that—'

Lucy tensed, braced for impact.

Under the table, the grip of Chris's hand on hers hurt.

'—she wasn't the only one,' Denise finished. 'She said there were other women being held there too.'

# Lost and Found

Angela sat at her desk in the Missing Persons Unit, staring at a Tupperware container full of limp carrot batons, trying to fathom what on earth had made Night-time Angela think that that was what Daytime Angela would want to eat.

For months now, these two parts of herself had been locked in battle. Night-time Angela would carefully measure out a cup of porridge oats and leave them to soak in a pan overnight. She'd poach a chicken breast and put it in a fancy bento-box-thingy she'd ordered online along with a few spoons of (massaged) kale salad and put *that* in the fridge, ready to grab. She'd slip her work shoes into a tote bag and leave her trainers and running gear laid out on a chair in her room – she wouldn't even need to think about pulling them on in the morning – and set her Fitbit and AirPods to charging.

Night-time Angela did things like maintain a skin-care routine, keep a gratitude journal and go to bed early. Daytime Angela would sleep through at least two alarms and wake up too late to have a healthy breakfast – or any breakfast – and with nowhere near enough time to run into work. Instead, she'd hop on the last Luas that would get her there on time and grab an oversized, flavoured coffee on her way into the office where, just as she sat down at her desk, she'd remember that her expensive water bottle and fancy lunchbox were both still sitting in the kitchen at home.

At least today she'd remembered to bring the carrots. Now, she just needed to find the motivation to actually eat them.

When the phone on her desk began to shrill, Angela answered it with a 'Missing Persons Unit.'

'There's a woman here in reception who wants to speak to you.'

Before Angela could say, *Well, that's nice, but this isn't a walk-in clinic, tell her to go home and call us or, better yet, her local station or the Garda Confidential Line*, there was a rustling noise and then a woman's voice saying, 'Hello?' uncertainly.

Angela rolled her eyes. They'd handed her the phone. *Great.*

'Hi,' she said. 'How can I help you?'

'To whom am I speaking?' The woman on the other end of the line sounded older, posh, prim.

'This is Angela.'

'*Angela?*' The caller made the name sound like an affront, and Angela knew why: because there was no title before it. 'Well, I need to speak to a guard. A detective, ideally.'

*Well, you're shit out of luck, lady.*

Angela was a civilian – they were supposed to be called *Garda staff* these days, but whenever she used that term she felt like she was trying to make herself sound better, like the teenager on the petrol-station forecourt who'll fill up your car for you claiming he's a *fuel injection technician* – and part of her job was to take calls like this so the actual guards wouldn't have to be bothered by them.

'Can I ask what this is in relation to?'

'A missing person,' the woman said. She left a dramatic pause before adding, 'I may have some physical evidence.'

*Physical evidence.* Someone had been watching too much TV. Angela rolled her eyes a second time and thought, *And so it begins.*

At pre-shift that morning, Don – Detective Sergeant Donal Byrne, the head of the MPU – had warned them that with potentially big news coming out of Operation Tide, the investigation into the missing women, the cranks would soon follow suit. People would suddenly be seeing the women everywhere, or remembering seeing them months ago, or accusing their neighbour of having all the women buried in his back garden because, you know, the timing of him laying down those new patio slabs was a *bit* of a coincidence, now, don't you think?

What the general crackpot population didn't understand was that the MPU had nothing to do with all that. They were an in-house service, providing backroom support to Gardaí at stations around the country and liaising with (translation: *bitching about*) Interpol. They dealt with people whose locations were unknown, not cases where something criminal had clearly happened. Most of their job was just keeping track of things, maintaining records.

'If you have any information that you feel may assist an active investigation,' Angela said, 'you need to report it to your local station or call the—'

'I've *tried* that,' the woman interrupted. 'Several times.' There was a rush of air on the line as she exhaled in frustration. 'Look, *Angela*, if you won't help me, my next call will be to her family, and I'd really rather not have to do that. But I'm prepared to, if you're not prepared to do *your job*.'

Angela looked at the carrot batons and wondered if this was the universe's way of punishing her for not eating them.

'I brought it with me,' the woman said. 'I can just leave it here. But before I do, I want some assurances that someone is actually going to *do something* about it.'

Angela hesitated. She shouldn't encourage this, but . . .

'You have what with you?'

The woman muttered what sounded like a string of mild swear words and then said, '*My name is Rosemary Barry-Hayes*,' as if she was being forced to explain a simple concept for the hundredth time. 'I volunteer three days a week in a charity shop on George's Street. I was sorting through donations when I found a handbag with a wallet, keys and a card in an envelope inside. A greeting card. The name on everything was Kerry Long. Kerry as in the county. I looked her up online thinking I'd try to contact her and tell her we have her things, and that's when I found out that she's missing. I've been calling and calling about this, and no one seems . . .'

Angela tuned out. She'd typed *Kerry Long* into Google and was scanning the search results. She could've searched for it on PULSE, but searches were monitored and she'd prefer to know what she was dealing with before she set off any alarms higher up.

At the top of the page was a link to a brief article on ThePaper.ie from around three and a half years ago.

**Gardaí seek public's assistance in finding missing Wexford woman**
*27 January 2019, 4:13 p.m.*

GARDAÍ ARE SEEKING the public's assistance in tracing the whereabouts of a woman missing from Enniscorthy, Co. Wexford.

23-year-old Kerry Long has been missing since Thursday. Kerry is described as being 5 feet 5 inches tall, with a slim build, blonde hair and blue eyes. She was last seen wearing black trousers, a white shirt and a beige trench-coat.

Anyone with information is asked to contact the Garda Confidential Line on 1800 666 111 or any Garda station.

Standard low-risk missing person fare. The accompanying photo showed a smiling twenty-something in a champagne-pink strapless gown, holding a bouquet.

Angela returned to the search results, looking for a *missing Enniscorthy woman found safe and well* companion piece, but there was none.

Her impression was that this was an elective leave-taking. An adult was technically missing because their loved ones didn't know where they were, but there was no evidence or indication that they had come to harm. Personal items surfacing in a charity shop years after the fact wouldn't change that, but Angela couldn't in good conscience send the woman who'd found them back on to the street when her plan was to start bothering the family about it.

'Stay there,' she said into the phone. 'I'll come down.'

When she stood up, Don called to her from the back of the room. 'What's that all about?'

She relayed what the woman had said. 'It's safer to go and get the stuff off her, isn't it? Keep the peace.'

Don nodded. 'What did you say the name was again?'

'Of the missing person? Kerry Long.'

'Kerry Long,' he repeated, like he was trying the words out for size. Then he waved a hand, dismissing her.

Angela took the stairs, feeling pious for choosing to descend two flights when she could have taken the lift.

There was only one woman waiting in reception.

Angela would've guessed Rosemary Double-Barrelled was in her sixties, although she seemed to be doing everything she could to age herself more. Her hair was teased into a bouffant Princess Anne would've approved of, and she was wearing a white polo-neck under a bright-pink cardigan decorated with a string of pearls. She was standing next to a chair with a small cardboard box on its seat.

'Rosemary? Hi. I'm Angela.'

The other woman looked her up and down. '*You're a guard*?'

'I'm with the Missing Persons Unit.' It wasn't a lie. 'Is that it?' She pointed at the box. 'Well, thanks for bringing—'

'I'd rather you look at the contents now,' Rosemary interrupted, 'before I leave, so there can be no confusion. I don't want to be, you know, *accused* of anything down the line.'

This must be punishment not just for the uneaten carrot batons, but the forgetting of the prepared lunch as well.

Angela reached for the box.

'Aren't you going to put on some gloves first?' Rosemary said, aghast.

The carrots, the prepared lunch *and* the water bottle, then.

There was a box of gloves on the reception desk. Angela pulled two – cloudy white latex, her favourite – and made a show of putting them on, snapping the cuffs loudly against her wrists. May as well give Rosemary the episode of *CSI* she clearly wanted.

'I have no idea when it came in or where it came from,' Rosemary said. 'Before you ask. We don't keep track of donations. It wasn't even something new; it could've been in the back room for months. I was just moving it from one shelf to another when I heard the keys rattling.'

Angela had lifted the bag out of the box. It was tan in colour and made of soft, real leather; left to its own devices, it had started to fall in on itself, collapsing like a half-deflated balloon. It looked as good as new, no visible dirt or scuff marks on the exterior.

This clearly wasn't an item that had spent any considerable time outdoors.

Inside were two open compartments, divided in the middle by a slim, zipped pouch. Angela reached in and started pulling out the items in there one by one.

A set of keys.

Three different types on one ring that reminded her of the ones she had for her own apartment: main door, door to the apartment and post box. There was no electronic fob, which made her think that these weren't for a new-build. The keychain was a souvenir from the National Gallery of Ireland.

'When was this?' Angela asked, placing the keys back into the now empty box. 'That you found it?'

'Two weeks ago, now.' Rosemary folded her arms. 'I've been trying to get through to someone here ever since.'

A small, fabric wallet.

It was stitched in the shape of an envelope, with a single snap-fastener under the flap. Floral design. Just about big enough to hold its contents: nearly fifty euro in tens and fives, a learner driver's permit granted in September 2018 and a debit card. The cards were both in the name of Kerry Long, and the photo on the permit looked like an unflattering angle of the same woman whose picture Angela had seen online.

'That's her,' Rosemary said. 'Isn't it? There was a photo on the internet.'

Angela made a *hmm* noise as she put the wallet in the box and returned to the bag to extract the next item.

A cream-coloured envelope with a greeting card inside.

*Mam* was written on it in loopy cursive, above a decorative line with neat curls on both ends. When Angela turned it over, she thought she could make out the word *birthday* through the paper.

'Her poor mother,' Rosemary muttered, pressing a hand to her chest.

Angela pulled the sides of the bag apart and angled it so the ceiling light was pointing straight into it.

Only then did she see a small pouch, credit card-sized, attached to the interior lining. When she pulled it open with a finger, she caught a flash of white: a Q-Park ticket for the multi-storey at Stephen's Green Shopping Centre, time-stamped 11:02 a.m. on 3 March 2018. That was here, in Dublin city centre, only a few minutes' walk away from where they stood.

She put the ticket with the other items and then unzipped the central pouch.

At first, she thought it was empty. It was a narrow, tight space; it wasn't easy to see all the way to its depths. But when she slipped her hand inside and reached her fingers right down into its corners—

There *was* something in there.

She lifted it out.

It was a bra.

Originally pastel in colour, with lace detailing. Small, padded cups. One strap was twisted while the other dangled free from the back loop. The underwire looked bent out of shape and maybe even broken in the middle, at the spot where the two cups met.

Rosemary gasped as Angela silently thanked her for suggesting that she put on gloves, because the bra was completely covered in blood.

As Don pointed Angela towards the Missing Persons Unit's conference room, her stomach whined loudly, as if it knew it was gone noon and that they weren't going to get to take a lunch break.

'Is there time for me to make a cup of coffee?' she asked.

'There is if you make two,' Don said, checking his watch. 'But be quick. She's never late.'

Angela was already moving towards the door. 'Milk and two sugars?'

Don nodded. 'And see if there's any biccies about, will you?'

There was no need to tell him that that was the whole idea. But all she could find in the kitchen was a Tupperware container marked VIC SUPP – DO NOT TOUCH! in aggressively large capital letters, wherein lay three unexciting supermarket packets in various stages of depletion. Angela stuffed two digestives into her mouth, reasoning that the people who availed themselves of the Victim Support Service had suffered enough without having to eat dry, dusty off-brand digestives too.

By the time she returned to the conference room, Detective Denise Pope was already there.

'. . . but we're trying to keep that on the down-low,' she was saying to Don. 'The down-*very*-low. Make him nervous. Hope he makes a mistake.'

'Ah, here she is now,' Don said unnecessarily loudly, clearly trying to signal to Detective Pope that she should stop talking about whatever she was talking about. 'Dee, this is Angela. Angela, this is Detective Pope.'

Detective Pope gave Angela a nod and said, 'Denise is fine.'

'Hi,' Angela said.

She only knew Denise by reputation, which was stellar. The daughter of a former inspector and a chief superintendent, legend had it that she'd wanted to be a guard for so long, she'd hand-sewn blue uniforms for her Barbies. She'd started her meteoric rise back in Templemore when she won the Gary Sheehan, awarded to the best all-round student in any given phase, the one who showed themselves to be both academically excellent and an excellent leader while also earning the respect of their fellow trainees, which was no mean feat when you were already doing the first two. One of her first assignments after passing out was a stint in the Missing Persons Unit under Don, who only ever talked about her short tenure with a glassy-eyed reverence as if he was describing being in the audience when U2 played their first ever gig at a Dublin school's talent show in 1976.

Angela wanted to be Detective Denise Pope when she grew up.

Which meant she had to pass the Physical Competency Test. Which she was definitely going to do on her second go, because she was totally going to start actually bringing her water bottle and eating her carrots and going *up* the stairs as well.

Angela was on a mission to graduate from Garda staff to actual member of An Garda Síochána. Unfortunately, the application process wasn't going as smoothly as she would have hoped. She'd failed the PCT, which consisted of running around a room full of obstacles before having a go on a push-and-pull contraption, sup-posedly designed to simulate a foot chase, and then restraining the guy after you caught his arse. It was all timed, and Angela's time hadn't been good enough, because she hadn't been fit enough.

They'd notify her of the date of her second attempt any day now. She really had to start getting ready for it. Hence, the carrot batons.

'Would you like a coffee?' Angela asked Denise as she handed a cup to Don.

Denise wrinkled her nose. 'God no.'

It wasn't entirely clear who or what the ire in that response was directed to, so Angela didn't ask a second time.

She took her seat directly opposite Denise, then a quick sip of her coffee. At least her stomach was quiet now. It seemed like the stolen pair of horrible diges-tives might have done the trick.

'I thought you lot were getting turfed out of this shithole, no?' Denise said to Don.

'We were,' he said. 'But it's taking them so long to build the new shithole, we outgrew it in the meantime. Anyway, thanks for coming in.'

'Well, I was free. I was just leaving our old friend Roland Kearns.'

'Ah, the world's most innocent man,' Don said with a wink. 'How is he holding up?'

'He's taken up oil painting. To deal with the stress.'

'Good choice.'

'I thought so too,' Denise said. 'Because he'll still be able to do it—'

'—in prison,' they said in unison.

'You're still doing his FLO-ing?' Don frowned. 'Surely you could've passed it on to some other poor sod by now?'

'I am for now. I like to finish what I start, and the powers-that-be were only too happy to leave me there.' Denise paused. 'I'm still doing it for the O'Sullivans too. I was there first thing, talking to the sister and the boyfriend – who's still living with the sister, by the way.'

Don raised his eyebrows. 'Are they . . . ?'

'Couldn't tell.' Denise looked at Angela. 'Anyway, why the summons? What's happened?'

The sudden attention caught Angela off-guard. She'd been silently watching their exchange, eyes going from Don to Denise like she was following the ball in a tennis match, beginning to believe that they'd both completely forgotten she was there.

She straightened up, cleared her throat, pushed her cup of coffee away.

'Tell her,' Don prompted.

And so Angela did – about Rosemary Double-Barrelled, the charity-shop discovery, the bag and its contents.

'I called the charity's head office,' Angela said. 'They confirmed that she works there. And there's lots of stuff online about her, with pictures. Local golf club, that sort of thing. She seems legit.'

'Where are these items now?' Denise asked.

'Locked in my desk drawer,' Don answered. 'For the time being.'

Angela knew enough to know that they were never going to whisk her bloody discovery off to the lab with a label screaming RUSH; Kerry Long's disappearance was well over three years stale and low-risk, and so didn't warrant the cost of the tests. Unlike TV detectives, real ones had budgets. You couldn't order a battery of expensive forensics tests for every lost button you found in the street.

Or bloody bra you found in a handbag.

But for some reason he hadn't yet shared with Angela, Don had been eager to tell Detective Denise Pope about what they'd found.

'I took pictures,' Angela said.

She pulled out her phone and swiped to bring them up. She'd taken them at the same table they were sitting at now, before Don had locked the items away. There was one of each item and the bag itself, and a number of close-ups of the bra. Angela had put a ten-euro note from her pocket next to them for scale, swapping it out for a two-euro coin in the close-ups, and made sure to get the tag on the bra (Primark, 36A).

And she was feeling very smug about having done all those things.

She slid the device across the table to Denise, who picked it up and started studying the pictures.

'The bag is in excellent condition,' Angela said. 'It

looks like it's been barely used, let alone been outdoors for any length of time, so I think we can assume this wasn't an item someone found left in the street or thrown in a ditch. And is it even Kerry Long's? Its condition and the Q-Park ticket suggests to me' – at *suggests to me*, something crossed Denise's face and Angela immediately regretted deploying that level of GardaSpeak – 'that the bag might not even be hers, that her things just ended up in it somehow. There was cash in the wallet, so this clearly wasn't about getting rid of items after a theft. And Rosemary said they don't track donations.'

Denise slid the phone back across the table.

'She's on your list,' Don said to her. 'Isn't she?'

'What list?' Her eyes flashed him a warning before she turned back to Angela. 'You're not a guard, are you?'

Unexpectedly, the words stung like a jagged knife-edge drawn against her skin. Angela swallowed hard, readying herself to respond, but Don got in there first with—

'She will be once she passes the PCT.'

—and then Angela could only hope that he'd leave it at that, because that could mean that she hadn't taken it yet, but of course he felt the need to clarify that—

'She failed it the first time.'

Angela's cheeks felt as if they'd suddenly been set ablaze.

'But she's bound by the same Official Secrets Act we

are, Dee,' Don went on. 'And while she mightn't have the qualifications – yet – she's got more cop-on in her little finger than some chief supers we know.' He paused. 'She reminds me of you, I dare say.'

Denise pushed back her chair.

'Well,' she said, 'in that case, can I borrow her?'

# Base Camp

*Where did it all start?* That's always what people want to know, isn't it? Where it began.

I have to say, I never really understood this obsession with the beginning until I inadvertently developed it myself, watching true-crime documentaries.

Surreptitiously watching them, mind you. I never do it openly. Not because it would, you know, arouse suspicion or anything. *Please.* I just don't want to be known as someone who does that. Because let's be clear: I have no interest in it as a genre. The vast majority of what gets lumped under 'true-crime documentaries' is, in fact, sensationalist shit. Talking heads who have absolutely nothing to do with anyone involved, pointlessly pontificating. So-called criminal profilers spewing pseudo-scientific bollocks. Re-enactments so bad, the actors aren't even worthy of their job title.

Anyway.

I don't watch those. I watch the *actual* documentaries, made by real filmmakers with something to say, the ones that air on prestige channels at primetime. Well, my wife watches them while I sit beside her, occasionally turning the pages of some thick historical biography I know she won't ever ask me about, one eye on the screen.

And I must admit that, yes, I often find myself sitting there, through the opening credits – flickers of a moody landscape, Ken Burns-effect on a vanilla corner of a crime-scene photo (nine times out of ten: a bare foot), grainy baby picture – wondering if they'll even be able to take us to the beginning, if they'll know where it is.

Because you really need the man himself to bring you there, don't you? Only he really knows where everything began. Will they have him? Will there be mumbling audio recorded long ago on Death Row? Chicken-scratch diaries helpfully explaining everything? Inadvertently revealing statements made by a guy still proclaiming his innocence, idiotically thinking that participating in a documentary about the crimes he's suspected of will be the best way to prove it?

What I really want to see is someone just telling the truth, but if they're lucky enough to actually have the guy, to be able to interview him, they're always so bloody *tentative* about it, aren't they?

They don't want to piss him off, I suppose. If they have him, he's almost certainly already in jail and won't have anything to lose by cutting the interview short and refusing to cooperate. They have to tread carefully. I get that.

But it seems to me like they never even *try* to ask the questions that would quickly and efficiently lead us all back to the start.

For instance:

Did you just wake up one morning and decide you wanted to kill someone? Was that it? Or was it more like, overnight, something appeared that had never been there before? Or was it something that was always there, always in you, and you were just waiting for the right time to act on it? And was that when you said, *Fuck it, I'm not resisting this any more, I'm just going to do what I want, regardless of the consequences for me*? Or did someone do or say something that set you off and you found that doing whatever you did to them was something you wanted to do again, to other people, even if they hadn't pissed you off? Or was there never any beginning, just an always, and trying to figure out when things changed is like searching for the start of a circle?

I'm the last one, if you're wondering.

Also, I wish they'd ask: what *specifically* about it do you like?

I like my wife. I really do. I like her the most. Sometimes I even think there's a little streak of darkness in *her* too. I mean, this is a woman who will routinely turn to me with a big smile on her face to say things like, 'You know me, I bloody *love* a good sex cult,' and, 'Yeah, yeah, but when are they going to get to the actual murdering?' and, 'I'd have killed her too, she's so bloody annoying.'

And yet *I'm* supposed to be the deviant one?

That was a joke, by the way.

A lot of the time, when I meet new people, I find that needs pointing out.

To be fair to my wife – her name is Amy; to be fair to Amy – she doesn't just watch documentaries about murderers. She'll watch anything that qualifies as a senseless tragedy. A minute-by-minute examination of a ghastly terrorist attack as described in great detail by the survivors, authorities and animated graphics. Three interminable hours about a greedy pharma dynasty whose drug ruined millions of lives and claimed a few hundred thousand. All the risks of summiting Everest, but with a deadly weather event thrown in too. A sex cult masquerading as self-improvement. Another cult masquerading as a religion (special guest star: ancient volcano aliens). A man who loved bears, finding out they definitely didn't love him back when one of them ate him and his girlfriend. Oh yes. Sign her up!

That last one was quite good, actually. Werner Herzog.

Before you ask, no. She doesn't know. What I find fascinating, though, is that she seems to think that she would, that it would be obvious.

We were watching – she was – that one about Ted Bundy's girlfriend, the woman he was with during his killing years, and Amy kept throwing up her hands and saying, 'Oh, come *on*!' and of course I had to say, 'What? What's wrong?' because I was supposed to be enthralled by *Hero of Two Worlds: The Marquis de Lafayette in the Age of Revolution*, which actually wasn't a great choice because Amy had recognized the name from *Hamilton* and started asking about it.

'He moves to Utah,' she said, waving at the screen, 'and then the murders move to Utah. They're out on the water one day and his eyes go black and he pushes her in. The police sketch looks exactly like him, the suspect drives the exact same car *and* they know the guy's first name is Ted. And yet she's trying to claim that she *didn't know*? Seriously?' She folded her arms, shook her head in disgust. 'Please.'

But I disagreed with her assessment of what was happening on screen.

*I* saw a woman saying that she didn't *want* to know, that she was too terrified to go there, that she couldn't bring herself to face up to the reality that the man she loved and knew to have kindness and joy and laughter in him, the man she was sharing her life and her heart and her bed with, was also a prolific serial killer who had murdered a large number of young women, often ending multiple lives over the course of a day or even an evening, and always with such a ferocious brutality that even the documentaries about him, including this one, didn't dare go into too many details about what kind of state he'd left his victims' bodies in.

Did you know, for example, that one of the survivors had been discovered in her bed, rocking back
and forth, with her jaw distended? As in, it had become
unhinged on one side. It was only attached to the rest
of her at one end.

Inside the skin of her face, her jaw was *hanging loose*.

I couldn't say any of that, of course. I certainly couldn't
tell Amy that I knew for a fact that she wouldn't know.
And, anyway, I was supposed to be enthralled by *Hero
of Two Worlds*. So I just made a *hmm* sound and said
something about hindsight being twenty-twenty.

I really liked that Everest documentary, actually. So
much so that, about fifteen minutes in, I put down
*Napoleon: A Life* and watched it openly. It was safe
enough, what with it being about mountaineering.

I suspected Amy was secretly pleased that I was
interested, that I'd put down my book and joined in.
We even started talking about it, commenting on the
people in charge, marvelling at the scenery, pretending
that maybe one day we would do something as adven-
turous as hiking to Base Camp, which is a thing people
really do. Can you *imagine* the eye-rolling of the actual
summiteers when those eejits arrive into camp, taking
up space and resources for a *stroll*, just so they can go
home and tell people they've *seen* a *mountain*?

I learned a lot from it. The documentary, I mean.

For starters, I had no idea that the real danger of a
summit attempt is not the trying to get to the top, but

the getting back down the mountain afterwards. I didn't realize how long people spent at Base Camp. Months, usually, acclimatizing and waiting for the weather gods to align. And until I watched it, I had no idea why anyone in their right mind would risk doing something so dangerous, so reckless, so overwhelmingly likely to end in failure, injury or even death.

Were they mad? Or just stupid? Or was this all about ego, less about actually wanting to do something and more about being able to *say* you'd done it?

But now I do understand. I understand completely.

They do it because when they're doing it is when they feel most alive. They can't understand why the rest of us *aren't* trying to summit Everest, how we can possibly be content without trying to. The way they see it, yes, they *might* die on the way up or down from nearly six miles closer to the sky, but they know that. They accept it. For them, it's a risk worth taking. Because not to try to conquer that mountain, not to aim for its peak, not to stand on the top of the world – literally – will bring certain death, albeit of a different kind.

And you know what I realized, watching that documentary?

That that's how I feel about *this*.

I know there's a very real risk it won't end well for me, but I've no interest in a life where I don't do it. The first time I made it to the summit, it was a feeling like I'd never known. As if there'd been a hole inside of me all this time and that feeling was the missing piece. It was the exact right shape and size. It filled me up.

For the first time, I really did feel *alive*.

(I know, I know. Bit cheesy.)

And, better yet, I managed to get off the mountain. I practically *glided* down the bloody thing, that time. Even though I'd barely prepared for the ascent. Even though the timing of my summit attempt was entirely opportunistic.

But once I reached Base Camp, I couldn't bring myself to pack up my stuff and fly home. I wanted to go up again. So I stayed there, waiting and preparing, until one day the skies cleared and the opportunity to set off on another summit attempt arrived.

And I survived *that* one too.

Like any good mountain-climber, I didn't assume it was because I was especially talented at it, that the accidents and tragedies that had befallen other climbers couldn't possibly affect me. I knew they could – and likely would, at some point. I acknowledged that the thing I was best at was being lucky.

But so long as I was . . .

Of course, the more times I do it, the riskier it gets. It's just maths. Every time you get in your car, you increase your chances of being in a car crash. This endeavour will almost certainly be the reason my life as I know it ends. And I might *actually* die. Those SWAT guys – what do they call them again? The Gardaí version? ERU? That's it. Emergency Response Unit, yeah – but it always makes me think of the word *emu*, which is an animal that's very hard to take seriously.

Anyway.

Those guys have guns and you can tell by the way they walk around with them, like they're extensions of their dicks, that they'd bloody love to use them.

But at least, if that *does* happen, I'll die doing the thing that made me feel the most alive. I'll die on the mountain.

Here's what I wonder, though. This is the great unknown: will it be on the way up or on the way down? Will it be this time? And if it's not, how many more summits will I see?

Are you even listening to me back there?

Look, if you can't stop screaming, I'm going to have to make you.

# Past Lives

Chris got up to see Denise out, leaving Lucy alone in the kitchen with the horror of what they'd just been told.

She took Denise's glass to the sink and turned it upside-down to let the remaining water drain out, just to have something to do other than imagining where Nicki might be now, alive, and what might be happening to her.

But her hands were shaking and the glass slipped, hitting the stainless steel with a loud crack, shattering.

In its aftermath, the house felt aggressively silent. The sound of voices retreating down the hall had disappeared outside. Lucy needed noise. She went into the living room and grabbed the TV remote.

When the screen came to life, it was with the sights and sounds of an episode of *Air Crash Investigation*.

She immediately identified the episode: American Airlines flight 587. Queens, New York; two months and one day after 9/11; wake turbulence. When planes punch through the air, they leave a temporary disturbance behind them in the form of wingtip vortices and jetwash. Aircraft following too closely behind can fly straight into it. 587's first officer, due to a quirk of his training, totally overreacted to it, putting so much pressure on the vertical stabilizer that it broke clean off. Two thousand feet above a stretch of suburbia, an Airbus A300 with 260 passengers on board dropped out of the sky like a stone.

Lucy knew this because she had already seen this instalment, twice if not three times. She'd already seen all of them, more than once. In the deepest, loneliest hours of the night, she found this show inexplicably soothing.

Maybe it was because of all the technical lingo, the *flaps* and the *pitot tubes* and the *trim* and so on, the terminology that turned the emotion of death and destruction into science, engineering and cold, hard facts. Or maybe it was that you could watch it safe in the knowledge that whatever the conclusion of the air-accident investigation team (which was, presumably due to the show's low budget, invariably re-enacted as three men in shirtsleeves gesticulating at a whiteboard), the cause was never going to involve a rapist, serial killer or abductor of women.

Or maybe Lucy just liked watching it because it

offered some kind of cruel perspective. After all, here she was, paralysed over one missing person, when there was a tragedy that had rendered hundreds lost in a single moment.

And she thought it was nice that they always referred to the dead as the *souls*.

The living-room door swung open and Chris came back in, and when she turned to face him she noticed for the first time how he was dressed: bare feet, jeans, a T-shirt on inside out and back to front. He must have still been asleep in bed when Denise knocked on the door.

'Did she just show up here?' Lucy asked. 'She didn't call ahead?'

'She called you,' he said, 'but you didn't answer. She didn't try me because she said she guessed I'd have been working until late, which I was. I suppose she assumed that this early in the morning, you'd have been at home.'

Perhaps she was imagining things, but to Lucy's ear the *home* sounded pointed.

'Are you OK?' Chris asked.

In this house, they both knew that that question should always be taken as if a *relatively speaking* had been tacked on its end.

'I was going to give up,' she said. 'I'd decided to. I was going to accept that she was gone and wouldn't be coming back. I was going to sell the house, open the cafe, move on. And I actually meant it, this time.'

'You still can,' he said. 'We don't even know if that Lena girl is telling the truth. This might all just be some story she made up to avoid getting into trouble with her parents. It might have nothing to do with Nicki. It's entirely possible that absolutely nothing's changed.'

'Or maybe we just found out that Nicki is still alive and has been held prisoner by some sadistic fuck less than half an hour's drive from here all this time.'

Chris shook his head. 'Don't do this to yourself.'

'Tell me how to stop, then. Because all I can think about is her tied up somewhere, being . . . being . . .'

But she couldn't say the words. She didn't even want to think them.

And then Chris was in front of her, reaching for her, pulling her into his arms.

She let him, burying her face in his chest, drawing in a deep breath and holding it, hoping it would hold in all the parts of her too, all the feelings that were popping and bursting and threatening to turn themselves into tears.

'We can't wait for ever,' he whispered into her hair.

'Exactly.' She pulled away, moved away. 'Exactly that. I can't wait for ever. I can't wait any more. I need to know what happened to her.'

'Luce, we've been through this. There's nothing you can do. There's an entire team of Gardaí whose full-time job it is to try to find her, and we just have to wait and let them do their jobs. Our only choice here is what we do while we wait. And I know it feels impossible, but it's been over a year; you need to start—'

'Don't,' she said, holding up a hand. 'I don't want to hear it again. I can't move on – because this is what happens. I really *was* going to stop living in this . . . this paralysed hell. I was going to call that annoying prick from the agency and tell him we can have viewings all next week if he wants. I was going to set an opening date for the cafe. And then this morning I have Denise sipping her glass of water in my kitchen telling me, oh, by the way, maybe Nicki is alive actually, and being held somewhere, and stand by for more on that in due course.'

During that speech, Lucy's voice had risen in volume to a shout.

It made Chris's sound all the quieter when he said, 'But what can you possibly do? Because if this is some justification for you continuing your little night-time excursions after you swore to me that you'd—'

'No,' she said, not wanting to get into all that again. She took a deep breath. 'I want to do an interview. And not another bloody community-radio phone-in tour. I mean something big. Something national. That will actually get people to care.'

Now Chris was looking at her with something that felt like pity, and it stung.

'But they won't,' he said gently. 'They don't. Because to them, Nicki wasn't some innocent, doe-eyed teenager *just* out walking her adorable dog in bright daylight. They think she was staggering around town on a Saturday night, drunk and alone, in a short skirt, after she'd ditched her friends. You're not going to be able to change their minds, and no one's going to give you the airtime to try in the first place.'

He was right. When Nicki first went missing, Lucy had tried everything to get the media to care. She'd called in to radio stations, messaged any email address she could find under a byline and even attempted to contact the producers of daytime TV and magazine shows.

It was a slow and painful realization that, in real life, *gone girl* wasn't anywhere near enough of a story. Thousands of adults went missing in Ireland every year and Nicki was just one of them, and she was one who'd apparently wandered off into the night, drunk.

No one had cared about her at all until Jennifer Gold went missing six months later, clutching a sheaf of Gone Girl Golden Tickets® in her hand: young, beautiful and totally innocent.

Within twenty-four hours, she was the subject of press conferences, column inches and primetime. When she was only seven days gone, there was a candlelight vigil in the grounds of Our Lady of the Wayside Church in Kilternan, a famously bright-blue clapboard structure built to a New England aesthetic – and so utterly alien to Ireland – that had been featured by *Accidentally Wes Anderson*. The following Friday, her mother was the subject of a sombre segment of *The Late Late*, a talk show guaranteed to get at least one in ten people living in Ireland tuning in. Both the president and the

Taoiseach took the time to pay tribute to this teenage girl they'd never met.

It wasn't an exaggeration to say that Jennifer's King Charles, Walter – whom she'd been walking when she'd disappeared and who had subsequently trotted back home alone, his lead trailing on the ground, inadvertently raising the alarm – had got more attention than the other two women's cases combined. Since he was in Jennifer's official photo, you could argue that Walter had been on the front page of all the newspapers before Nicki had even been mentioned inside them.

'Well, maybe what I should do,' Lucy said, 'is point that out. Call the media and the public out on their hypocrisy. Guilt them into caring about *all* the missing women.'

'I think that would be a very bad idea,' Chris said. 'What would you even say? "The missing seventeen-year-old girl doesn't deserve that much sympathy?" We need to keep the public on side, Luce. That's definitely not the way to do it. Jennifer Gold has practically been canonized. Christ, we'd probably start getting hate mail . . .' He sighed. 'Look, I'm going to get dressed. I'm not working tonight. Do you want to do something? Go for a drive?'

'Ah, maybe later,' Lucy said, waving a hand. 'I'm going to go back to the cafe.'

Before he could make a comment about her claim that she was going *back* there, she turned and went into the kitchen.

The first thing she saw was the stack of envelopes she'd swiped off the table and on to one of the chairs. She picked up the thick business envelope with the red IMPORTANT stamped on it and the barcode sticker showing that its journey to this address had been tracked. She ripped a corner open just enough to see the logo for her bank, the one the mortgage on the cafe was with, and then put it back with the others on the chair.

It was then she saw the little business card on the floor. It must have been with the envelopes, but had fallen when she'd transferred them to the chair.

Lucy bent to pick it up.

It belonged to Jack Keane, former crime correspondent for one of the tabloids, now self-styled true-crime expert who made a living churning out salacious non-fiction about high-profile cases that seemed to be trying to upset everyone involved, and getting hired as a talking head on the kind of documentaries you didn't want to tell your friends you'd watched.

He had tried to contact most if not all of the missing women's family members at one point or another, but no one wanted anything to do with him. Trusting him with the story of your missing loved one was like going to Jerry Springer or Jeremy Kyle to sort out your family feud.

Lucy was about to take the card to the bin under the sink when she saw that it had something handwritten on the back of it.

*You're not being told everything. Call me and I'll tell you.*

She read the sentence three times, then tucked the card into her pocket. She grabbed her keys and her phone, and left the house.

Before she got into her car, Lucy gripped the stake the FOR SALE sign was attached to with both hands, yanked it free of the garden wall and flung it on the grass.

A year and a half ago, another FOR SALE sign had got Lucy into this mess.

She'd been driving by the old butcher's shop on Clonskeagh Road when it caught her eye, hanging in the window. By that stage, the premises had been sitting empty for months. It was a small, narrow, two-storey house whose entire ground floor had been the butcher's shop, with space for three cars to park outside. Every time Lucy passed it, she'd added another detail to her daydream of buying it, renovating it and turning it into a cafe.

Lucy had spent most of her professional life working in the food-and-beverage side of hospitality management, most recently as an events coordinator for a city-centre hotel, but she fantasized about one day opening a small, welcoming neighbourhood cafe, the kind that served excellent coffee but didn't judge you for how you liked to drink it, that was friendly to dogs and laptops, and whose food offering was one thing done exceptionally well, like donuts or cupcakes or cheesy toasties.

That morning, as she'd sat in her car waiting for the lights to change, looking at the FOR SALE sign, a little voice had whispered, *Why one day? Why not now?* That night, she'd sat down and done the sums – and then done them again and again, until they gave her the answer she wanted.

Then she'd sat Nicki down and pitched her plan. Lucy would take out a mortgage to buy the butcher's, using all her savings as the deposit. Going by recent sales in the area, their house was worth at least one and a half times what the butcher's shop was asking; they'd sell it, splitting their share. Lucy would use hers to reno- vate the studio above the shop so she could live in it, and invest the rest in getting the business off the ground. Nicki wasn't enthusiastic, but Lucy pulled every trick she could think of to persuade her – pointing out that she could use the money to go travelling, or do that ceramics course she'd been talking about, or just take a few months off to do nothing much at all – and, even- tually, she'd come round.

Just a few weeks later, Lucy had the keys to the butcher's and there were two offers on the house, both of which were above the asking price. She'd handed in her notice at work. Nicki's intentions were still vague, but Chris had sorted them a room in a friend's house that they could move into if the house sold before they'd made other plans.

Then Nicki left the house to go to a birthday party and never came home again.

Now, just over a year on, Lucy was unemployed, defaulting on her mortgage and unable to pay her bills. She hadn't sold the house. This was partly because she couldn't bear the thought of her sister somehow finding her way home only to have the door answered by a stranger, and partly because after the one and only viewing she'd allowed since Nicki's disappearance, Lucy had found weird little prayer cards tucked under all the pillows on the beds. Clearly, at least one person hadn't been as interested in buying the house as they had in getting into the house of the woman who was missing.

Lucy couldn't stomach having another one, no matter how much the estate agent promised he'd thoroughly vet future house-hunters.

But she desperately needed to do *something*. Sell the butcher's or sell the house. Or sell the house and open the cafe. Or sell everything and go somewhere else to start a new life for herself. In the meantime, the cafe – or rather, the butcher's shop with its linoleum floor removed, newspaper blocking the view out of its floor-to-ceiling window and a few mismatched patio chairs arranged in a circle around an upturned tea chest – was a physical manifestation of where she was in her life: trapped in a useless, desolate limbo.

'Lucy?'

She had the cafe's door propped open for air, and

now when she turned she saw a man standing just inside it.

He was in his forties and wearing jeans, a faded blue T-shirt and a pair of mirrored sunglasses he was in the process of taking off. She could smell his cologne: something musky and pungent that must have been sprayed on recently, perhaps as recently as just before he got out of his car. His face had the strange, porous sheen of too much Botox and his skin was so tanned that, as he smiled now, the contrast between it and his teeth was genuinely alarming.

She'd never met him in person, but she recognized Jack Keane from his TV shows.

Or the ads for them, anyway.

Jack lifted the hand that wasn't holding the sunglasses to show her what he'd brought: a cardboard tray with two takeaway coffees on it. 'Cappuccino on the left, latte on the right,' he said. 'Take your pick. I know it's a bit strange to bring coffee to a cafe, but I did a search online and found nothing, so I guessed it wasn't open yet, so . . .'

'Thank you,' she said, taking the nearest cup. 'And thanks for coming so quickly.'

'Not at all. Thanks for calling me.'

'We can sit here,' Lucy said. She motioned to the motley crew of chairs. 'If you don't mind a little dust.'

When they were both seated, she asked him if anyone else had called him too.

'You mean any of the other families? No.' A brief

smile. 'Not yet.' He arched an eyebrow. 'Why did *you* call me, Lucy?'

She took a sip of the – bad – coffee while she considered her answer.

'Because I want to know what you know,' she said. 'What they aren't telling us.'

Jack nodded. 'I imagine you do.' He set his coffee down on the tea chest and relaxed into his chair, crossing his legs and leaning back. 'You said on the phone you'd already heard about Lena Paczkowski?'

'Yes. Our FLO visited us this morning.'

'Is that Denise Pope?'

'It is, yeah.'

'What did she tell you, exactly?'

Lucy repeated what they'd been told: about how Lena had gone missing two weeks ago, re-emerged miles away near the Great Sugarloaf only to get hit by a car and, before she fell unconscious from her injuries, told the paramedics that she'd been held in a place where other women were being held too.

'There's a bit more to it than that,' Jack said.

She waited for him to elaborate, but instead he sighed deeply.

'Look, Lucy. I'm going to be blunt with you, OK? This isn't a gift. It would have to be an exchange. I'm here because I want an interview. Now, I know what you're thinking: *asshole*. And I get it. But you wouldn't be the first person to call me that. You wouldn't be the first person to call me that *today*. But I'm the asshole with the information no one else is going to share with you, least of all your so-called friends in the Gardaí. I will tell you what Denise Pope won't, or can't. And trust me, you're going to want to hear it.'

Lucy was a little lost. Jack was saying all this as if he was breaking news to her, but she'd assumed that that's what he'd come here to say.

Of *course* he was trying to get an interview with her. Why else would he have put his business card through her door in the first place? And if she wasn't prepared to give him an interview, would she have bothered arranging to meet?

'I'm not going to pretend I don't have a job to do,' he was saying now. 'And a mortgage to pay. *Two* bloody mortgages, since the wife decided she couldn't stand the sight of me any more. And please don't say it.'

'What?'

'That you're on her side.' He smiled briefly, then returned to Serious Face. 'And what you need to know is that this wouldn't be for my . . . let's say, usual fare. This won't be *Murder on the Motorway*.'

'What's that?'

'That was my last show,' he said. 'Craig Lewis? The guy who murdered that woman at the tollbooth? Still annoyed they wouldn't let me call it *Horror on the Hard Shoulder*, to be honest. But anyway, no. This would be for a special edition of the six o'clock news. We're going to do a full hour with some pre-taped reports on Operation Tide, and the interview would be the centrepiece. This would be worth doing, Lucy. I promise you.'

She nodded her head like she was taking all this in, carefully considering it.

She was starting to understand what was happening here now. Jack Keane didn't understand that Lucy had moved into a new phase of desperation, one in which she was perfectly willing to talk to the likes of him if he was the only way she could get on the national news.

He thought he was up against the same brick wall with the families of the missing women that he'd been dealing with since the commencement of Operation Tide, and he was doing his best to put a crack in it.

If she didn't disabuse him of that belief, she might find out what the Gardaí were keeping from them right now.

*And* get what she wanted: a national TV interview.

'I don't know,' she said, trying to look conflicted. 'I'm still not sure.'

'I know. Of course. Yes. And it would certainly be a challenge.' Jack straightened up. 'Look, the reason we're doing this show is *because* of what they're not telling you. What they haven't told anyone. Which is that Operation Tide isn't fit for purpose.'

Lucy felt a chill, even though the cafe was warm.

'What do you mean?'

'The guy heading it up, Superintendent Colin Hall – he loves the limelight. Facts, though, not so much. Seems like our crack team of detectives on one of the most high-profile investigations the state has ever seen have a serious case of confirmation bias. They went looking for more missing women to connect to Jennifer Gold so they could meet the quota for bringing in the big guns, but we're not sure they properly investigated the ones they got. If you need something to fit in a round hole, you're not going to stick on some edges, now, are you?'

'I'm sorry.' Lucy frowned. 'I don't really . . .'

'What if,' Jack said, leaning forward, 'they could solve one of the cases right now? What if they have enough circumstantial evidence to make a case?'

'Which one?'

'Tana Meehan,' Jack said.

Lucy's throat was suddenly bone dry. 'So . . . are you saying . . . Roland Kearns . . . ?'

Jack held up his hands. '*I'm* not saying anything. That's just what I'm hearing. That's what we're digging into right now. That they don't want to charge Roland Kearns with his ex-wife's murder because that'll be the end of Operation Tide's bottomless budget, and it'll therefore make it – they say – more difficult to solve the other two. Or three, potentially, if you include Lena. We think we have a Garda source who'll go on the record for us on that.'

Lucy thought about the hope she'd felt surge in her chest the day Denise had first come to the house, said a glass of tap water would be fine, thank you, and then told them about Nicki's case being upgraded and joined with the two others under the remit of Operation Tide. It had felt like the answers were not only there all of a sudden, but within her grasp. But what had they learned since then?

Absolutely nothing.

It hadn't made any difference at all.

'And,' Jack said quietly, 'I know what Lena told the paramedics. What *else* she told them. Do you want to know?'

Of *course* she wanted to know.

'Yes,' she said, nodding.

'You sure? It might be upset—'

'Just tell me.'

'I can't tell you everything,' he said. 'And not just because I'm trying to convince you to do this. Some of the information . . . Well, we haven't made a decision yet on whether we're going to report it. But I will say this. Lena was in a nightdress that neither her parents nor boyfriend recognized, one of those long cotton ones, so someone had given her clothing since she'd disappeared. And she kept saying something about a pink house. *The* pink house. She repeated it, over and over. That's what the boys in blue are out searching for as we speak.'

A pink house, in the Wicklow Mountains? Surely the guards could find that. The area was huge, yes, but how many actual homes were there?

And how many of them were pink?

Hope bloomed in Lucy's chest and took off surging through her body.

Finally, something tangible. Something that might actually bring this nightmare to an end.

'Look, Lucy. I'll level with you, OK?' Jack was standing up now, collecting his sunglasses from the top of the tea chest. 'I want this interview because it'll make fucking great TV, and that'll make me look fucking great. But if this is all out in the open, if Operation Tide's shit is exposed for all to see . . . It could change everything. It could break open this case. These cases. Which maybe aren't connected at all. Which might get solved if that didn't matter.'

'So when would this happen?' she asked. 'I mean, if I went ahead.'

'In an ideal world? Tomorrow. I'm not going to pretend I don't want to be the first to break this, but the only way I'm going to get to do it like this is if I get this interview to go along with it. The powers-that-be don't want a story about potential corruption in a task force, they want to see the pain it's causing on the faces of real people. But ultimately, when – and if – we do this depends on you. And your powers of persuasion.'

Lucy was lost again.

'I know it'll be a challenge to change the others' minds,' Jack said.

The *others*?

He saw the look on her face.

'Oh, sorry,' he said. 'Wasn't I clear? My apologies. It's not just you that I want for the interview. It's all of you. All three families. Tana's parents, Margaret Gold and you. You and Chris, if you want. But as you know, the others have always steadfastly refused to deal with me – and they continue to. That's where you'd come in. I'd be relying on you to talk to them about this and change their minds.'

'But . . . But I don't think that's even possible.' Lucy had thought she was getting exactly what she wanted, and easily, but now it was sprinting well beyond her reach. 'Why can't it just be me?'

Jack's eyes met hers and she read the answer in them.

Because she wasn't enough.

Because Nicki alone just wasn't *enough*.

'Well,' Jack said, moving to go. 'I'll leave you to it. You have my number. Do what you can and, well, you can let me know.'

# Gone Girl

The only house Kerry Long had ever lived in was your typical uninspired seventies Irish bungalow, sitting on a rise close to the road, somewhere in the Wexford countryside south-east of Enniscorthy. Its pebbledash was painted the colour of undercooked salmon, in jarring contrast to its pitch-black PVC window frames, and most of the front garden had been sacrificed to the concrete gods, affording all the rooms to the front uninterrupted views of the occupants' two parked cars. A similar bungalow sat directly opposite, but level with the road and mostly hidden behind a line of trees.

It had taken two hours to drive down from Dublin and at no point had Denise told Angela that this was where they were headed. Instead, she'd asked what time Angela was due to finish work and then, after she'd got an answer, if getting home late today would pose a problem. When Angela had said no, it'd be fine, Denise had turned on the radio at a level that discouraged conversation, and then there hadn't been any more for the remaining seventy miles.

Not that Angela was complaining. She was out of the office on one of the warmest days of the year and she was doing some actual police work with none other than Detective Denise Pope.

Or at least she hoped that that was what was about to happen.

Denise had parked right outside the house, alongside the other two cars. All the blinds at the front of the house were down and the windows were closed. There was no sign of movement, or any noise coming from within.

'Do they know we're coming?' Angela asked.

'They certainly don't know *you're* coming,' Denise said, getting out. 'And no.'

'How come?'

Angela got out too, the heat a surprise after the artificially cold air inside the car. She immediately started sweating. Denise was heading for the front door now and Angela hurried to follow her.

'If I'd called ahead,' Denise said, 'they might have rung the local boys to ask what was going on, and I don't want them knowing I'm here.' She pressed the doorbell; it chimed loudly inside the house. 'Let's just see what we can get before we draw *them* on us.'

'What are we trying to get?'

Through the frosted panes in the front door, they both saw a shadow move inside.

'Look,' Denise said, her voice low. '*I* do the talking here, OK? Consider yourself on mute. We won't under any circumstances be mentioning the items from the charity shop. And if you're offered anything, say you'd love a glass of tap water. Don't refuse and don't ask for something else.'

The door opened to reveal a small, neat woman in her fifties. She had too much clothing on for this weather: a long dress, nude tights and a cardigan.

Just looking at her made Angela sweat even more.

Denise stepped forward. 'Mrs Long?'

But there was no question that this was Kerry's mother. The two women were so similar, it was like looking at Kerry's photo in that article Angela had found online, only age-progressed.

Mrs Long frowned. 'Yes?'

'I'm Detective Garda Denise Pope.' Denise took her ID from her bag and flipped it open. 'And this is my colleague Angela . . . ah, Murphy.'

'Hi,' Angela said, smiling until it occurred to her that that might be inappropriate in a situation like this.

And her last name was actually Fitzgerald, but sure.

'We're from the Missing Persons Unit,' Denise said smoothly. 'We were hoping we could have a few minutes of your time . . . ?'

A look of total alarm took over Mrs Long's face.

'It's just a routine matter,' Denise added quickly.

'We're not here with any news or developments, I'm afraid. We're in the process of conducting a review of all outstanding missing person reports from the last five years and we wanted to ask you some questions about how you came to file one for your daughter, mostly to ensure that we have all the information we could possibly have and that everything is up to date.'

Now Mrs Long was looking uncertain. 'My husband is due home soon,' she said, peering over their shoulders as if hoping that he was already there, so he could deal with the visitors.

'We could wait for him?' Denise suggested.

'No, I . . .' Mrs Long reluctantly opened the front door wider and motioned for them to enter. 'It's OK. Yes. Come in.'

Crossing the threshold was like walking through a thick wall of cloying heat. It felt as if every window and door had been shut for a very long time, not just for these last few exceptionally hot days. In some distant room, country music was on low. The air smelled of cleaning fluids.

And Angela had never, ever seen so much pine.

The hall ceiling was clad in it. The interior doors were made of it. Through the open one at the other end of the hall, she could see pine kitchen units and a pine dining table and pine dining chairs. They were directed to the first – pine – door off the hall, which led to a living room with a pine fireplace, pine built-in shelving units on either side of it, and a pine coffee table.

Everything was just so, down to the throw cushions which had been fluffed up, carefully placed in a standing position and then expertly karate-chopped. There wasn't a single item that could conceivably be classed as clutter or mess, or even evidence that anyone actually lived here.

Angela wondered if this was the Good Room, or if the entire house was just this pristine. Show-house vibes. Although, with the pine infestation, for a development that had gone on sale at least thirty years ago.

Mrs Long motioned for them to sit down. 'Will you have a cup of tea?'

'A glass of tap water would be great,' Denise said with a smile.

Mrs Long looked to Angela.

'Same for me,' Angela said. 'Thank you.'

Mrs Long left the room, and they both stayed silent until they heard her footsteps reach the kitchen floor.

Then Angela whispered, 'I think they like pine.'

Denise pointed at the shelves bordering the fireplace. 'What else do you think?'

The shelves were home to an extensive collection of framed photos. Small ones taken generations ago, in black and white. Faded ones of what were presumably Mrs Long's and her husband's parents, sitting in brown oval mounts with gold borders. Daintier, silver-plated frames engraved with cursive dates immortalizing various wedding days.

And traced in frames of various shapes and sizes, the

entire life of a man who had grown from a chubby, ruddy-cheeked baby in blue dungarees to a tall, skinny twenty-something in a cap and gown, with a Holy Communion and a Confirmation and various sporting achievements and a Grads ball along the way.

'There's no photos of Kerry,' Angela said.

'None at all.'

'Maybe they're somewhere else? Or hidden away, because it's too painful?'

'Maybe,' Denise said.

There were footsteps in the hall and then Mrs Long was in the doorway, holding two matching glasses of water with ice cubes in each. She set them down on the coffee table and took two coasters from a drawer. She put the coasters on the table, moved the glasses on to them and then wiped away the rings of condensation their first positions had left with the cuff of her cardigan.

Angela immediately picked hers up and started drinking it, hoping it would help cool her down.

'So, Mrs Long—' Denise started.

'Maisie,' she corrected. 'Please.'

She'd taken a seat on the armchair directly opposite, her back ramrod straight, her expression tense.

'Maisie. As I said, we're conducting a review into Kerry's case – into all outstanding missing person reports from the last five years. I want to be very clear that that's all we're doing. Unfortunately, we have no new information to share.' While Denise was saying this, she had pulled a notebook from her bag, and was now poised with a pen hovering over a fresh page of it. 'What we'd like to do, if you don't mind, is just hear the circumstances of her disappearance, from you, in your own words. So we can be sure that the report contains all the detail and information that it possibly can, and that that information is correct. Would that be OK?'

Maisie said, 'Yes, fine,' but her body language and facial expression didn't appear to agree.

'Why don't we start with when you last saw her?'

'It was when she left for work that morning,' Maisie began. She was wringing her hands together in her lap, her knuckles white. 'Kerry worked in Wexford town, in an estate agent's. She used to get a lift in with one of our neighbours who worked near by, but she'd have to get the bus home. The nearest stop was about a mile down the road, so she'd walk the rest of the way – or ring me for a lift if the weather was bad. She was always home by six, but that night she never arrived, and we couldn't get in contact with her and she never contacted us.'

Denise scribbled something in her notebook.

'What did you do before you called the Gardaí?' she asked. 'Did you try friends, her office, other family members?'

Maisie nodded. 'Everyone I could think of. I rang Wendy – that's our neighbour that she'd get the lift with – and she said she'd dropped her that morning like always. The office was closed by then but her boss was in the phone book, so I rang him at home. He said she'd been at work all day. He'd gone home before she did, but he gave me the number of one of the other girls and she confirmed that Kerry had left at her usual time and walked in the direction of the bus stop. Like always.'

'Did they actually see her reach the bus stop, or . . . ?'

'No, it was a ways away from the office. But she went left out the door, as per usual. I asked how the form had been, and she said Kerry had seemed great, that they were chatting and laughing all day. We rang a couple of girls around here who she'd meet up with from time to time, but no one had seen her. So then we rang – well, my husband rang – the local station, just to get some advice, really. They said she's probably just decided to head out on the town and to call them again if she hadn't shown up by the morning. And, well . . .' Maisie paused. 'She didn't, so we did. But even then there wasn't much, you know, *action*. We just filed a report and they called us a few times, and that was it.'

Denise scribbled down something else. Angela tried discreetly to read what it was but her handwriting looked like the output of a malfunctioning EKG machine.

'Mrs Long,' Denise said then. 'Maisie. Why did you ask Kerry's colleague about what sort of form she'd been in? Had she been . . . ?' Her voice trailed off and she let the implication dangle in the air between them.

'Well, Kerry had had . . .' Maisie shifted her weight. 'She'd had some struggles. Over the years. Mostly when she was a teenager. We had some issues with her eating for a while, and then there was . . . the, ah' – she absently traced a finger across her inner arm – 'hurting herself, and we had to admit her for that . . . Three months, she was in that time. Missed the Leaving Cert over it. But then she started seeing this new therapist, and she had new medication, and she really improved. She hadn't had any issues for, I don't know, a couple of years.' She paused. 'Hasn't had.'

'There was an article online,' Denise said. 'An appeal for information. Generally those occur at the behest of the family, so at some stage you must have . . . ?'

'That was her brother's idea. Michael.'

The golden boy in all the photos, Angela presumed.

'Does he live here too?' Denise asked.

'No, he's in Melbourne.'

'Is he older or younger?'

'Older by eighteen months.'

'Was he in Melbourne when Kerry disappeared?'

'He's been there for nearly ten years. He flew home, of course, when he heard, but after a few weeks . . . He has a very big job, you see. An important job. Lots of responsibility. He couldn't stay, and we told him there was really no point.'

'Did the appeal generate any helpful information, can you remember?'

Maisie said, 'No.' She had started playing with a little silver locket she had on a chain around her neck, threading it from side to side. 'The thing is, my husband, he's a very private person. Doesn't like everyone knowing our business, you know? And he didn't want to cause a fuss. So we sort of said, look, if she wanted to run off, let her.'

'Had Kerry ever left like that before?'

'No, but she'd threatened to. I mean, back when she was ... God, fifteen? Sixteen? Teenage tantrums. She didn't mean it, I don't think, it was just in the heat of the moment. They didn't get on, you see. Her and her father. Too similar.' Her face changed then, and she let go of her chain to put her hands in her lap. 'She wanted to move to Dublin, but he thought that would be a waste of money – the rent. They were at loggerheads over it.'

'Did Kerry drive?'

That question had come out of Angela's mouth, and she was just as surprised as Denise to hear it.

'Sorry, I—' she started.

'She'd taken the theory test,' Maisie said, 'but not any lessons, not yet. She was waiting until she could afford a car.' The woman's eyes narrowed. 'Why?'

'It's just a routine question,' Denise said, flashing Angela a warning look. 'Maisie, do you by any chance still have Kerry's possessions? Personal items, clothes, that sort of thing?'

'Ah, yes. Some of it. It's all in boxes, but . . .'

Maisie was still looking at Angela, as if trying to figure something out.

Denise stood up. 'Do you think we could possibly take a quick look at them?'

\*

Maisie led them along the hall that ran from one end of the bungalow to the other, to the (pine) door that opened into a garage with cinderblock walls, a dusty cement floor and a mess of things – tools, chopped wood, a light-up reindeer – pushed up against its walls.

'Here you are,' she said, pointing to a small, somewhat haphazard pile of boxes tucked into a back corner. 'Those are Kerry's things.'

Angela counted five boxes. Just five. Three of which were archive boxes, the kind documents came in, and so not very big. The remaining two were a box that had once housed a microwave and a large one designed specifically for moving house – it had the name of a moving company printed on it – but still, this paltry collection was surely not big enough to hold all the possessions accumulated by a twenty-three-year-old woman. Not even one who watched all those organizational Netflix shows hosted by smiling people with alarming fetishes for throwing things out.

'Are you looking for something in particular, or . . . ?' Maisie asked.

'No,' Denise said. 'It's just helpful sometimes, to get a feel for the person.'

This was a weak cover story, especially by Denise's standards, but Maisie seemed to buy it.

She also seemed to read Angela's mind.

'We, ah, we gave away her clothes,' Maisie explained. 'And got rid of a lot of the . . . Well, you know. The rubbishy stuff. This is what's left.'

The words *Gave away as in donated to charity shops?* were forming on Angela's tongue, but another warning look from Denise ensured that they would stay there.

'Can I leave you to it?' Maisie asked. 'It's hard to, you know, look at it.'

'Of course,' Denise said. 'We'll only be a minute.'

Maisie turned on her heel and disappeared back into the hallway, closing the door behind her.

'What the—?' Angela started.

'*First of all*,' Denise said in a furious whisper. 'What part of *be mute* didn't you understand?'

Angela's cheeks coloured. 'Sorry,' she said. 'It just slipped out.'

'Don't be sorry, be *silent*. Now she's wondering why we asked about her driving specifically, what information we might have, when I told her this was just routine. She's probably on the phone to the local boys right now, checking up on us. And you're not even supposed to be here. *I'm* not even supposed to be.'

'Sorry,' Angela said again.

Denise held up a finger. 'Strike one. Two strikes and you'll be getting a bus back to Harcourt Square. Got it?'

Angela nodded.

This was going great. About as well as the PCT.

Denise lifted the top box off the pile, set it on the floor and bent to open it. Inside was a jumble of mostly anonymous personal-possession detritus: paperback books, DVDs, souvenir mugs, plush toys and a tangle of old charging cables. Angela, afraid to do anything now, just watched her.

'Anyway' – Denise pulled out a battered copy of *The Secret History*, thumbed through it – 'what were you saying? What the what?'

'Well, it's just that . . .' Angela wasn't sure how to put it. 'It's like they don't really *care* that Kerry has disappeared.'

'Elaborate. And go through a box while you do.'

Angela pulled one of the archive boxes close and lifted the lid, revealing a mess of perfume and make-up bottles, an acrylic storage case filled with congealed cosmetics, a broken mirror, some birthday cards and a tangle of cheap necklaces.

A plume of some pungent fragrance rose up from it and tickled her nose.

'Well, there's the no photos,' she said. 'On the shelves. And if all this stuff is here, I'm guessing they aren't keeping her bedroom ready for her return either. They donated her clothes. If this is everything that's left of hers, they must have thrown away most of it – and they haven't taken any care with the stuff they did keep. Like in here.' Angela tilted her box so Denise could see into it. 'It looks like someone went to her dressing table, held this at one end and just swiped everything off it with an arm. And did they really look for her? It doesn't sound like they made much effort. They seemed to accept pretty quickly that she wasn't coming back.'

'Or?'

'Or what?'

'If I forced you to come up with an alternative theory,' Denise said. 'Think back. Run through the entire interaction. From the moment Mrs Long opened the door. What did you see?'

Angela quickly replayed everything in her head.

'The husband,' she said then. 'Kerry's father.'

'What about him?'

'This is his doing. Their attitude towards her disappearance, I mean. Father and daughter didn't get on, and she'd had issues before, when she was younger. He didn't want everyone knowing their business, so he's certainly not going to want his daughter's face splashed all over the news. He thinks she's run off and he's saying, *Well, let her go, then. Feck her, if that's what she wants to do to us.* So they put away the pictures, throw away her things, and the golden son is elevated to only child.' Angela paused, thinking. 'Maybe Mrs Long *can't* look for her daughter, or keep out pictures. She seemed nervous about the husband coming back, and about us being here without him. And this house is insanely pristine. And she has a long-sleeved cardigan on and it's an absolute sauna in here.'

'Don't get carried away,' Denise said. 'Not everything is a crime waiting to be uncovered. The house could just be clean and Mrs Long might just feel the cold. But otherwise, yeah. That's what I'm thinking, too.' She straightened up with a groan. 'There's no clothing in here. Have you got any? I was hoping to find something with a bra size, or at least a few things that might tell us how much she tended to spend when she shopped. That bag you found was real leather. She definitely didn't pick *that* up in Penneys.'

'No. Nothing in here.' Angela poked around inside the archive box, just to be sure she hadn't missed anything that fitted the bill. 'Maisie said they gave away her clothes. We could ask if that was to charity shops. And we could show her the bag, ask her if she recognizes it.'

Denise shook her head. 'We can't do any of that, because we're just here conducting a routine review, remember? I don't want to risk upsetting anyone. Not until I'm sure, anyway.'

'Sure about what?'

But instead of answering, Denise jerked her head towards the door and said, 'Come on. Let's go,' and although Angela hadn't spent that much time with Detective Pope, she already knew enough about her to know not to ask her question a second time.

They went back into the hall and found Maisie waiting for them at the other end of it, by the front door. She was still tugging on the locket around her neck and, now, Angela wondered if there *was* a photo of Kerry Long here after all.

'Thank you so much for your time,' Denise said to her. 'We'll head away now, but . . . Maisie, can I ask you what might be a difficult question? It's just that you seem fairly certain that Kerry left of her own

accord. Is there a specific reason why you think that?
Is it because of her past troubles, or . . . ?'

There was a long, pregnant silence.

'I think she's in Dublin,' Maisie said then, her voice
just above a whisper.

'And what makes you say that?'

Her fingers closed around the locket. 'Hope, I
suppose.'

Denise nodded. 'I under—'

'And the phone.'

'Sorry – the phone?'

'Yes,' Maisie said. 'Kerry's phone.' She turned to the
console table behind her and opened the little drawer
underneath it.

Behind her back, Denise and Angela exchanged a
glance.

Angela's said, *Is* this *why we're here?*

Denise's said, *Don't say a* word.

'We found it here the following day,' Maisie said,
withdrawing a crumpled ziplock bag and holding it up
so they could see inside: an old, muddy iPhone whose
glass had been splintered in intricate webs, front and
back, although no shards appeared to be missing. 'She
didn't want to be contacted, you see. Kerry didn't just
leave her phone behind, she smashed it up and left it in
our garden.'

# Acclimatization

That's better. Now try and stay that way, OK? We've a while to go yet and I could do without a thumping bloody headache.

Anyway.

Where was I? Oh yes . . .

One night Amy was channel-surfing and I was reading *Team of Rivals* when she stopped on a panel show, the kind where they stick two people you vaguely recognize and one person you've never seen before behind a desk, and get some guy who's mostly on the radio to sit at another desk and react as they read the newspapers that you can read yourself the following day or even right now if you go online.

She only paused on it for a minute, but that was long enough for me to catch a woman who the brightly coloured band at the bottom of the screen alleged was a *bestselling crime writer* saying that if these missing women cases were the plot of a novel, your editor would make you rewrite it. 'It's unfathomable that he hasn't been caught,' she said, as if making up crime novels qualifies you to know anything about committing crimes in real life. 'Or even *seen*. How has he done this that many times without anyone seeing it happen? And in a country this small, with all the technology we have now . . . I just don't get how he can still be out there. I mean, it sounds to me like the guards know about as much now as they did when—'

Amy changed the channel, landing on an old episode of some painfully unfunny sitcom, and I went back to actually reading my book.

But I know that silly crime writer is not alone in thinking that my still being out here, free and unidentified, is *unfathomable*. I've caught snippets of similar discussions on phone-in radio, across the opinion pages, in the comments. (I know, I know – never read the comments. It's hard not to, though, isn't it?) At a bus stop once, I eavesdropped on two teenage girls who were talking about it. About me. They said there was some crazy theory on Reddit that explained everything, but I didn't want to search for it on any of my devices. And anyway, it *must* have been crazy, because no one can explain everything except me.

But it's a valid question.

How *am* I getting away with this when so much of the technology that permeates our daily lives has a tracking component, and criminal detection, in terms of both training and tools, is probably as good as it's ever been?

And still, now, three women later?

Although, as of tonight, I suppose it's technically four women.

I'd be remiss if I didn't point out that my getting away with this – thus far – isn't unique to me. This happened before, three decades ago, and whoever he was, he still hasn't been caught. They never even found his bodies. You're probably too young to remember it actually happening, but I'm sure you've heard of it.

After all, isn't it your generation that are so obsessed with true crime that you listen to all those grisly podcasts while you're putting on your make-up and doing your hair?

What's *that* all about, eh?

Now, I know what you're thinking: things were different then. And they were. A lot different. Ireland was. Hitchhiking was practically a sanctioned form of public transport. My parents lived near Cork airport, and I remember there being young people stood on the hard shoulder on Airport Road with monstrous bags on their backs, crude cardboard signs in one hand, thumb up on the other. Outside of cities, there was no CCTV – and I'll tell you this much, even now, there isn't nearly as much CCTV in cities as you might think. You were mainly reliant, after the fact, on footage from private security cameras, all of which were pointed somewhere specific, like at an ATM. That's why so many of the last images of the missing women from back then are grey, grainy stills taken from footage captured by cameras mounted on the ceilings of banks, post offices and corner shops, all of it impossibly pixelated on our modern screens.

And, of course, no one had a mobile phone, but we'll come back to that.

I think it's important to remind you at this juncture that I'm not trying to get away with it, remember? That was never my goal. Certainly not in the long term. I know that, some day, I will be caught. It's inevitable.

One morning, I'll be awoken by an exceptionally heavy knock on my front door and Amy will turn to me and say, *Who's that at this hour?* and I'll kiss her and say, *Stay here, I'll go check*, and then I'll take a mental picture of the way she looks at me because I know it'll be the last time she ever does it, that she'll never look at me the same way again, that I might not even *see* her again after that, and I won't be sad about many things when all this ends but I think there's a good chance I'll be sad about that.

One of these times, I'll perish on the mountain. If I keep going up, that much is true.

All I'm ever trying to do, really, is delay it.

To avoid it being *this* time, if I can.

Luckily, I've learned a lot from Amy's documentaries. Over the years, and especially with the more recent ones, I found myself keeping a mental list of how those guys got caught. I watched and I took note and I learned. Now, I don't think I can outsmart the authorities completely – and I think, actually, it's fucking idiotic to think that – but I don't want to make things easy for them either.

You *do* have CCTV now, obviously. Although, like I said, it's not as widespread as you might think. And there's things like automatic licence-plate readers and cell-tower data. But we are also helpfully tracking ourselves. Did you know, for example, that unless you've turned it off, your Google account tracks your every move? Yes, your Google account. Your *email* is following you everywhere you go and remembering where you were.

Did you know that?

Granted, you don't need to concern yourself with that kinda thing any more.

My point is, if you're trying to hide, technology is not your friend. Take that guy . . . Oh, what was his name again? The architect. You're old enough to remember that one, surely? The trial was . . . what? 2014? 2015? The guards had text messages between the victim and the man they were coming to believe was her killer, even though initially they'd put her death down to suicide. So they get the cell-tower data from the presumed killer's phone and it shows them that, during the day, the phone is mostly in Dublin 2 and that, in the evenings, it's mostly in a South Dublin suburb. They figure this man, then, whoever he is, works in the first place and lives in the other. They also have data that shows that, on one particular day, the phone was in Dublin in the morning and in Galway city by the afternoon, which means its owner probably went through a certain tollbooth during a certain window of time.

Did you know what they did with that information?

Someone sat down at a computer and went through every *single* licence plate that used the tollbooth, looking for a driver who fitted the bill.

Imagine how long that took, how many man-hours. And it was only going to work if he actually had taken the main road and not some other, roundabout scenic route *and* if the owner of the car was the one driving it.

But it did work.

I remember reading in the papers that they knocked on his door at 6:30 a.m.

Once you leave urban areas and stay off major roads, the chances of you encountering a camera or a licence-plate reader drop dramatically. Yeah, there's still a chance some rich guy with a gaudy mansion in the arse-end of nowhere will have a camera on the gate, or that you'll whizz past a speed van parked up on some potholed road, or that you'll pass some wanker with a dash-cam at the worst possible moment, but that would be some very bad luck. The countryside is your friend, basically, is what I'm saying.

That's why we're out here.

But I went a step further than simply sticking to the sticks. I went analogue.

First, I traded in my car. I had only one requirement beyond it being within my budget: it had to have a dash that didn't look like the cockpit of the Space Shuttle. I wanted a dumb car, with no built-in GPS or any other kind of internal computer system. What good would it do to avoid the powers-that-be if *my own vehicle* was recording everywhere I went and when? So I ended up with this, which – I don't know if you noticed before you got in – is a one-three-one reg. With what I got for my old car – which was practically new – I was able to pay off what remained on the car loan *and* cover the cost of this, so I could tell Amy I did it because I wanted to reduce our outgoings.

And we needed to do that because, let me tell you, the mortgage is *killing* us.

Which reminds me: life assurance. I've been trying to find out for months whether Amy would get a payout on my policy if I was found, after the fact, to have committed crimes. You wouldn't happen to know that, would you? It's not the sort of thing you can ring up your broker and ask, you know?

Anyway.

After that, all I needed to do was to leave my phone at home. But here's the thing: I do that regularly. At least two or three times a week, I leave the house without my phone – and when I do have it on me, I rarely use it. I've cultivated the persona of someone who doesn't like smartphones, and I've made sure that everybody in my life knows about it, so my not having it doesn't raise eyebrows or cause me any undue stress. Because people lose their goddamn minds when you go somewhere without your phone, when you render yourself uncontactable. Isn't that mad? Considering that until ... what? Twenty-five, thirty years ago, for all of human existence we'd managed just fine like that.

Now it's a cause for immediate panic.

I give myself no reason to have it outside of texts and phone calls. I don't use social media, or convenience apps, or even Google Maps. I use road signs.

Road signs!

Imagine that.

So I'm always driving this dumb car and I'm regularly away from home for long stretches without my phone, and I know if I'm in the countryside, sticking to local roads, I'm unlikely to be caught on any camera.

Now, this is going to sound like a total contradiction of everything I've just said, but the next most important thing – and, in some ways, I think this is even more important – is not to plan it in advance. No *tonight's the night*. I don't decide that I'm going to go out and find someone, that before I get into bed I'll have taken one more. I don't prepare.

What I am is always prepared – so I can do it at any time.

Think of it this way ... Every now and then, you like to go for a swim in the sea. But you're not a great swimmer and the waters can be rough, so you only ever go in when conditions are exactly right. When the water is calm. When the weather is good. When the tide is at a certain point of retreat, and you feel strong enough for the swim, and when being soaking wet afterwards isn't going to feck up your plans for the day. But that's a lot of what-ifs, so you can't really know in advance when all those things are going to come together for you. Your house is a ways from the beach; you don't know before you leave home whether or not you're going to be able to have a dip. So you keep all your swimming gear in a bag in the boot, always. You drive past the beach regularly. And, occasionally, maybe one time out of ten or fifteen or even as much as twenty, you stop and park up and get out and go for a swim.

It's safer that way. You're never disappointed that you didn't get to go for a swim, only happy that you unexpectedly did. And if, say, someone was watching you, trying to figure out how often you go for a swim, if there's a schedule or a pattern to it, if maybe the next time you go they can fix it so they're there too and they catch you in the act, well . . .

They can't.

Because even *you* don't know when the next time will be.

Things with you were different, of course. But then, they had to be.

When she opened her eyes it was to a darkness so complete that when she closed them again, it made no difference. Her mouth and throat were dry and her lips felt rough and sticky at the outer corners; the airless heat had silently invaded her insides while she slept. There were pools of slick sweat in the folds of her body and at the places where her bare limbs touched, and her hair was stuck to the back of her neck, her cheeks, her forehead. She felt nauseous despite her empty stomach and the skin on her face burned like she'd sat too long in the sun.

*This is what it feels like*, she thought, *to be cooked*.

She licked her lips and swallowed and gathered all her hair in a bunch behind her head, but it made no difference. She needed water and fresh air and to not be in this room, but she couldn't just get up and go get those things.

Not any more.

Not here.

Not with all his *rules*.

Elsewhere in the darkness, a body stirred. Three women slept in here, which was the half of a derelict stone cottage that had been made slightly less derelict. Its walls were solid and thick, the expert work of some long-ago builder, but the roof of corrugated steel sheeting was a more recent addition installed by someone who was no expert at all. The glass in the windows was long gone, the portals left behind covered with thick, cloudy plastic that had been nailed into place. The only thing new and solid and fitted right was the door. As a home, its most impressive feature was that it managed to be completely unsuitable to live in no matter what the weather.

He kept promising they wouldn't have to stay here for much longer, but it had been months since she'd believed him.

She'd already spent a summer here, but that one hadn't been as hot, and anyway, she'd been too pre-occupied with just making it from one day to the next to complain about the conditions. The winter months had been the worst; there was nothing you could do to get the place to hold any heat. Her bed had been a wedge of what might have been insulating foam thrown on the rotting wooden floor and a cocoon of old but thick sleeping bags, and even though back then they were still allowed to build a fire in the cottage's hearth, she'd woken up on too many mornings with ice crystals in her lashes and pain in her limbs from the cold.

In the spring the rain came, and it came *in*, dripping

constantly and sometimes even pouring through the gaps in the roof, and of course there was always at least one more leak than they had receptacles to catch them with. Sometimes, during stormy nights, the buckets and pans or whatever they had would quickly overflow, the rain drenching them from both above and below. They'd be constantly cold and wet, their skin damp, their fingertips forever shrivelled like prunes. For weeks, everyone had had a cough or a fever or a sore throat.

Summertime had been the promise of some comfort and for a few weeks it had brought a little relief, but the intense heat of the last few weeks had been a torture. Hot air began pushing its way inside shortly after sunrise and got trapped there, building and thickening all the while, so that it was a suffocating, solidified thing come the night.

One night of such temperatures was an anomaly; they could take solace from the fact that it'd feel better tomorrow. Two in a row was uncomfortable, guaranteeing a night of sweaty and broken sleep. But yesterday had been the third day the mercury had stayed past the thirty-degree mark and in here, now, it was absolutely unbearable.

She closed her eyes and imagined diving into cool, clear water, hoping her subconscious mind would steal a few details for her dreams, but thinking about feeling that way only made her feel worse.

And anyway, she couldn't dream if she couldn't sleep. They all had different names for who they'd been and how they'd lived before they'd come here. The Before. The Outside. The Previous, as in *my previous life*. But on the whole, they tried to avoid talking or even thinking about it.

It was best to forget.

Easier.

Necessary, in the long run.

But now, when she wondered what the hell she was doing here, how she'd ended up in this situation, why she continued to stay . . .

She *had* to think about Before, to remind herself that she'd no choice in the matter. She couldn't leave.

She was trapped here.

# Kin

The hum of polite chatter. Unobtrusive background music. The clink of a teaspoon hitting off the inside of a ceramic cup. Water coming to the boil with a hiss. Chair legs scraping and shifting across the floor.

If Lucy closed her eyes for a second, she could imagine that the cafe was open, that she had resumed and rebuilt her life, and that she had been able to do that because she had the answers to all her questions about where her sister had gone. But this afternoon, the place sounded like that because she *didn't*.

She'd gathered the families of the missing women to discuss Jack Keane's interview request, a summit of tragedies.

Behind the old counter, Lucy absently arranged some biscuits on a plate and surveyed the odd scene.

Sarah and Tommy Meehan were sitting side by side

in chairs that they'd pulled close together. The last time they'd seen their daughter, Tana, she'd been leaving their house to catch a train into Dublin city centre over a year and a half ago. She'd moved back in with them when her marriage to Roland Kearns had broken down. Like most of the country, Tana had been working from home for months by then, but needed to collect some items from her office.

They never saw their only child again.

Now Tommy was on a cocktail of medication for his heart and Sarah had just completed a course of treatment for a cancer she'd beaten before Tana's disappearance that had since returned. They'd had Tana late in life; they were both edging towards seventieth birthdays they wouldn't have any desire to celebrate. And even though Sarah was the one on the far side of chemotherapy, it was Tommy's appearance that concerned Lucy. Every time she saw him, it seemed like his eyes had sunk a little deeper into his skull and his pallor was another shade closer to grey. He seemed to be slowly *succumbing*, helpless to stop his physical being from being eaten alive by his grief.

Lucy didn't worry at all about the woman sitting to Tommy's left, and she knew that Margaret Gold didn't spend a single moment of any day worrying about her or the others.

Today, Jennifer Gold's mother was as made-up and shiny as she always was, wearing a linen shirt in a shade of hot pink that reminded Lucy of bubblegum and Barbies, with a pair of designer shades on her head. Perched there, not pushed into her hair, because that would mess up its careful styling.

Eight months ago, her just-turned-seventeen-year-old daughter had left the house to walk the dog in chilly winter sunshine but, fifteen minutes later, the dog had returned alone. Just a few yards from their front gate, Margaret had found Jennifer's damaged phone.

Immediately, she was a presumed abduction. She got detectives, search teams and an incident room. For days, a Garda helicopter had droned over the area while civilian volunteers moved over the land-scape below like lines of crawling neon-yellow ants. After a week of blanket media coverage, vigils and even presidential concern, public demand had forced the authorities' hand.

Without Margaret, there would probably be no Oper-ation Tide, and Nicki would still be a flimsy report at the back of a filing cabinet somewhere. But it was hard to feel grateful when the woman consistently acted as if Jennifer was the only missing woman worth finding.

Worse yet, the general public seemed to agree. They weren't even half as bothered about what had hap-pened to the twenty-nine-year-old overweight woman who'd moved back in with her parents after her mar-riage failed, or the drunk one in a short skirt who'd abandoned her friends on a night out.

It was, to say the least, depressing.

Today, Margaret had an air of barely contained

impatience and looked like she'd got lost on the way to a Slimming World meeting she was only attending to make sure she stayed at her goal weight. Lucy watched her take a sip of the (instant) coffee she'd been served and then turn the corners of her mouth down in disgust. She was also sitting on her own cardigan, which she'd made a point of taking off and laying on the seat of her chair before she sat down.

Lucy had to remind herself that this woman was missing her young daughter, and that she deserved sympathy and compassion.

Margaret just made it so hard to remember that.

Finally, there was Caroline. She was approaching Lucy now and making a face, unseen by the others, that silently said, *Good luck with this lot.*

Out loud she said, 'Is there anything I can do?'

'I'm all set here,' Lucy said. 'And you've already done enough.'

It was Caroline she'd called when she knew she needed to get the family members together, and Caroline who'd got everyone here, and quickly.

She'd been an old school friend of Tana's and had, by chance, seen her waiting at the bus stop in Kildare town on the evening she disappeared, having got off a commuter train from Dublin. It would turn out to be the last positive sighting of Tana Meehan. Since then, Caroline had become Sarah and Tommy's unofficial helper, doing things like managing social-media accounts and fielding media requests: the logistics of having a missing daughter that neither Tommy nor Sarah was in good enough health to do themself.

'I've been meaning to ask you,' Caroline whispered. 'Are you still . . . ?' She raised her eyebrows meaningfully.

'What?'

'You know . . . Going out *there*, at night?'

She was the only person Lucy had told about what she'd been doing these last few weeks.

She hadn't meant to; it had just slipped out on a night when Caroline had called over with a birthday card for Lucy from Sarah and Tommy and a bottle of wine from her, and they'd sat in the uncut wilderness of the back garden, talking about the case until the sun set.

But Caroline hadn't reprimanded her, or tried to persuade her to stop. She hadn't pointed out that it was stupid and pointless and possibly dangerous. She'd just said, 'You do whatever you feel you have to do,' and then told Lucy to call her, any hour of the day or night, if she got in trouble out there and needed help.

'Last time was the night before last,' Lucy said, her eyes on the three around the tea chest, making sure they couldn't overhear. 'And that *was* the last time. I'm going to stop. It's not going to achieve anything. But if I can get everyone to agree to do this interview, that actually might.'

'Just a heads-up,' Caroline said, 'but I don't think Sarah and Tommy have the stomach for it. But then, at the same time, I can't see them outright refusing your request, you know? Not if it's something you're telling them will help.'

'Did they get a card from Jack too?'

'If they did,' Caroline said, 'I didn't see it when I came round to pick them up, and they didn't mention it to me. I just mean in general. They're both exhausted. And now with all this stuff about the Polish girl . . .'

Lucy nodded. 'Yeah, I know.'

She actually didn't know if Lena Paczkowski *was* Polish or if that was just an assumption Caroline was making, but she let it go.

'Sorry, Lucy?' Margaret called out, tapping her spoon against her cup like she was asking for quiet before a speech. 'Could we get started, do you think? I have to be in Donnybrook in half an hour. What's this all about?'

'Yes, yes, yes,' Margaret said impatiently before Lucy had even finished explaining why she had gathered them here. 'The card from Jack Keane. I presume we all got it?' She looked around and either didn't see or chose to ignore Sarah's and Tommy's blank faces. 'But it's just amateur dramatics. He doesn't know anything.'

'Actually, he does,' Lucy said. She turned to Sarah and Tommy. 'He said there were things the guards weren't telling us, and he was prepared to share them with us because he wants us all to go on the news tomorrow at six and give him an interview. A joint one. Together.'

Sarah looked alarmed. 'Things like what?'

Margaret scoffed. 'What kind of person would with-hold details from the families of missing women in order to get something in return? It's preposterous. And it's all a manipulation. Jack Keane is a charlatan. He doesn't know anything.'

It was no secret – because she kept mentioning it – that Margaret's brother was a friend of Superintendent Colin Hall's. That was one of the reasons why, Lucy believed, Jennifer's case had got immediate and plenti-ful attention, and how Margaret always seemed to have more details than anyone else.

She claimed it was because Patrick, her FLO, just did a better job than Denise of keeping her in the loop, but Lucy had her doubts. Margaret was getting infor-mation by other channels.

How was that different to talking to the likes of Jack Keane, who must have got it from the same place?

It was *all* coming from the guards, after all.

'He hasn't withheld it,' Lucy said. 'He told me what it was when I met with him this morning.'

Margaret rolled her eyes.

Everyone else in the room leaned forward, waiting.

Lucy, who had just realized she was going to have to share nightmarish information with Sarah and Tommy, right here, right now, swallowed hard before continuing.

'He, ah, he said that when Lena was found, she was in clothing – a nightdress – that wasn't her own, and that she kept talking about a pink house. *The* pink house. He said that's what the Gardaí are doing now: searching for something that matches that description in and around the area in which she had the accident.'

Silence.

Without looking down, Sarah reached out, immediately found Tommy's hand waiting for her and clasped it tightly. Lucy had to avert her eyes because the tenderness of it, the togetherness of it, was enough to break her.

'God,' Caroline said. 'Really?'

Margaret shrugged one shoulder. 'That's not what I'm hearing.'

*But of course*, Lucy thought.

'What did you hear?' Sarah asked.

'Yes,' Lucy snapped. 'Please do share with the group.'

Margaret glared at her. '*Excuse* me?'

'We'd just like to hear what it is too,' Caroline said, in an obvious attempt to defuse the tension. 'Is there a reason you can't tell us?'

Margaret narrowed her eyes at Caroline.

Before Nicki disappeared, Lucy could never have imagined that a meeting of people who were missing people would play out just like any other assembly of randomly connected strangers tasked with making a collective decision: very badly.

Even when traumatized, people were the worst.

'*I* heard,' Margaret said, 'that that girl has nothing to do with us. That she ran away from home after a fight with her parents and rather than face the music, she's come up with this elaborate story about being kidnapped – because she knew people would believe it, because of *our* girls.'

On *girls*, something unusual happened: Margaret's voice caught. She rarely showed emotion and had in fact been lauded by the public for being such a steady pillar of stoic strength. Lucy started to feel bad about her own lack of compassion towards the woman, but then—

'Her mother is Iranian,' Margaret said pointedly. 'So, you know.'

'No,' Lucy said. 'I don't know. What's *that* supposed to mean?'

'Just that that household is more than likely very strict. Very conservative. Especially with girls. You can see how arguments would arise, and how a situation like this might occur, especially when she was raised here.'

'We don't know any of that,' Caroline said. 'Actually.'

She looked at Lucy as if to silently say, *What the fuck?* and Lucy returned one that said, *I can't even with her.*

'So there was no house?' Sarah asked. 'I'm sorry, I'm not sure I . . . ?'

'We're getting off track here,' Lucy said, holding up a hand. 'The bottom line is it doesn't really matter whether or not Lena ran off, or whether Jack has the facts. What *does* is that he's asked us to do this interview and I think we should. Of course we should. It's a chance to keep Nicki, Tana and Jennifer's faces fresh in the public's minds. Why wouldn't we? We should be taking every chance we get to do that.'

Caroline nodded in agreement, while Sarah and Tommy looked lost in thought.

Margaret pressed her lips together and Lucy knew exactly what she was doing: trying to stop herself from saying that she didn't need to, that she could pick and choose her chances, because she had got plenty of them.

Because the woman *she* was missing was Jennifer.

'I don't know,' Sarah said. Her voice was weak, wavering. 'I agree with what you're saying, Lucy, but I just don't know if I'm up to doing anything like that.' She glanced at Tommy, who was looking at the floor. 'We're not in the best form at the minute, either of us, you see, and, well, you know me.' She smiled briefly, sadly. 'I'm no good with this kind of thing. I can't even say her name without . . . You know . . .'

'What if,' Caroline said, 'I sat in for you?' To Lucy, 'Would he go for that, do you think? Me representing them?' Back to Sarah, 'You could write down whatever you'd like to say about Tana, and I could read it out for you.'

Sarah brightened. 'Would you?'

'Of course. Whatever you need.'

'That's a good idea,' Lucy said. 'I'm sure that'd be

fine.' She knew it would be, because when Jack said he wanted all of them, they both knew who was the most important one. 'And what about you, Margaret?'

'No,' she said, folding her arms. 'Not for him.'

Sarah frowned. 'What do you mean?'

'It shouldn't matter who is doing the interview,' Lucy said. 'It's all publicity. And he said *this* is going to be on the six o'clock news.'

'He's not serious,' Margaret said. 'His *viewers* aren't serious. They want drama and blood and salaciousness. So if we go on, that's what they'll want from *us*. What Jack Keane will. Haven't you seen what kind of programmes he makes? They're horrendous. Sorry, but I will not get my Jennifer involved in something like that. Not all publicity is good publicity.' She paused. 'And actually, I've decided to take a break from interviews. I've been doing so many of them lately . . .'

Lucy closed her eyes and began counting to ten, lest she stand up, grab the plate of biscuits and hurl them directly at the head of this woman whose daughter was missing.

'Why can't you do it yourself?' Margaret asked her. 'If you're so keen?'

'Because they want all of us,' Lucy said. She'd only made it to four.

'Well, some of us will just have to do.'

Margaret stood up then, preparing to leave.

Caroline stood up too.

'Margaret,' she said, 'that's not really fair. You know things are different for you. And Lucy is asking you to do this. If you asked her to do something that would help Jennifer, you know she would in a heartbeat.'

Tense, awkward silence.

Margaret fixed Caroline with the kind of stare super-villains display right before their eyes glow red and murderous laser-beams shoot out of them.

'*You*,' she said through clenched teeth, 'shouldn't even be here. What's any of this got to do with you? We've lost daughters and a sister. What have you lost? Someone you used to know when you were in school that you hadn't talked to in years? This isn't even any of your business. How bloody *dare* you.'

Caroline paled, and her bottom lip began to tremble.

Tommy said, 'There's no need for that language,' and everyone startled and turned towards the sound of his voice because they heard it so infrequently.

Lucy stood up too.

'Look,' she said, 'I think we could all do with taking a breather here. Calm down a bit. Let me make more coffee and we can just have a think about this, OK?'

She needed a breather herself. She was going to go out the back and find something that would muffle a scream. She couldn't stay in this room of broken people a moment longer, or she'd break herself.

She didn't have the energy to remain afloat in this

ocean whose surface was littered with the debris of these poor people's lives, and her own.

'I can't stay,' Margaret said, going to the door. 'And my answer is no. You do whatever you have to do, but I won't be a part of it.'

# Official Secrets

An hour closer to Dublin, Denise pulled off the M11 and straight into a McDonald's drive-thru.

It crossed Angela's mind that since she'd answered that call from reception this morning, her PCT prep had completely fallen by the wayside, and yet spending time doing what felt like actual police work with Detective Denise Pope made her want to become a fully-fledged member of An Garda Síochána more than ever.

She opted for a chicken salad and a pineapple stick, then watched as Denise demolished a Big Mac in what seemed like the qualifying time for advancing to the next round in a competitive eating event.

How on earth did she look the way she did, eating like that?

After the case of why Denise was so interested in a

three-and-a-half-year-old low-risk missing person report, that was the next mystery Angela wanted to solve.

'So,' Denise said, crumpling her empty McDonald's bag into a ball. 'Tell me. What do you know about Operation Tide?'

Angela happily abandoned her salad. She'd already eaten all the chicken pieces out of it anyway.

'It's a special task force,' she began, 'set up to investigate the three missing women cases from the last two years—'

'Which are?' Denise interrupted.

Unlike the PCT, this was a test Angela actually had a chance at passing. But she had to be careful to separate the cold, hard facts from the office whispers and overheard phone conversations that had added details she most certainly wasn't supposed to know.

'Chronologically,' Angela started. 'Tana Meehan was the first. She was, ah . . . twenty-nine.' She hoped – although Denise didn't correct her, so she must have been. 'Disappeared in December 2020, last seen at a bus stop in Kildare town. She'd just got off a train from Dublin. She and her ex-husband, Roland Kearns, were legally separated at the time. He's been questioned but never charged.' Angela figured she probably shouldn't say, *And everyone thinks he killed her in a jealous rage because he thought she was having an affair with a friend she had visited that night in Dublin, and as Kearns is* such *a creep and a complete narcissist who* cannot *seem to keep his mouth closed around the press, it's very easy to believe.* 'Her phone was found the following day, on the road close to the bus stop, by a member of the public. And she had the bad luck to go missing the day before Covid cancelled Christmas, so her disappearance barely made the news.'

'*Two* days before,' Denise corrected. 'She was last seen on December nineteenth. The government announced new restrictions on December twenty-first, and that's all anyone cared about from then on. And, according to Kearns, she was pregnant.'

'Really?' Angela did her best Surprised Face, even though that fact was common knowledge around the water coolers of Harcourt Square. The metaphorical ones; they didn't actually have water coolers in the building. 'How far along?'

'You tell me.' Denise raised an eyebrow at Angela as she plucked her Coke out of the cup holder between the seats and sucked noisily on the straw. 'For your sake, I hope you don't play poker.'

Angela blushed. 'I heard ten weeks.'

'That's what Kearns told us, yeah. And that it was his. They'd reconciled, he said. Conveniently. But we don't have any evidence of a pregnancy. Tana spent some time in a friend's apartment near Spencer Dock on the night she disappeared – we ruled him out – and he said she'd had a couple of glasses of wine, which of course doesn't mean much in itself. But she hadn't visited her GP either. She had, however, told at least two other friends that Kearns had been abusive throughout their relationship. Psychologically *and* physically.'

'That doesn't make him a m—' Angela started.

'It makes him a lot more fucking likely to be a murderer than a man who *hasn't* pummelled his wife in the face with his fists,' Denise said, her voice rising slightly. 'You know, it drives me absolutely fucking nuts when people say that. As if a man who's violent, not only at *all*, but to the woman he supposedly loves the most, is our baseline for normality, and a man who does it until his victim dies is some other species entirely. They're one and the same, for fuck's sake. The only difference is one of them got angrier than the other.'

Angela looked down at her grease-stained cardboard box of limp salad leaves and resolved never to say such a thing again.

'Anyway,' Denise said. 'After Tana was . . . ?'

'Nicola O'Sullivan,' Angela finished, more tentative now, lest she say something else that would make Denise's nostrils flare. 'Ah, Nicki. Twenty-five when she disappeared in June 2021. Living with her sister in Dundrum. Last seen leaving the Duke pub on Duke Street late on a Saturday night.'

'Technically she was last seen on CCTV walking towards Grafton Street,' Denise said, 'but OK. She'd been in the pub with friends, drinking enough to make her at least a little drunk. She didn't tell any of them she was leaving, and when she did, she turned right out of the pub instead of left – when left would've brought her to a Luas stop within seconds, and the Luas would've brought her all the way home.'

'And they found her phone the next day, in a laneway near the pub.'

'Yes,' Denise said, nodding. 'Her sister did. After she went into the pub to ask the staff if they'd seen where she'd gone.'

'Was she meeting someone, maybe?'

'There was nothing on her phone to indicate that, and the CCTV lost her in the late-night crowds on Grafton Street, and none of the surrounding streets picked her up again. We got a few reports of sightings of her at various places down the east coast, but none of them ever panned out.' Denise sighed. 'What else do you know about her?'

There was a beat of silence while Angela tried to think of something.

'That's it, really,' she said. 'Unless you count the fact that Nicki O'Sullivan's disappearance didn't really make the news until Jennifer Gold went missing that Christmas, and Operation Tide put them and Tana Meehan together.'

'And what do you know about Jennifer Gold?' Denise asked.

'Presumably snatched just yards from her home on the Enniskerry Road in broad daylight last December, while walking her dog. She'd just turned seventeen. Her phone was found thrown into a bush. She'd been WhatsApping with a friend who'd seen a *Jennifer is typing* message but then nothing more.' Angela paused. 'I think the dog was called Walter.'

Denise looked at her with such disappointment that Angela coloured.

'Do you think it matters what the dog is called?'

Angela shook her head. 'But you asked what I knew—'

'So we have our three missing women,' Denise said, cutting her off. 'Tana Meehan, Nicki O'Sullivan and Jennifer Gold. Disappeared in December, June and then December again. From Kildare town, Dublin city centre and the Enniskerry Road, around ten p.m., around midnight and in broad daylight just after three. When Jennifer disappears, the three cases are linked and Operation Tide is established. But what links them? Evidentially?'

'The phones,' Angela said. 'All three of their phones were found thrown on the ground near to where they were last seen or, in the case of Jennifer Gold, presumed snatched, bundled into a car or something.'

Denise took another noisy sip of her Coke, then pointed the straw at Angela.

'And you think that alone is sufficient? Do you think the phones are enough tangible evidence to say these three disappearances are definitely related to each other and *un*related to all others?'

It was obvious from her tone that the answer was *no*.

But why? Angela sensed she should at least attempt to come up with a reason.

'I, ah, I don't know,' she said. 'But I suppose . . . Well . . . The phones were all found discarded in public places, right? So isn't it possible that there's a missing woman whose phone we just didn't find? Like one that ended up slipping down a drain or getting flattened by a truck or picked up by someone who didn't realize its significance?'

Denise nodded, encouraging her.

'And then there's the fact,' Angela went on, 'that thousands of adults are reported missing by their family or friends every year who have actually *decided* to leave, for whatever reason, and if you wanted to disappear, surely the first thing you'd do is get rid of your phone. Or one of the first things, anyway. So how do you differentiate between a phone thrown away by its owner and a phone that someone potentially *took* off its owner and threw away because he was bundling her into the back of his van or whatever and didn't want to be tracked?'

'Do you know Superintendent Colin Hall?' Denise asked.

Angela was thrown by the sudden change in direction and before she could answer *no*, Denise had carried on.

'You'd recognize him if you saw him, because he's never met a camera lens he didn't love. Well, Jennifer Gold went missing from his jurisdiction and her uncle is one of his golfing buddies. Hall is at least partly responsible for the circus that followed Jennifer's disappearance – and he's wholly responsible for the establishment of Operation Tide. Which he thought he should lead, needless to say. Have you ever read *Jurassic Park*?'

Angela blinked at Denise. 'Have I . . . ?'

'And I do mean *read*. Seeing the film doesn't count. It's not just about dinosaurs, you know.'

'I didn't say it w—'

'There's a scene in the book,' Denise said, 'where they realize that their computer program, the system that runs the park, isn't doing what it's supposed to do. It isn't counting all the dinosaurs. They have it set up so that, say, there's supposed to be ten raptors or whatever, and every so often it checks that there's still ten raptors, that none of them have escaped. But Ian Malcolm – that's Jeff Goldblum in the film – realizes that the system has a fatal flaw. If you tell it to look for ten raptors, it'll look for ten raptors. But then it'll stop. It won't let you know if there's eleven, although it will alert you if there's nine. Once it finds what it expects, it's satisfied. So it's not really counting the animals in the park at all.'

Angela wondered if there'd been some kind of hallucinogen in her salad, or perhaps salmonella in the chicken. Was she really sitting in Detective Denise Pope's car parked just off the M11, eating McDonald's and talking about counting the dinosaurs in *Jurassic Park*?

And if so, where the hell was Denise going with this?

'*That's* Operation Tide,' Denise said. 'Hall wanted

his little glory op. He needed enough missing women to justify it, so he went and found them. There's no question that Jennifer Gold was abducted, but one missing woman does not a high-profile operation make. He needed more. But he *only* needed two more, and he stopped once he had them. And look, maybe I'd have done the same. It's no bad thing that everyone is now looking for two women who no one was looking for before. The problem is, there could be more raptors out there. And the three he has might not even be raptors at all. One of them might be a T-Rex. One of them might not even be a dinosaur, but a cow or a sheep or something. And if he proves that, what happens to his op? It gets junked. So you'd have to ask, how thoroughly has he checked?'

Angela was too busy trying to track the metaphor to answer.

'Do you like Don?' Denise asked then. 'Like working with him?'

'Yeah,' Angela said. 'He's great.'

This conversation was giving her whiplash.

'Well, he vouched for you, so if you repeat any of what I'm about to tell you to anyone else, it's him that'll get in trouble.' Denise met her eye. 'Do you understand that?'

Angela nodded vigorously. 'Yeah.'

Denise gave her one last lingering glare.

'I have a list,' she said then. 'Disappearances that I think could possibly – *should* possibly – be under the remit of Operation Tide. All it was before today was a list of guesses. Possibilities. Because I can't go reinvestigating cases, and I can't go to the Super and tell him I think him and his Tidies should do it. And I'm only tangentially on Tide, because I happened to be the FLO for both Tana and Nicki's families. When Kearns started looking shady, they put me on him too. Figured it was no harm to have a detective around him. But Hall could kick me off at any moment, and then I can't do anything. So I have to tread very carefully and move quickly, before anyone starts asking why I'm helping a paper-pusher in the MPU' – Angela tried not to react to this – 'chase down something we can't use in court anyway on a three-year-old missing person report that not even the family want to keep active.'

'So Kerry Long was on your list?' she asked.

Denise nodded. 'She was at the top of my list, actually. I didn't really have anything tangible on her one way or another, but I don't know . . . I just had a feeling. Sometimes that's all you have, and you have to trust that that's enough of a reason to do a little more digging. That's why Don called me about it – about what you found.'

'And now her phone being in the front garden—'

'—confirms my suspicions, yes. Her mother said Kerry would get a bus out of Enniscorthy but she'd have to walk the last bit of her route home. In January, she'd have been doing that in the dark. She could've been snatched off the road by someone who took her phone and threw it over a hedge, not realizing it was *her* hedge. Not realizing that he'd taken her from right outside her own house.'

'It's just like Jennifer Gold,' Angela said. 'It could be just like her.'

'Only in this case, we have physical evidence. Nothing that we could use in court, of course – our continuity of evidence is completely fucked – but we might be able to use it for something all the same.'

'January 2019, though.'

'What about it?'

'If it was the same guy who did the other three,' Angela said, 'that would mean there was a two-year gap between victims one and two.'

'So?'

'So . . . That seems ages,' she said lamely.

'But we don't know she's victim number one, do we? And we don't know that Tana Meehan is actually number two. There could be more out there we don't know about. I'm not sure we even know that the three we do have are linked to each other. And I presume that, whoever he is, he got about as much done in 2020 as the rest of us.'

'Right. Yeah.'

They lapsed into silence.

'What about Lena Paczkowski?' Angela asked then. She figured there was no point pretending she hadn't heard the chatter about her around Harcourt Square; she'd only made it as far as the lift that morning before she overheard her first conversation about it. 'I know what she said. To the paramedics. About being taken and held at a place where there were other women.'

Denise gave her a sideways glance. 'That all you heard?'

'Yeah. Why? Is there more?'

'Official Secrets Act or no, there's some things I really *can't* tell you.'

They both fell quiet again.

'For Jennifer Gold,' Angela said, 'the alarm was raised immediately. But it was months before Tana and Nicki's disappearances were flagged as possible abductions. Lena was gone two weeks and she still hadn't been. And if there's more victims like Kerry Long, women we don't know about *at all* . . .'

Angela looked to Denise, certain she was about to point out something the other woman had already thought of.

'There's no telling how many women he's taken,' Denise finished. 'And for all we know, he could have someone right now.'

# Ice Fall

What really gets me is when people say things like, *She just disappeared off the face of the earth. It was as if the ground opened up and swallowed her whole. Vanished without a trace.* The guards, the media, the general public – it seems like no one can understand how a woman can be there one minute and not there the next, and there's no flashing neon arrow pointing in the direction she went.

Like you, tonight.

It's the same when someone dies suddenly and you can count on at least one idiot to say, 'But I just saw him yesterday!' Bloody hell, you don't say? You're telling me that up until the moment his heart stopped working, it *was* working, and he was alive? Mind-blowing!

I guess I just wasn't expecting the whole *mystery* of the thing.

Take my obligatory media moniker, for instance. The Phantom, they were calling me, until that opinion piece about foregrounding the victims and not their killer. Did you read that? It was by that girl – sorry, *woman* – who wrote that book, *The Nothing Man*. Which is a bit ironic, don't you think? She called her book after *her* guy. Suppose she's safe to publicly regret that choice now that it's sold thousands of copies for her.

Would it have sold even half as much if it were called, I don't know, *Several People Who Were Murdered*?

Would it, fuck.

But the Phantom. I mean, come *on*. It sounds like a villain in a Marvel movie. A guy with superhuman powers, abilities that no ordinary man has, because he got accidentally pushed into a nuclear experiment with, I don't know, a fruit-fly or some shite.

And look, I get why that happened. I understand that people want there to be some sort of dark magic involved, because they don't want to think about the ordinariness, the banality, the *availability* of what is. I have no special skills or superpowers. Theoretically anybody could do what I've done, if they wanted to. That's what's really terrifying to people, so they prefer to think that some mysterious force is at work.

But it's just violence.

And speed.

Politeness. Both my own, and my taking advantage of theirs.

I always knew the key to it would be speed. Whatever I did, it had to be quick. A snatch. She couldn't know what was happening until it already had. She'd have to be caught off-guard. Too stunned to cry out or fight back or think about leaving helpful evidence, and in no position to escape from the car. But most importantly, it had to be fast to avoid there being witnesses.

Before I ever did anything, I spent a lot of time thinking about safety. I would ask myself, *When am I safe? When is it OK for me to be seen?*

There's two crucial . . . let's call them *safety zones*.

The first is just before it happens. All there is then is a woman, walking by herself down a road. All is well. All is normal. I'm just a man driving a car that's presumably about to pass her. Nothing to see here.

The second is the first moment after I take her when everything is *back* to looking that way. When it's just me again, driving my car down a road. So long as I'm not speeding or driving erratically, and my face doesn't have any injuries another motorist might see if they pulled up alongside me at a traffic light, and there's nothing odd about the exterior of my vehicle – no bloody streak on the side, no woman pounding on the window in the back, no thumping noise from inside the boot – then I'm OK. I'm safe again.

The key to all this, then, I knew, would be to let as little time lapse between those two points as possible.

Which meant I had to get her into my car as quickly as I could. And locked in there, secure.

But before that, I had to get rid of her phone.

*How is he choosing them?* That's another needless mystery that no one can figure out. I really hope there's some poor guy buried in the bowels of Garda HQ who's been staring at a corkboard of paper scraps and maps and string for months on end, trying to figure out what links my victims. Is it something physical, like how they wear their hair? Or is it something hidden in the patterns of their lives, like how they frequent the same coffee shop or bank branch or gym? Or are they getting so desperate that they're trying to match things up with pagan festivals, or the phases of the moon, or Catholic feast days? Or – God, I'd love this – have they already resorted to bringing in a white witch or a psychic? But it's so simple, actually.

Are you ready for it?

All the women I took were women *whose phones I could see*.

That's it.

That's the connection.

I was out, driving around rural or relatively rural roads, in my dumb car and with no phone, not planning to do anything, not committed to it, but prepared to take advantage if an opportunity presented itself, and then it did. I saw a woman walking close to the road, alone, on a quiet stretch of it, with very little, if any, passing traffic, away from houses and intersections and other people.

And she was holding her phone.

Looking down at it, ideally. Distracted by it.

She has to be shorter than me and skinny, not because I care about how she looks or I have a type or whatever, but so that I can be confident I can physically overpower her and, later on, carry her a distance.

Although . . .

Well, I suppose I *do* have a type, because I like them to be around my own age or a little younger. Not a lot younger, and certainly not young. This isn't *that*, OK? I'm not one of those sickos. One of them was much younger than I thought, actually. Too . . .

She was too young, to be honest with you. When I read her age, later, in the papers, I felt a little . . .

I don't know.

Not great. But I didn't know how old – young – she was. She didn't seem like she was only seventeen, like she'd only just turned that.

If I'd known, I wouldn't have taken her. I swear.

And I didn't know about her dog either. *That* was a bloody surprise. When I first saw her, he was under a hedge, probably taking a shit, and I suppose the lead was hidden on her other side or something.

But it could've been worse. At least he was a small, docile little thing who didn't react at all to his human getting into a strange car and driving away, leaving him behind. He didn't even chase after us, from what I remember.

So, yeah. I have to be able to see her phone, to know where it is *before* I stop. There's going to be no time to dig through her bag or her pockets looking for it, and of course she'll tell me she doesn't have one if I ask, thinking there'll be an opportunity to use it later, or at least to track her location after the fact.

What happens then?

You know, in a weird way, I'm kind of excited to tell you. I've never told anyone this. And with you, of course, things were different, so . . .

Right. So. Here goes.

# Intrusion

When she got home, Lucy stood at the kitchen counter and poured herself a cold glass of white wine. She drank half of it immediately, imagining that she could feel its effects instantaneously, that as it slipped down her throat it was already working to blur the sharp edges of this awful, awful day.

Then she refilled her glass almost to the brim, and carried it into the living room.

Chris was on the couch, watching the opening titles of the evening news. The *proper* evening news, the one with actual, serious journalists, that aired on the kind of channel that wouldn't let the likes of Jack Keane make the tea.

'I just thought there might be an update,' Chris said. 'I can turn it off if you want?'

'No,' she said. 'Leave it on.' She sat down on the

couch beside him as he turned the volume up. 'Let's see what they're saying.'

She almost added *and what's been made public* but she swallowed the words back just in time. She hadn't told Chris anything about today. Not about what Jack Keane had told her, or what had happened at the meeting. As far as he knew, since she'd left the house this morning she'd been at the cafe, listening to music and cleaning. He'd called her phone around six to check where she was, and she didn't have the energy to tell him the truth, then or now.

Lena Paczkowski was the top story.

The male anchor in the studio spoke directly to the camera. 'Gardaí investigating the disappearances of three women from the east of the country are tonight searching a new area in the Wicklow Mountains, having received what they describe as significant new information. A spokesperson said no further details would be provided for operational reasons, but Garda sources quoted in tomorrow's *Irish Times* suggest that detectives have spoken to a possible survivor of an abduction, who told them she'd been in a location where other women were also being held.'

'The news is out, then,' Chris said.

Some *of it is*, Lucy corrected silently.

The screen cut to a shot of rolling fields, while a voiceover by a different man said pretty much the same thing, only with some added colour. '*As the sun sets this evening on the Great Sugarloaf, this car park is, like always, a hive of activity – but on this warm summer's night, there isn't a hillwalker in sight. Instead, dozens of specialist Garda search teams assemble to receive their instructions, ready to search this terrain for any trace of Jennifer Gold, Tana Meehan or Nicola O'Sullivan . . .'*

'She hates being called Nicola,' Lucy muttered.

It was enough of an insult that the media didn't talk about her sister as much as they should, but then, when they did, they didn't call her by her name.

On screen, footage of chains of neon flak-jackets moving across scrubland was replaced by a woman in her fifties walking under some trees on what was clearly the grounds of the RTÉ studios in Donnybrook. She was coiffed and glossed and wearing a pressed linen shirt in a shade of hot pink that reminded Lucy of bubblegum and Barbies, and she was managing to look like she'd naturally been captured out for a stroll instead of asked to walk from point A to point B while a camera filmed her for some 'candid' shots.

'You have got to be fucking kidding me,' Lucy said.

The voiceover returned. *'Margaret Gold's daughter, Jennifer, had just turned seventeen when she went missing only yards from their home in Kilternan, County Dublin, one sunny afternoon last December. Soon after, Operation Tide was established to investigate possible connections between Jennifer's disappearance and those of two other women. But this evening, her mother, Margaret, is calling on authorities to do more.'*

Lucy couldn't actually believe this.

When Chris turned and looked at her, she realized she'd said that out loud.

'What's the problem?' he said. 'Isn't she always giving interviews?'

Margaret was standing still now, facing the camera and holding a large, framed photograph of her daughter dressed for her Debs ball: a strapless black gown, tacky corsage, unimaginative up-do. Her skin was perfect and her hair was shiny and her teeth were straight and white. There was no TikTok-thick make-up, fillers or fake tan on display here. Jennifer was a natural beauty who looked like she was somehow lit up from within.

'Well, yeah,' Lucy said. 'That's just it.'

The sunshine Margaret was walking around in outside the news studio looked low enough to be late afternoon and, at the cafe, she'd said she was on her way to Donnybrook, where the studios were.

*That bitch*, Lucy said silently, then felt bad for thinking it.

'Any attention on any of them is good,' Chris said. 'We just have to think of it that way.'

But Lucy wasn't sure that was true.

'I just want to know where my daughter is,' Margaret was saying on screen, clutching the photo frame tightly. Her fingernails, Lucy noticed, looked as if they'd been professionally done. She hadn't noticed that at the cafe. 'I just want my Jenny home.'

'I'm surprised to see the Debs photo,' Chris said. 'She doesn't use that much.'

They were more used to seeing Jennifer in her school uniform, being presented with a certificate she'd been awarded by the Department of Education for six years of unbroken attendance, meaning she'd never missed a *single* day of secondary school. Or Jennifer holding her Leaving Cert results, a photo which had been taken by a press photographer because she was one of only seven students in her year to achieve a result of eight H1s, and in which her Pioneer pin was also clearly visible. Or Jennifer in athletic shorts and a tank top, her long hair in a ponytail frozen in mid-swish, looking flushed and happy and wearing a medal around her neck.

Either Margaret had no photos of her daughter without some tangible evidence of her exceptional achievement in her hands, or she was out to prove a point with every choice: out of the three, Jennifer was by far the biggest loss. When Lucy had been choosing Nicki's official 'missing' photo, she'd only considered what she'd been told: that it needed to look as close as possible to what Nicki had looked like the last time she'd seen her. The only shot of Nicki's newly purpled hair was a blurry selfie she'd sent Lucy via WhatsApp, so she'd gone with that.

What she *didn't* consider was that that photo would be everything that anyone else knew about her sister: who she was, what she was like. From this single image of one moment, people would extrapolate an entire life. And that photo made Nicki look like a woman who coloured outside the lines, who didn't abide by society's rules, and who might well just decide one day to walk away from it all.

Even the poor quality of the image, the low pixel count, the fact that it blurred whenever it was blown up for an online article or a newspaper page – it suggested an irreality. It helped promote the idea that Nicki just wasn't as vibrant and substantial and *alive* as Jennifer had been and, therefore, not as important.

On screen, the news bulletin moved on to flooding in Pakistan.

'Well,' Chris said, handing Lucy the remote. 'I'm wrecked. I'm going to bed.' He stood up. 'Luce, tonight, please, can you just—'

'I'm not going anywhere,' she said. 'I promise.'

And that was the truth.

'Glad to hear it.' He smiled a little, reached out to squeeze her shoulder. 'Goodnight, then.'

The tenderness of this gesture took Lucy aback and her breath caught in her throat, forcing a splutter that she tried to cover with a cough.

'Ah, yeah,' she said, her eyes watering a little. 'Goodnight.'

She watched him go into the hall, then switched the TV to a channel number she knew by heart.

An episode was just starting.

British Airways 5390, June 1990. Window in the

cockpit blows out at 17,000 feet and sucks the captain out with it. A flight attendant manages to grab the man by his belt and they descend with him outside the aircraft, incredibly landing safely and with him suffering only minor injuries. Cause: the window hadn't been fitted correctly.

She really should've told Chris about Jack and about the meeting. Why hadn't she? There was more to it than her just feeling too tired to: she knew he'd try to talk her out of what she was planning to do tomorrow.

Her Plan B.

And maybe she should let him.

She poured more wine as a second episode began.

Aloha Airlines 243, April 1988. Another explosive decompression, only this one took an eighteen-foot section of the roof from the cockpit to the wing and a flight attendant whose body was never found. Sixty-five other people were injured, eight seriously. Cause: metal fatigue.

Or maybe, before she did anything, she should call Denise. Just be honest. Tell her everything. Ask for her advice.

But then, Denise wasn't being honest with them, was she? She'd held back that detail about the nightdress and the pink house.

As a third episode started, Lucy drained what was left in the bottle into her glass.

Air France 447, June 2009. An Airbus A330 stalls over the Atlantic and then plunges into it, killing all 228 souls on board. By the time the three men in shirtsleeves were gesticulating theatrically at their whiteboard, Lucy was struggling to keep her eyes open.

She finished her wine and lay down on the couch, intending to close her eyes just for a moment.

When she opened them again, it was completely dark.

Lucy felt woozy and disorientated, and it took her a beat to remember where she was and how she'd got there: an exceptionally shite day, a whole bottle of wine on an empty stomach and at least three episodes of *Air Crash Investigation*. She'd fallen asleep on the couch, but how long ago? The TV had turned itself off – she didn't know it even did that; it hadn't before – and it was deathly quiet, and she was a little cold, and everything just felt . . .

Different, somehow.

She sat up and patted the surface of the coffee table for her phone. Its screen lit the room with an eerie blue glow, telling her it was 2:03 a.m.

She'd been asleep for a couple of hours, three at the most.

Jack Keane had sent her a text at 00:23 a.m. *Only saw your message now. Can't promise anything but I'll run it by my boss. Call me first thing and we'll discuss.* Caroline had sent her one just before ten. *Sorry about today. Saw MG on the news. I shouldn't be shocked but . . . JFC. You OK? What's your plan now? Let me know if I can help.* She swiped the notifications away, making a mental note to respond to them in the morning.

Lucy stood up, waited a beat for the room to stop spinning, and then went to the wall to switch on the ceiling light. Its bright glow turned off the dark, instantly vaporizing the shadows, but still, even now, there was something that just wasn't right, something that had caught on her subconscious . . .

But what?

She scanned the room, picturing it from earlier, from before she'd fallen asleep, and compared the two. A real-life game of Spot the Difference.

And then it came to her: the light.

She hadn't been sitting here in the dark, but it hadn't been this bright either. The floor lamp had been on, and so had the lights in the kitchen.

But now, both were off.

They'd been *turned* off, while she slept.

*Chris*, Lucy thought, reaching to collect her empty wine glass and the empty wine bottle from the coffee table. He must have woken up at some stage, heard that the TV was still on, and come down to turn it and the lights off.

That's all.

She went into the kitchen, flicked the lights on in there. Put the empty glass into the dishwasher. Left the bottle by the back door so she'd remember to put it in the recycling bin first thing. Turned the lights off again. Went back into the living room.

But still, something felt off.

She scanned the room once more and, this time, caught a ripple of movement behind the curtains, the floor-length ones that hung across the patio doors.

*What the . . . ?*

For one moment, Lucy was paralysed with pure, abject terror, convinced that someone was hiding behind the curtain, that an intruder had gained access to the house, that something terrible was about to happen—

But in the next, an explanation came to her.

*The patio door was open.*

She and Chris had started doing that in the evenings lately, since it was so warm outside: opening the sliding door a few inches to let the air into the room, but pulling the curtain across it to stop moths flying in.

Lucy rolled her eyes as she crossed the room to yank back the curtain before her imagination had a chance to overtake her again, and saw that she was right: it *was* open, but only a few inches.

She slid it closed, pushing the latch on the handle down so it locked, too.

She should get a glass of water, she thought, and find something with paracetamol in it to take before she went to bed. She couldn't have a hangover tomorrow. She needed her wits about her, for what she was planning.

She went back into the kitchen, got a glass and started filling it from the tap in the sink. Her gaze drifted upwards, to the window directly in front of her.

And then something very strange happened.

Her reflection moved, but she didn't.

Jesus, how quickly did she drink that wine? She shouldn't be drinking at all with everything that was going on. It wasn't safe. It wasn't smart.

And then she realized—

*There was someone standing outside the kitchen window.*

A figure dressed in dark clothing with something on its head. A baseball cap. Or a hood. Or both.

Lucy caught the scream that was about to launch itself out of her throat and told herself no, no, it couldn't be, it was just shadows, it was too much wine and not enough food, it was the patio door's curtains all over again.

The glass in her hand was overflowing now and she let it drop into the sink and reached instead for the light switch on the wall.

*Click.*

The inside and out swapped places. Now the kitchen was dark and the back garden was bright, because the light over the back door was on.

And there was still a man on the other side of the glass.

Facing *in*.

Staring right at her.

Lucy finally let the scream out and he turned and ran.

# Lines of Enquiry

Angela watched the clock mounted on the wall high above the door to the Missing Persons Unit as it ticked towards three o'clock. She looked at the door to the MPU, willing Detective Denise Pope to come walking through it. Then looked back at the clock.

This was the longest day she had ever had at work, maybe even in her entire life.

The problem was, Denise hadn't actually said anything yesterday about whether or not Angela would get to continue to work the Kerry Long case today. Denise hadn't said anything at all. She'd stopped the car at a red light near the Luas stop in Carrickmines and said to Angela, 'You'll be all right getting back from here, won't you?' and then driven off before Angela could ask any questions of her own.

She'd managed to kill a good chunk of the morning

by creating a spreadsheet with the address of every charity shop, clothing bank and vintage store she could find in Dublin and its surrounding counties. She'd typed up a letter explaining that the Missing Persons Unit was appealing for reports on any personal items found in bags or other women's accessories that may have been donated, and to be on the lookout for them going forward. She wouldn't do anything until she got permission, and she didn't want to ask Don for it until she was sure she wouldn't get an opportunity to ask Denise, but having everything ready to go at least felt like doing *something*.

Now, Angela drummed her fingers on the desk.

'Don't you've anything you could be doing over there?' Don called from the back of the room. 'Because if you're looking for something, I've got a cup of tea you could make.'

*Good question*, Angela thought.

*Was* there something she could be doing? Something *else*?

She took out her phone and swiped through the photos she'd taken of Kerry Long's things, stopping when she got to the Q-Park ticket. She didn't think it was Kerry's, but she did think it could belong to the person who'd owned the bag, which she didn't think was Kerry's either. It was stamped with the address of the Stephen's Green car park and the time and date – 11:02 a.m. on 3 March 2018 – in small black type, alongside what must be some reference numbers and a barcode.

152

The car park itself was only a few minutes' walk from Harcourt Square, but Angela figured it was wiser to ring the company rather than visit the facility itself. She had a much better chance of someone believing she had any authority if she was only speaking to them on the phone. She found a number for Q-Park Ireland's head office online and called it to try her luck.

'Ah, hi,' she said when someone answered. 'My name is Angela Fitzgerald and I'm calling from the Gardaí's Missing Persons Unit in Harcourt Square.' Which was all true. If someone mistook her for a guard, that wasn't her fault. 'I'm wondering if you can help me with something. We have a ticket here for your Stephen's Green car park that may be relevant to one of our cases. Is there any way to get a registration number or a name or debit card info from that ticket?'

The woman on the other end said, 'Well, that depends. What's the date on it?'

'March 2018.'

'Oh no,' she said with a little laugh. 'Not a chance. Since GDPR came in, we have to delete everything after eleven days.'

'So there's no way?'

'No way at all, no.'

'No way to do what?' a new voice said.

Angela turned to see Denise sitting down in the chair of the unoccupied desk directly behind hers. She thanked the woman on the phone and ended the call, and tried not to look too pleased that Denise was here.

'That was Q-Park,' Angela explained. 'I called them to see if the parking ticket we found in the bag could give us any information about the car's owner.'

'With data protection laws, not a hope,' Denise said. 'Not for something that far back. But good thinking.' She pointed at the open Word document on screen. 'And that?'

'Oh. Well, I had an idea—' Angela started.

'To ask charity shops to tell us if they find any wallets or keys or anything like that, in case there's more out there belonging to the other women, waiting to be found?'

'Um . . . Yes.'

Angela's sense of pride at having thought of it was already draining away.

'They already do,' Denise said. 'Effectively. Most people who find lost wallets either try to get in contact with the owner, or hand them in to their local station. As your friend from the charity shop did yesterday.'

'Oh,' Angela said, minimizing the letter on screen. 'Right.'

'And I'm sure if any of our three families had been contacted about something like that, they'd have told us. Likewise if something arrived at a station.'

'What about the public? Is there any point trying to get a message to them, like through the media or something?'

Denise shook her head. 'There's no need. The names and pictures of these missing women have been plastered all over the place for over six months. If a member of the public came across something like a wallet or an ID card or a keychain with one of their names on it, they'd tell us. And if they wouldn't, we're not going to make it happen with an appeal.' Denise paused. 'But you know what? You do have a point on the charity shops. They could have donations they haven't sorted through yet. We could ask that, if they have unsorted stock and they have the time, they go through it. But the thing is, we couldn't do this officially. If Colin the Showboat found out, I'd be in trouble. If you want to take a piss on this op, you have to ask him first. Which is why I have you.'

'Me?' Angela frowned. 'What difference does that make?'

'You found the bag. You told your boss about it. Your boss told me – not officially; it just came up in conversation' – Denise winked – 'and I offered to help you out, because Don let you run with it a bit, because you want to be an actual guard and not just a paper-pusher with clearance. We're not investigating the missing women, Angela. We're just taking a closer look at a three-year-old missing person report no one else gave a shit about, who may or may not turn out to be one Operation Tide missed.'

'I see.' Angela was feeling more and more deflated by the minute. 'Yeah.'

'But,' Denise said, 'we *could* do a social-media appeal. Maybe. Community Facebook groups, Twitter, etc.

That kind of thing. But not one that links to us directly. We'd have to give it to someone else, a civilian, to post it and get the ball rolling.'

'Like who?'

'I might have just the person, actually. Caroline O'Callaghan.'

Angela frowned. 'Why do I know that name?'

'She was a friend of Tana Meehan's,' Denise said. 'Actually, she was the one who positively identified her at the bus stop in Kildare town that night. When the cases got joined up, she became a sort of *de facto* organizer for the families. Tana's parents aren't up to it, and Roland Kearns can hardly chip in, so it all sorta worked out. She's a bit of a busybody, but she'd be useful to us on this. Do you have a Gmail account?'

Angela nodded.

'And that's just in Word, is it?'

Angela nodded again.

'Recreate it on your home computer and send it from your own email to hers. Here, take this down.' Denise had been scrolling on her phone while she talked, and now it was showing a contact for *Caroline O'C (Tana M)* along with an address and phone number. Angela hurried to copy the information on to the nearest piece of blank paper she had on her desk. 'But wait until after I speak to her, OK? No offence, but we can't have some rando civilian ringing her up about this. I'll explain everything first, so she'll be expecting you.'

The contact information abruptly disappeared from

the screen, because the phone was pulsing with an incoming call from DUNDRUM.

'Hang on,' she said, rolling her eyes.

Angela did her best to finish scribbling down the contact info from memory. She might double-check it again later.

'Yeah?' Denise said, having put the phone to her ear.

The only people in the MPU were Angela, Denise, Don and another civilian Garda staff member, and he and Don were at Don's desk at the back of the room, talking in low voices about a folder that was open in front of them. There was no radio, no key-clacking and no one else talking, so it was quiet enough for Angela to hear the other half of Denise's phone conversation clearly.

'*Hey, can you talk?*' A male voice.

Denise made a face at Angela as if to say, *This fucking guy*. 'I wouldn't have answered if the answer was no, DFS Dineen.'

'*Lucy O'Sullivan called 999 last night to report an intruder in the garden. A man dressed all in black, she said.*'

'Did he have a press pass?'

A snort on the line. '*If he did, he didn't flash it.*'

'Please tell me he didn't flash anything else . . .'

'*She said he was outside the kitchen window looking in, watching her, but he ran away when she saw him.*'

'What time was this?' Denise asked.

'*Ah, around two.*'

'I take it she didn't recognize him?'

'*It doesn't say she did, no.*'

'I take it we sent around some uniforms?'

'*They didn't find anything. Some scuff marks on the fence. There's no side access there, so he'd have had to go through the neighbour's garden to get to her.*'

'All right,' Denise said. 'Probably just some teenager on a dare. I'll give her a call later. Hey, is the sale still on?'

'*Fuck off.*'

She laughed to herself and then ended the call.

'Everything OK?' Angela asked, even though she'd heard the entire conversation. It seemed like the polite thing to do to pretend she hadn't.

'Someone was in Lucy O'Sullivan's back garden last night, apparently. A man dressed all in black. Any time there's news in this case, the looney tunes come out to play.'

'What's a DFS? I don't think I've heard of that rank before . . . ?'

Denise frowned. 'What?'

'You called that guy DFS Dineen.'

'It's not a rank,' she said, laughing. 'It's a furniture shop. The place that sells sofas? The one with the interminable sale?'

Angela was following this about as well as the *Jurassic Park* reference.

'It's his nickname,' Denise explained. 'Because he has zero per cent interest. In the job. Get it?'

'*Oh*. Yeah, that's . . . That's funny.'

'Come on, then,' Denise said, standing up. 'I need to go see Mr Roland Kearns, and Don says that I can take you with me.'

Denise took them off the M50 at an exit promising a place Angela had never heard of. The slip road didn't just take them off the motorway, but all the way back to 2008, the year the Celtic Tiger choked and died, to what was surely supposed to have been just the first phase of an entirely new community, full of hopes and dreams and overstretched mortgage-payers, but which, in the economic carnage that followed, never made it past that.

Enormous apartment blocks, apparently inspired by the Soviet era, towered behind rows of tiny, boxy houses, glued together in never-ending rows without so much as a grassy verge between their driveways, on a bleak, desolate landscape of burnt grass, weeds and bare soil. To get to them, you had to pass a U-shaped retail park that, at first glance, looked completely empty but, on second, at least had an Aldi. A huge flag-like sign lied that the other units represented a PRIME RETAIL OPPORTUNITY! as it flapped in the wind, its end ripped and fraying.

'It's pretty bleak, isn't it?' Denise said, glancing at her. 'There's a place up the country where they house post-release sex offenders in an effort to rehabilitate them, and it looks just like this.'

'Lovely,' Angela said and Denise laughed.

They were driving deep into the development, to the

apartment blocks at the rear. On the right, they passed an upturned washing machine that someone had just left on a corner.

'Actually, I used to work with a guy who lived here. A detective. Well, *former* detective now. Ever hear of the Canal Killer case?'

Angela nodded. 'Yeah, of course.'

You could count Ireland's confirmed serial killers on one hand, even if you'd been in some traumatic vegetable-chopping accident, and the Canal Killer was one of them. He'd targeted students at St John's College on the south side of the city, knocking them unconscious before leaving them to drown in the muddy waters of the Grand Canal.

'He was on it,' Denise said. 'Helped solve it, basically. Remember the ex-girlfriend? Alison Smith? Well, they're married now.'

Angela raised her eyebrows. 'Really?'

'Hence former detective. And, luckily for him, former resident of this shithole.' She cut the engine. 'I think they live abroad.'

Denise had parked outside the block furthest from the entrance. She got out of the car and walked to its main door, and Angela followed her. There was a high-tech-looking intercom system with a digital display and lots of buttons, but someone had taped a hand-written note over it: BROKEN.

When Denise pushed a hand against the door, it swung open easily.

'It's been broken for weeks,' she said. 'We'll just go upstairs and knock.'

They got into the lift, which smelled of spilt milk and had a streak of something wet and brown in the corner.

Denise jabbed the button for the third floor and then turned to Angela.

'Now look,' she said. 'This time, I can't tell you not to say anything. You're going to have to say *something*. He'll address you directly. Try to get you to engage. He'll think he's charming you. You can respond if he does. You should. Talk to him like you would anyone else. The more you talk to this guy, the more *he* talks, and the more he talks, the more likely he is to say something he shouldn't.'

The lift doors opened again and Denise started leading them down the hall. Its carpet was dotted with unidentifiable stains and the track marks of bicycle tyres criss-crossed the magnolia walls.

'I'll introduce you as a trainee,' Denise continued. 'He doesn't know how things work; he'll buy it. But he'll also assume that you don't know shit.'

*Which I don't*, Angela thought.

'Which you don't,' she added. 'Not yet, anyway.'

They stopped outside a door with a 27 on it.

As Denise knocked, it occurred to Angela that you would only be hoping someone would say something they shouldn't if you thought they'd been holding back until now.

Or lying.

'Do you think he did it?' Angela whispered, just as the door opened, quickly and with a flourish, as if Roland Kearns had been standing on the other side, waiting for them.

He looked just like he did whenever Angela had seen him in the press repeatedly protesting that he was innocent of the crime no one had ever charged him with: tall and broad-shouldered, physically imposing, with a full head of jet-black hair which he'd let grow until it was almost touching his shoulders. He was exceptionally attractive, and smiling now, friendly and looking pleasantly surprised to see them on his doorstep, even though the smile didn't seem to reach his eyes.

'Denise!' he said, as if a detective involved in the investigation into his wife's disappearance was an old, beloved friend. 'To what do I owe the pleasure?' Before she could answer, he turned his attention to Angela – *all* of his attention, his gaze laser-focused on her. 'And who's this?' He extended a hand. 'I don't believe we've met?'

Angela shook it limply, half expecting him to lift it to his lips for a kiss.

'This is my colleague Angela,' Denise said. 'She's in training with the Missing Persons Unit. Do you mind if we come in?'

'Never,' Roland said warmly, and stepped back so they could.

The interior of the apartment was furnished in the

Uninspired Single Man Special of beech-effect flat-pack, classic framed movie poster (*Goodfellas*), glass-and-chrome coffee table that didn't go with anything else, and a glossy black leather couch and matching armchairs that were patently too big for the space.

But it was clean and neat, not too warm thanks to the balcony doors being wide open, and it smelled better than the building's common areas.

'Can I get you lovely ladies anything?' Roland asked. To Angela, 'This is where Denise will insist that all she wants in this world is a glass of tepid tap water, but I have a very good coffee machine with lots of buttons on it, if I can interest you in a cup?'

'We're fine, thank you,' Denise said.

'I'm fine, thanks,' Angela chimed in, even though she was thirsty.

'Not even water today?' Roland put a hand to his chest in mock shock. 'It *must* be serious.'

He waved them towards the couch and took a seat himself on one of the armchairs, reclining, relaxed, folding one leg over the other. His socks, Angela noted, had little cartoon ice creams on them.

'So, what's up?' he said to Denise.

'I just wanted to check in,' she said.

Roland raised an eyebrow. 'Twice in two days?'

'Well, I was passing. We're just on our way back from Wexford.' Denise flashed a look at Angela that said, *Just go with it.* Presumably she was pretending their trip had been today and not yesterday so she could casually bring it up in conversation. 'Aren't we, Angela?'

Angela nodded. 'Yep.'

Now Roland seemed bemused. 'Oh?'

'Just outside of Enniscorthy,' Denise said. 'Lovely area.'

Very deliberately, Roland brought his hand up and looked at his watch.

'You've been to Enniscorthy and back already today? Gosh, you must have started off *very* early.'

'We did. And we got lucky with the traffic.'

'How lovely for you both.' Roland looked to Angela. 'Are you having a nice day?'

He asked it in the same tone you'd ask a child if they were looking forward to Christmas. Angela's skin felt like it was in the process of detaching itself from her soft tissue and rotating one-eighty degrees around her body.

Thankfully, Denise asked him, 'Ever been?' before she had to answer.

Roland laughed, then wagged a finger at her in playful reprimand. 'Now, now, now, Miss Denise. That sounds like something you'd have to ask in a formal interview.' He turned up his palms, looked around, feigned confusion. 'Is *this* a formal interview?'

'So you *have* been to Enniscorthy?' Her tone was getting sharper,

'Is this how you talk to all your charges?'

'I'm just asking, Ro.'

*Ro*, Angela noted. He looked pleased that she'd

called him that, not because it was friendly or familiar, but because it meant she needed something from him and was buttering him up to try to get it, that he had the upper hand.

'What about Ballinteer Road?' Denise asked. 'Ever been there?'

Roland did a pantomime frown. 'Where's that?'

'Dundrum.'

'If it's near the shopping centre, then quite possibly. Why?'

'Lucy O'Sullivan had an intruder in her garden last night,' Denise said. 'Or very early this morning.'

'Oh.' Roland smiled, satisfied. 'Oh, I *see*. But you're just here to check in.' To Angela, 'This woman can't lie for shit.'

'I don't know what you mean, Roland,' Denise said evenly. 'Lucy O'Sullivan *did* report an intruder in her garden last night. I'm here to check you haven't had any similar trouble. It's this Lena Paczkowski news, of course. It churns everything up again. Gets out all the crazies. And you're such a recognizable face, it wouldn't surprise me if some of them came your way. Has there been any strange or nuisance activity that you'd like to report? Did you notice anyone outside your property last night?'

Denise and Roland held each other's gaze for an uncomfortably long moment.

Then he said, 'I was too busy in here to notice anything out there. Do you want her number?'

What Angela wanted, at this juncture, was a shower. If not a power-wash.

'That won't be necessary,' Denise said.

Roland's face changed then, into a genuine frown, and when he spoke again, his tone was totally different.

The smarm was gone.

'Could it have been a woman?' he asked. 'This intruder?'

Denise hesitated. 'Possibly . . . Why?'

He stood up and went to the window, stuck his hands in his pockets and looked out. If you ignored the boulevard of broken dreams and abandoned washing machines and focused on the green hills rising up behind them, Angela thought, the view actually wasn't that bad.

'What is it, Ro?' Denise said.

A long beat passed before he responded.

'Maybe it was Caroline,' he said without turning around. 'The intruder in Lucy's back garden.'

Angela thought, *Who the hell is Caroline?*

'Caroline *O'Callaghan*?' It was clear from Denise's tone that she thought this was a preposterous suggestion.

Angela remembered now: the friend of Tana Meehan's who helped out with the families. That was the woman she was going to email her charity-shop appeal to once Denise had had the chance to explain their plan to her.

'That woman is unhinged.' Roland came and retook

his seat on the armchair, but the reclining was gone. Now he was sitting forward, elbows resting on his thighs. 'I've told you before: she's obsessed with me. She's convinced I killed Tana and that she'll be the one to prove it.' To Angela, 'It wasn't me, for the record. Yes, we fought and, yes, I didn't want the divorce and, yes, a couple of times things got heated. But' – back to Denise – 'that doesn't mean I killed her, so maybe you should go *just check in* on Crazy Caroline and tell her that.'

'Yes,' Denise said, sounding bored, as if this was a rant she had heard from him many times before. 'But what does that have to do with someone being in Lucy O'Sullivan's garden?'

'Because Caroline has been hanging around here. She parks her car outside' – he pointed towards the balcony – 'and she just sits in it all night, watching me. A couple of nights ago, I got up at, like, I don't know, three or four, to take a piss, and I saw someone standing out there, completely still, just, like, looking up at my window.'

'And you think it was Caroline?'

'Who else would it be? She's a bloody nutjob. And maybe it's not just me she's doing that to. Maybe she's watching all the families.'

Denise and Angela exchanged a glance.

'What?' he said. 'You don't believe me?'

'OK,' Denise said. She stood up, then jerked her chin at Angela, motioning for her to get up too. 'I'll have a chat with Caroline about this—'

Roland looked surprised. 'Really?'

'—and see what she says, but in the meantime, if you see anyone you don't recognize hanging around outside, you should report it.'

Roland narrowed his eyes at her, suspicious.

He probably should be, because Angela didn't think for one second Denise had any intention of actually bringing that accusation to Caroline.

Denise and Angela went to the front door; Roland followed them.

'Thanks for all your help,' Denise said pleasantly. 'Don't forget to call me if you need anything.'

'Ah, nice to meet you,' Angela said.

'It was a pleasure to meet you,' Roland said, meeting her eye. 'Until next time.'

Neither of them said anything until they were back in the lift and the doors had slid closed in front of them.

'Jesus Christ,' Angela said, exhaling deeply. 'What a creep.'

'He'd love that you said that. That's what he wants. To unnerve people. Fucking prick.' Denise rolled her eyes. 'And that car wasn't Caroline, it was *us*. He's been under surveillance. But his ego is so enormous that he's insisting it must be his missing wife's friend who's quote-unquote *obsessed* with him.'

'What about that figure he said he saw the night before last?'

'That's just plain old bullshit.'

The lift doors opened.

'He doesn't like Caroline,' Denise went on as they exited the building. 'I would go so far as to say he hates her. He thinks she's the one who turned Tana's parents against him. When Tana was alive, he had a great relationship with them. Because of course he turned on the charm. They probably never met the real Roland. They were shocked when Tana announced she'd left him, and I don't think she told them the real reason why. They heard it after she disappeared, presumably from friends of hers – but he's convinced it was Caroline who told them.' Denise rolled her eyes. 'And not the whole, you know, his relishing being a suspect in whatever did happen to their daughter.'

They were at the car now, and as Angela reached for the passenger door, something occurred to her.

'You never said it was the back garden.'

Denise stopped too. 'What?'

'You never said it was the back garden an intruder had been in, but he did. Was it?'

'It was outside the kitchen window, so yeah . . . it was.' She frowned. 'But then, I suppose that's an easy assumption to make.'

'Maybe,' Angela said.

They both got into the car.

'What did you think of him – apart from being a creep?' Denise asked.

'I think he's a sociopath,' Angela said confidently. 'A narcissist.'

'He's definitely that.' She started the engine and put the car in gear. 'And if he was physically abusive to his wife, that makes him a violent one. But he has an alibi for Jennifer Gold. So if he did kill Tana – which no one has been able to prove one way or the other yet – that means she isn't connected to the other cases, and if he didn't, he doesn't have anything to do with this at all.' Denise turned to look at her. 'So yeah, he's a bloody sociopath, but is he the sociopath *we're* looking for?'

# Valley of Silence

She has to be walking against the traffic so she's facing me but when I pull up beside her, she's on the passenger side of the car. A couple of times I've seen someone and considered driving on, swinging around and coming back so she'll be in the correct position, but I've never actually done that yet.

I stop, roll down my window and call out to her, 'Sorry – do you live around here, by any chance?'

Already, the clock is ticking.

Five seconds gone.

There is a car stopped in the road with a man behind its wheel alongside a woman who is about to disappear. Anyone who passes by and sees us could, potentially, retain enough information in their brain to lead the Gardaí straight to my door, starting with my licence plate. Someone who knows her could arrive upon us, making it what they call a 'positive sighting', one that everyone is certain is actually of her. They could even stop to say hi, forcing an end to our conversation, so that the next time I pull over on the side of the road to snatch a woman whose phone I can see, this woman will have a story to tell about a man who stopped alongside her a few weeks or months ago, and then *she* could be the one who leads the Gardaí to me.

It's the riskiest part of the whole endeavour. I have to move fast.

Whatever she says, or ideally before she can say anything, I go straight in with a, 'Do you know where Meadow Park is, by any chance?' Or Riverstick Road. Or Lakeview Lane. I just make something up. And she'll say no, she doesn't, because it doesn't exist, and then I'll shake my head and say something like, 'I'm going to be in so much trouble. My phone is dead so I'm just going off my wife's directions, and I was supposed to be there half an hour ago with the cake.'

And then I jerk my head towards the back seat.

Twenty seconds gone, if I'm lucky.

Remember how I said it was like swimming in the sea? That you don't go every time but you're ready to go any time? That you keep all your swimming gear in a bag in the boot?

Well, this is *my* swimming gear:

A glossy white cardboard box, the kind a cake comes in.

A waxed carrier bag from a well-known, high-end

department store with some tissue paper sticking up out of it.

A bouquet of flowers. Plastic, artificial flowers, but a mere glance at them isn't going to tell you that.

When I'm out on my drives, Amy thinks I'm at the gym, or gone for a hillwalk, or with my astronomy club (that last one is very useful for night-time excursions). That's what I tell her, and that's why – she thinks – I keep a black gym bag in the boot of my car. If she ever unzipped it, she'd find things like thermals, muddy trainers, waterproofs. But if she kept digging, underneath all that, she'd find the empty white box and the department-store bag, packed flat, and, underneath *them*, the bouquet of plastic blooms.

I stop in the car park of our local Aldi to take them out of the bag and set them up in the back seat – not because I'm planning to do anything, remember, but so I'll be ready if I decide to, if the right opportunity presents itself.

If it doesn't, I stop somewhere else to put them back.

I used to do it in the driveway before I left home at all, until one day Amy belatedly remembered that she needed me to pick up some milk and came hurrying out to say so. I had only *just* managed to get my jacket thrown over them when she reached my window.

Close one, that.

Although I'm sure I could've come up with something. I mean, it wasn't exactly a bunch of cable-ties and a crowbar.

You women aren't as trusting or naive as you once were, you see. Thanks to all those bloody documentaries and true-crime podcasts, you've wised up. You know now that men like me love to use your own sweet and generous natures against you, that we'll rely on your manners and pleasantness and your being nice, and prey on your fear that the absolute worst thing someone could accuse you of is being a bitch. And you know that serial killers love to pretend to need help, like Bundy and his plaster casts. So there has to be something in the car – in the back seat, so it's not overtly obvious – that telegraphs, somehow, that I'm not that guy.

Baby paraphernalia was an obvious choice. A baby seat. Baby toys. A 'forgotten' bottle or one of those stupid stick-figure baby-on-board signs, or maybe even a family photo tacked to the dashboard because, gosh, I'm just so in love with my family I need to be able to see their faces *all the time*, even when I'm driving the car and should really have my eyes on the road. But a baby seat is not only a tricky thing to hide, it's impossible to explain to your wife when you and she don't have any children.

And what I realized is that, actually, that's trying to solve the wrong problem.

What I needed to do wasn't to convince the women that I was a good family man and so would never hurt them – especially seeing as good family men hurt people all the time, sometimes even members of their own family – but that I was really doing what I *appeared* to be doing, what I said I was: asking for directions to a place I should've already been at.

I had to make it seem like I was, genuinely, in a hurry to get to a party.

And I knew exactly what to use.

We'll get to why I did.

But back to the roadside. She's standing there, holding her phone, and her gaze has travelled into the back seat. She's taking in the cake box. The birthday present that might be in that bag. The flowers, perhaps for the hostess.

Twenty-five seconds gone.

There's a *Collins Road Map of Ireland 2017* in the pocket of the driver's door. It's always there, folded neatly, and I grab it as I get out of the car. 'They wrote down some directions for me,' I say as I make my way around the bonnet to her, 'but I can't make head nor tail of it . . .'

Thirty seconds gone if this, so far, has gone well.

But another car could come along at any moment. The longer one doesn't, the more likely it is that one will in the next.

She might wait for me to get to her, to show her what I have in my hand, what I've implied are the written directions. Or she might say, 'Why don't you give me the address and I'll look it up for you?' Or she might apologize and say she has to go and maybe even take a step or two away, but there's no abort button here.

We can't demote her from victim to witness. From the moment I stopped the car there was no choice but to follow through, so I ignore whatever she's said and hold out the map and while her attention is on it, I move.

Fast.

I bring my forearm up, connecting with her arm from underneath, knocking the phone out of her hand and sending it flying so it lands several feet away with a satisfying *crack*. I never actually touch the thing, so no prints. Before she has a chance to react – to her, it probably seems simultaneous – I bring up my other arm so I can put a hand behind her head and then I slam it as hard as I can into the side of the car, so she goes face-first into it. I aim for the part of the chassis just above the door, right at the curve of the roof. That, I've found, is the sweet spot. She's stunned now and almost certainly bleeding too, and I only have two or three seconds before her vision returns and the white, hot pain that's all she knows subsides enough to let some coherent thoughts in, one of which will be, *I'm in trouble here.*

Open the back door. Push her inside, on to the items that convinced her I wasn't a man who would do this, along with any bag she might have over her shoulder or be wearing across her torso on a strap. Close the door. Wipe any bloodstains off the passenger side of the car with my sleeve. Pick the map up off the ground along with any shoes that came off and put them in the boot as I walk around it.

On the driver's side now, open the rear door there and punch her several times on the side of the head. Take the nearest seatbelt and wind it around her wrists as many times as it will go, and then either tie it to another belt or clip it into the buckle, whatever's at the intersection of speed and function.

Close that door.

Get back into the driver's seat and go.

Sixty seconds gone, on a good day.

I know what you're thinking. What if she screams? Or what if she gets into her bag and is able to scratch you with her keys? And what about the blood she's leaving all over your back seat?

All fair, but also beside the point.

Remember, I'm not trying to commit the perfect crime here. There is no such thing. I'm only trying to delay the getting caught for as long as possible, to fit in as many summit attempts as I can before my luck runs out and I succumb to altitude sickness and perish in the Death Zone. So separating her from her phone, getting her into the car, doing it quickly enough to minimize the chances of someone seeing us . . .

That's good *enough*.

We have a ways to go yet, though, she and I, so the next thing is to find somewhere to pull in – a lay-by, a boreen leading into some forestry, a badly lit and empty car park – so I can transfer her from the back seat to the boot and ensure she's secure there for the rest of the journey.

Secure *and* quiet.

Which I do.

See? No superpowers required.

Of course, with you, tonight, it was different. You made it easy for me. All I needed to do to get you in my car was call out your name.

When the next night brought no break in the heat, it broke *her*, and she decided to break the rules. In that moment, it felt like the consequences could not be as bad as continuing to feel like this, like she was sitting in front of an open, blasting hot oven.

As quietly as she could, she got to her feet and manoeuvred her way around the sleeping bodies on the floor. She was barefoot and dressed only in her underwear; it was too hot to wear anything else inside this furnace. She moved in what she hoped was the direction of the door, keeping a hand outstretched in front of her, waiting for it to meet something solid.

She felt the stone first, unexpectedly cool, and then, a few steps to the left, the smooth wood of the door. She pushed on it before she could panic herself with the idea that he might have locked it from the outside.

But he knew he didn't need to lock it.

They all did whatever he said.

Until now.

A whisper from the dark. 'Where are you going?'

And then another. 'If he catches you . . .'

No one was sleeping in here, she realized. It shouldn't have come as a surprise. In this heat, how could anyone possibly?

'I'll be right back,' she said.

'Will you get some water?'

In her mind, she pictured their surroundings as they looked during the day. Turning left out of the cabin would bring her on to the path that led through the trees to the lake. It would be difficult to navigate in the dark but the worst thing that could happen was that she'd fall over.

The route to the tap, however, was to the right, down a steep incline and through an obstacle of gates and fencing, outbuildings and a series of steps badly built out of railway sleepers – and it went right past where *he* slept.

Wasn't this risky enough without risking waking him?

'I'll try,' she said, not meaning it.

And then she slipped outside, into the night.

# Promises

The two uniformed Gardaí who had arrived to check the house and take a statement from Lucy about the intruder hadn't ended up leaving again until well after 3:00 a.m. Chris *had* left the patio door open a few inches, it turned out, and he *had* come downstairs to switch off the lights and TV at some point, but there had also been a strange man outside the kitchen window.

They had physical evidence: in his hasty retreat, the shadowman had knocked over one of the pots in the house-plant graveyard Lucy had been assembling on the ground directly below the window.

Even though she and Chris had checked that everything was locked, and even though he had suggested that they sleep in the same room for the night, or what was left of it – the box room, which still housed the bunk beds Lucy and Nicki had shared when they were kids – Lucy hadn't been able to fall asleep until long after the sun had started to make its way over the horizon.

She was exhausted, even more so than usual, and not at all in the mood when Chris suggested they go for a drive. But he wouldn't take no for an answer. He was adamant that she needed to get out, to clear her head, to gulp down some fresh air.

But as they joined the hazy snake of slow-moving cars escaping the city southbound, all Lucy breathed in were hot exhaust fumes. Chris hadn't said he was heading anywhere in particular, and as the road began to rise, she thought for one crazy moment he was driving her to the scene, to the spot where Lena Paczkowski had reappeared. But he drove past the relevant turn-off and up higher into the hills, choosing the more elevated route at every crossroads, until eventually they found themselves at the peak of a sweeping landscape of rolling, sun-scorched mountains dwarfed beneath a dome of perfect cornflower-blue sky. Even the city was hidden from them up here.

They could've been the last two people on earth.

Chris pulled over, parking on the side of the road. He'd had the radio on since they'd left the house, tuned to a station that only used voices to intro songs, read out requests and promise they'd be back to intro more songs and read out more requests after the break, but when he cut the engine, it died too, plunging them into silence.

'Let's get out,' he said. 'Stretch our legs.'

He did that and, even though Lucy didn't feel like it, she followed suit. They met at the front of the car, rested themselves side by side against the bonnet.

No longer framed by the parameters of the windscreen, the landscape was even more impressive. Infinite, it seemed. Edgeless and endless.

It started to make Lucy feel a little light-headed. She wasn't used to this much . . .

This *much*.

For the last year, she realized now, her world had been steadily, physically shrinking. She rarely went anywhere that wasn't the cafe, her house or the supermarket.

'Isn't it beautiful?' Chris said.

She nodded. It truly was.

Then Chris ruined it by saying, 'Ah, look, Lucy . . .' in a tone that said he was gearing up to say something that would make them both uncomfortable.

Lucy sucked in a breath and held it, braced. They were standing side by side, leaning against the car.

No part of him was touching any part of her but she could feel him, feel the static charge in the few inches of clear air between his side and hers.

She had no idea what he was about to say, but when he said—

'I'm moving out.'

—she thought she'd misheard him.

'I don't want to leave you on your own,' he said, 'but I can't . . . I need to start moving on. Forwards.'

Her chest tightened, a ripple of panic.

'I've been offered a job in Amsterdam,' Chris went on. 'Manager of a new Irish bar that's opening in January. I know the owner, I used to work with him, and he knows I need . . . Well, he knows I could do with a fresh start. He wants me by December first, at the very latest. And I think I'm going to go.'

She said, 'Oh,' because she had to say something and that was the shortest thing she could think of.

'That way, you know, you can sell the house and not have to worry about where I'm going to go.' A pause. 'One less thing for you to deal with.'

'Yeah,' she said, because it was as short as *oh*.

Was he doing this for her, to lessen her burden? That somehow made it even worse. Because this wasn't what she wanted. But how could she say that? What reason would she give? And wasn't it totally unfair of her to ask her missing sister's boyfriend to stick around a bit longer just so *two* lives could be in complete limbo?

'You're disappointed in me,' Chris said.

Lucy shook her head, because she knew if she answered that, if she said, *No, I'm just disappointed*, her voice would crack and then the rest of her might too, and everything that she was holding in would come flooding out.

'You should open the cafe,' he said. 'I could help you. Before I go.'

'I need to sell the house first.' Her perennial excuse.

'Do you want me to put the sign back up for you?' His tone was pointed, almost mocking.

'Why?' she said, turning to glare at him. 'Did it fall down?'

'Luce, come on. You can't live like this. What if she never comes back?'

'I can't think like that.'

'But you can't live like this either. It's been so long, Luce. We have to be realistic.'

'And what about Lena?'

'What about her? We don't even know if she's telling the truth.'

She still hadn't told him about the extra details she knew, the ones she'd got from Jack Keane. If she did, she'd have to tell him where she'd got them.

And if they got on to the subject of Jack, she'd have to tell Chris what she was planning to do. Otherwise, there'd just be even more shouting later, after she'd done it.

But it was easier not to say anything.

Best just to get all the arguing done in one go.

'It's not like I'm expecting her to just walk through the door, Chris,' she said. 'I'm not an idiot. But I need to know. *I need to know.* Where she is. How she got there. Who took her there. *Why* he did. What happened that night, going all the way back to why she walked out on her friends at that bar. What was she thinking? Was she going to meet someone? Why didn't she get on the Luas and come home? I can accept that she'll never walk through the door, but not until I know *why* she won't.'

A beat passed before Chris asked, 'Why?'

'Why what?'

'Why do you need to know?'

She looked at him like he was insane. 'What kind of a question is that?'

'One I'm asking you to really consider. Why do you need to know? Think about it. You find out every single detail in the morning. Every single one. What will it change? How will it help?'

But Lucy had considered it, already, many times.

'This is like when people say money can't buy happiness,' she said. 'No, it can't, but you'll definitely be a lot bloody happier if you can afford food and light and heat, and you're able to sleep at night without worrying about being able to afford it tomorrow. If I know, yeah, OK, it won't magically make everything better. It won't make me happy. It probably won't bring anything like peace. But I will *feel* better because I won't have to deal with the . . . the torture. The endless, constant, excruciating torture of *not* knowing. I'll have some headspace. A little bit. And maybe I'll be able to keep a thought in my head for a minute that isn't about Nicki.'

Chris looked at her for a long moment and then sighed.

Mercifully, Lucy's phone rang.

'I have to take this,' she said, even though there was

no name on the screen, just a Dublin area-code number. 'Hello?'

'Lucy? It's Jack. Can you talk?'

'Um, hang on . . .' She walked away, far enough that Chris wouldn't be able to hear the other side of the conversation, but not so far that she could presume he couldn't hear hers. 'Not really. But I can listen. Or I can call you back in a while?'

'I talked to my news director,' he said, 'and we're go for launch.'

'Really?'

'So long as you agree to say you have concerns about Operation Tide, we're happy to go ahead with just you. You'll be live tonight on the six o'clock bulletin. You'll have about ten minutes, but it won't be me interviewing you. It'll be Rachel O'Leary – do you know her?'

'I know the name, but . . .'

'She usually anchors the ten o'clock,' Jack explained, 'but they're swapping things around tonight so she can talk to you. They think a woman will be better. I'll be doing the pre-recorded reports that will play before and after, but I can tell you more about them when you get here.'

Lucy groaned inwardly. If she'd known that yesterday, before the family meeting at the cafe, she might have been able to persuade them to do it. Although Margaret would probably still have found some excuse not to.

'Where do I go?' she asked. 'And what time do you need me there?'

'I'll text you the address. I'd say . . . five o'clock? You'll get hair and make-up. Don't wear any small patterns, prints or lines, they bleed on screen. We'll have a chat beforehand about what you'll be asked and what you're going to say.' He paused. 'I think that's it for now. Do you have any questions?'

Only: was she actually going to do this?

Really?

She looked back at Chris, who was leaning on the car, scrolling on his phone.

'And, ah, listen,' Jack said. 'There's something I have to tell you now, because it'll be in our report and I don't want you finding out live on air. Or just before you go on. It might be upsetting. I could've told you yesterday but I didn't know if we were going to report on it or not, and if we weren't . . .'

'What is it?'

'It's, ah, Lena Paczkowski. They've been trying to keep this under wraps for operational reasons, but . . . I'm sorry, Lucy, but she passed away. In the ambulance. She never even made it to the hospital.'

Her heart sank.

And then a crushing, suffocating disappointment settled on her chest, pushing it down deeper, making it difficult to breathe.

She wanted to sink to the ground, but she could feel Chris's eyes on her.

And this was another thing she couldn't tell him, unless she told him everything else first.

'Thanks for letting me know,' she managed to say into the phone.

Jack had actually just told her three things.

That Lena was dead.

That Margaret Gold's supposed source of Garda intel didn't know what the fuck they were on about, and Lena *had* been telling the truth.

And that Lena was never going to be able to open her eyes and tell them exactly what she'd seen, exactly what had happened to her, and lead them to where the other women were still, presumably, being kept.

Which answered Lucy's question.

She *was* going to do this.

She didn't have a choice.

# Rogues

On the drive back to Harcourt Square, Denise had an idea. She'd been looking at historical missing person reports, she told Angela, older than a year, to see if any other missing women might fit the Operation Tide profile. But she hadn't wanted to risk looking at anything more recent in case it drew attention.

Every search on PULSE was logged, and if a serving member or someone on the civilian staff was found nosing around reports or records they had no official reason to be, they could get hauled in by the superiors and made to explain themselves. You weren't allowed just to browse for shits and giggles, or because you had suspicions that one of the biggest dedicated operations in recent memory was fatally flawed. But Angela worked in the MPU, Denise pointed out, and they could get Don to OK pretty much anything, so why didn't *she* do a search of all missing persons in the last twelve months and see if there were any more for Denise's list?

'I have some time now actually,' Denise said, as they turned on to Harcourt Street. 'I'll come up with you and we can go through the reports together. You hop out and break the news to Don, and I'll follow you once I've found somewhere to park this car.'

It was past quitting time for Angela, but she didn't say so. She wanted to do this. But she'd only just started explaining everything to Don when Denise came running in, face flushed, and said breathlessly, 'Do you lot have a TV in here?'

Before either of them could respond, Denise must have remembered that there was one on the wall in the meeting room and hurried in there.

Don and Angela exchanged a glance before they followed her.

Denise was pointing the remote at the dead TV and muttering, 'How the hell do you . . . ?'

'What's going on?' Don said, hoicking up his trousers. 'Is it out about Lena?'

Angela frowned at him. 'Is *what* out?'

Denise managed to turn the TV on.

'There's that,' she said, flicking through the channels, 'and then there's a whole other pile of shite on top of that. Fucking Jack Keane. He's really gone and done it this time. That shiny little Botoxed prick.'

'What's it made of?' Don asked.

It took Angela a beat to realize he was referring to the aforementioned upper-tier pile of shite.

On the screen now was one of those flashy news studios, the kind that doesn't actually exist, the type that's only a giant green screen once you get behind the sofas.

Sitting on one of the sofas was a woman who looked to be in her late twenties. It was clear that she'd dressed herself and that someone else had done her hair and make-up; there was a total mismatch between the plain, casual, ill-fitting clothes and the furniture-polish-shiny hair, unnaturally tight curls and heavy make-up.

She looked vaguely familiar to Angela but she couldn't place her.

At that moment, a chyron helpfully appeared at the bottom of the screen informing viewers that this was LUCY O'SULLIVAN, SISTER OF MISSING NICKI.

Angela didn't immediately understand what the problem was. The families of the missing women talked to the press all the time. She hadn't seen Lucy O'Sullivan do it before, but why were both Don and Denise watching the screen, tensed like a bomb was about to go off?

Then Denise figured out how to turn the volume up.

'—understand why this hasn't been made public,' came Lucy O'Sullivan's voice, booming around the room. 'But the families should've been told. Now it's out there anyway and some of us are learning it from the news. That's just not good enough. It's very upsetting. And what about *Lena*'s family? Was this kept

from them, too? Like I said, I understand that sometimes these kinds of measures have to be taken. But if
you're going to keep something secret, you'd better
ensure it actually is that. I heard it's been all over
Twitter for more than a day, if you knew where to
look.'

'What has?' Angela asked, but Don just shushed her.

The screen changed to a wide shot which revealed a
blonde woman, the anchor, sitting on the couch opposite, holding an iPad and nodding thoughtfully. Her
hair was even shinier than Lucy's but poker straight
and seemingly frozen in place.

'And before this,' she said, 'would you say the families were happy with the way the investigation was
being conducted?'

'No,' Lucy answered firmly. 'I wouldn't say that at
all. I mean, it took three women to vanish before we
even *got* an investigation. Tana Meehan had been missing for a full year and my sister for six months before
either of them got upgraded from a missing person
report that nobody cared about. And here we are now,
eight months after the establishment of Operation
Tide – which has all the resources, the budget, the per-
sonnel they could possibly need, led by Superintendent
Colin Hall—'

'This might be the first mention of his name on TV
that he doesn't like,' Don muttered.

'—and we *still* haven't had a single arrest. We're not
even any closer to getting answers. No one has found

anything.' Lucy took a breath before adding quietly, 'Or any*one*.'

'Well, this is a right fucking shitshow,' Denise said, folding her arms.

Angela opened her mouth to try again to ask what was going on but this time Don shushed her before she even got out a syllable.

'But I want to say,' Lucy said on screen, 'there are three families involved here, and we don't all feel the same way about everything. We couldn't possibly. Even within families, there are differences of opinion. So I don't want to put words in anyone's mouth. I want to be clear: I'm only speaking for myself tonight. And for my sister, Nicki.'

'Tonight,' the anchor said, 'as we sit here, searches are ongoing in the Wicklow Mountains, near to where Lena Paczkowski was hit by a car after – allegedly – managing to escape an abductor who may or may not be related to the other three cases. Before she died—'

'She *died*?' Angela said. 'When?'

'—we believe she was able to give some detail to the paramedics who attended the scene.' The anchor paused, as if she was going to come up with her next question on the spot and not read it from the list on her trusty iPad. 'Does that give you hope?'

Lucy said, 'Not if Operation Tide are in charge, no.'

The anchor frowned, concerned. 'And why do you say that?'

'Because it seems like they don't know what they're

doing. We hear things – the families, I mean – outside of, you know, proper channels, and what I'm hearing is that there's a fatal problem with Operation Tide. That they were more concerned – that *Superintendent Hall* was more concerned – with collecting enough missing women to get himself a special op than he is with actually investigating their disappearances. So I'm calling on the Minister for Justice to meet with us and answer our questions about the professionalism and efficacy of Operation Tide. Because, based on what I'm hearing, we don't even really know how many missing women there are – or even if the three they have are connected to each other.'

'Fucking fuck *fuck*,' Denise said.

'Now, now, your mother wouldn't like that language,' Don said to her.

'What? The *English* language?' she spat back.

During this exchange, neither of them tore their eyes from the TV.

'That's a very serious—' the anchor started.

But Lucy was in full flow now. 'And are they going to admit if one or more of them isn't connected? Or are they mostly just concerned with keeping the budget for their special op? I mean, my first question is: why wasn't Lena Paczkowski included in their tally? Her phone was found at the side of the road too. She went missing two weeks ago. If she *had* been included, would she still be alive today?'

Don winced.

Angela tried again. 'Is Lena Paczkowski dead? Since when?'

But this time, no one even bothered to shush her, let alone answer.

'That's a very serious accusation,' the anchor said on screen, her eyes gleaming.

'What *I* think is serious,' Lucy said, 'is that in this day and age, three adult women can go missing – and a fourth can be abducted – in a country of this size, in this age of technology and surveillance and forensic science, and here we are, eighteen months after the first woman was last seen, and we're none the wiser about what happened to any of them. It just beggars belief, doesn't it?'

There was the briefest moment of dead air.

'And it means . . . ?' the anchor prompted.

'It means,' Lucy repeated, her eyes straying to the camera lens, 'if something did happen to them, whoever's responsible is still out there. He could be out there, right now, looking for another woman to take. He could take her tonight. How is any woman in Ireland, and especially in the Dublin area, supposed to feel safe, knowing that?'

The anchor took a beat and then looked directly to the camera herself.

'We'll have more on this,' she said, 'and the rest of the day's headlines, when we return.'

'Fuck,' Denise said again.

*

There was silence in the meeting room as all three of them digested what had just happened. Angela bit down on her lip to stop herself from asking all the questions that were bubbling up inside her.

The silence was broken by the sound of a phone ringing: Denise's.

'Shit,' she said, looking from the screen to Don. 'It's Hall.'

'*You're* his first call? Why?'

'I don't know, but it can't be good, can it?'

'You didn't . . . ?' Don paused, nodded at the screen. '*You* didn't do this, did you?'

'What? Leak to Jack Keane? Seriously?'

'I meant Lucy O'Sullivan. You're her FLO, aren't you?'

'Of *course* I didn't,' Denise snapped. 'Why would I tell her any of that? She must have got it from him, and I don't know who the fuck *he* got it from.'

Don held up his hands in surrender. Denise threw him a furious look and then hurried out of the room, presumably to answer Hall's call.

A cheery ad for car insurance was on the TV now.

Angela let its idiotic jingle fill the room for a few bars before turning to Don and starting to ask, 'What the—?'

'Lena Paczkowski died in the ambulance,' he said. He pulled out one of the chairs and sat down, facing the TV. 'She never even made it to the hospital. They were keeping it quiet in the hope the guy – if there *is* a guy – would get nervous and, I don't know, come back to the spot where he'd dumped the bodies to make sure they were still hidden or whatever. But he didn't. Or else, they're not buried anywhere near the Wicklow Mountains and the girl ended up there for some other reason. Or there are no bodies. The point is, the Tide lads did a piss-poor job of keeping their secret a secret, and now it seems like' – Don pointed a finger at the screen – 'the families found it out from the media.'

'Shit,' Angela said. She sat down too, exhaled.

'Shit indeed.'

'You seem pretty calm about this.'

'Well, this isn't us, is it?' Don said with a shrug. 'It's Tide. This is one of those times when I thank my lucky stars our main responsibility is filing things. Not my circus, not my monkeys.'

'But we're the Missing Persons Unit. Didn't we at least rent them the tent?'

He pointed at the screen. 'They're back.'

Angela turned towards the TV in time to catch the end of the news programme's titles and then a one-shot of the blonde anchor sitting on the couch.

'Welcome back,' she said smoothly, 'to our special report this evening into Operation Tide, the investigation into the missing women. We'll be looking at the rest of today's headlines later in the programme, but for now we're going to continue our conversation with Lucy O'Sullivan, whose sister, Nicola, known as Nicki to her family and friends, has been missing since June of last year.' She pivoted in her seat just as the feed changed to a two-shot, showing both women still sitting opposite each other in the studio. 'I'd like to switch gears a little, Lucy, if I may. What is it like, not knowing what happened to your sister?'

'Hell,' she answered immediately. For a moment it seemed like she might leave it there, but then she continued. 'The last time I saw Nicki was on CCTV footage that showed her leaving the Duke on Duke Street on Saturday the twelfth of June 2021, and walking out of shot towards Grafton Street. Every second of those images, every frame, is burned into my brain. And there isn't a moment of the day when I'm not wondering what happened next' – her voice caught here – 'and wondering why we don't have the answer. You try not to, but it's impossible to stop yourself from filling in the blanks, even if we don't actually know anything. I don't know if whatever happened happened there, or elsewhere. Did she get on a bus, or was she pulled into a car, or did someone push her into the river?'

Tears were dripping on to Lucy's cheeks now and the anchor had the sense to steer the conversation in another direction.

'This is the first national television interview you've given since Nicki disappeared,' she said softly. 'What do you want people to know about your sister? What was she like?'

Lucy wiped at her cheeks and then took a deep breath.

'I've been dreading that question,' she said.

The anchor blinked, as if taken aback.

'Nicki was funny,' Lucy started. 'And curious. And carefree. We had so much fun when we were children – on Saturday mornings, we'd make a sort of tent out of our bunk beds, and our mother would bring breakfast to us, and we'd all sit and have a picnic . . .' Lucy smiled briefly at the memory. 'And I don't know what I would've done without her when our mother died. Even though she was the younger one, she took care of me in many ways.'

The anchor nodded sympathetically, relaxing again now that she'd got the answer she was expecting.

'But she was also selfish,' Lucy continued. 'And she could be mean. She hurt the feelings of the people who cared about her, and she didn't even notice she was doing it. She was self-involved. She was always the most important person in her universe. She lacked direction, and she could be lazy, and she wasn't bothered about things like getting a job or keeping a job or how she would afford a roof over her head and all those, you know, *responsibilities*, because she was too busy living in the now, and living with me, and taking advantage of the fact that when our mother died, she left the house to us. Chris, her boyfriend, would tell you that when it came to deciding things – big things, like where to live, and small things, like what to watch – she would never compromise. Her way was the only way. And on the night she disappeared, her friends said she'd snapped at them over something minor and then just left, wandering off by herself, while drunk and wearing a short skirt and—'

The anchor glanced at someone off-screen, nodded almost imperceptibly.

'—*none of that should matter*. I've watched and read and heard Margaret Gold talk about Jennifer so many times, and she's able to say that Jennifer was incredibly kind and caring and her smile lit up rooms, and everyone who met her loved her, and she was so smart and hard-working and talented and she was going to do amazing things, and she'd already achieved so much, and Margaret has all these beautiful pictures . . .' Lucy exhaled. 'The best resource for finding a missing person is not the guards, but the general public. But it feels like the people of Ireland haven't' – another deep breath – 'bothered looking for my sister. That they don't care about her that much. And so I've been scared to tell the truth about her, in case it makes them care even less.'

The anchor inhaled sharply, evidently about to say something, but Lucy rushed on.

'Because that's what happened, isn't it? With these women. Tana wasn't even thirty and she was getting divorced in a country where *Friends* has been on TV longer than that's been legal. With Nicki, everyone just saw the purple hair and the short skirt and her supposedly stumbling around town. They disappeared, we filed reports, and nothing happened. Then the same thing happens to Jennifer Gold and within *hours*, she's front-page news. Why do you think that is? Yes, circumstances were a little different, but I think it's mainly because she was young and beautiful. Because she hadn't had time to do anything wrong yet, and everything she had done had been right. And she was walking her dog near her home in broad daylight. *Just* walking her dog. Isn't that what everyone said? As if Tana and Nicki had put themselves in harm's way, somehow. As if they got what they deserved.'

'Well, now—' the anchor started, putting a finger to her earpiece.

'And what about Lena Paczkowski?' Lucy continued, her voice rising. 'Her phone was found near where she was last seen, just like the others. *Two weeks ago*. But Operation Tide didn't think she was one of the missing women. Why? What was it that made the difference? Was it her name? Was it too hard to pronounce? Would she be alive today if her name was, I don't know, something like Sinéad McCarthy?'

'Oh my God,' Angela murmured.

'Girl has a point,' Don said under his breath.

'Lucy,' the anchor said firmly, clear now that she had all but completely lost control of the interview. 'We only have thirty seconds left but, very briefly, what do you want to see happen now? You mentioned the minister. Will meeting with him be your next step?'

Without hesitation, Lucy turned to look right down the barrel of the lens.

'My sister, Nicki, has been missing for more than a year. Every single moment – every *single* moment – that I'm awake, I'm wondering where she is. And I'm going to be honest: I can't take it any more. I'm telling *you*, I can't take it. I know you're out there. You're probably watching this. So please. I'm begging you. You don't need to confess.' She glanced at something happening off-camera, something that seemed to panic her, and when she spoke again it was in a rush. 'You don't need to go to the guards. I just want to talk. I just need to know. But please tell me. Tell me what you did. Tell me where you left her. Tell me where she is now.' Her eyes had filled with tears. 'Show me. Please. Come get me. I will go with you if you take me there. I will. I just need—'

Abruptly, the screen changed to an ad for breakfast cereal featuring animated chipmunk things singing about mornings.

Neither Don nor Angela said anything for a long moment. They just looked at the chipmunks and then at each other in stunned silence.

'They cut her off,' Angela said.

'About two minutes too late.' Don got the remote and muted the television. 'Every half-cracked eejit in the land will be packing a bag now, getting ready to head her way. She's just sent them all invitations.'

'Can we . . . Can we do something? Put a car on her or—?'

'No.' Don shook his head. 'You only get that if you're a witness, and even then only if you're an important one. I can ring ... Where does she live? Dundrum? I can ring the lads there and get them to put her house on their patrol routes, but we don't give private individuals protection, even if they go and do something as monumentally stupid as this.'

'Even if she doesn't get the crazies, she'll get the press.'

'She'd better hope she does,' Don said. 'At least if there's cameras on her, that offers some protection.'

Denise came back into the room.

'More good news,' she said, throwing up her arms. 'Roland Kearns called the incident room at Naas and demanded to speak directly to Hall to lodge a complaint about me. Said I accused him of trespassing and refused to take his concerns about his personal safety seriously. And he also managed to drop in that I'd mentioned I'd been in Wexford, which was news to my super.' She exhaled, annoyed. 'I'm due in his office at nine o'clock tomorrow to explain myself.'

Angela thought Denise looked paler than before, tired.

Beaten, even.

'So,' Denise said, looking from one of them to the other. 'What did I miss?'

# The Death Zone

The wanting was always there, like a figure standing perfectly still in the shadowy corner of a room. At first, you don't see them. You might not even sense their presence; you might presume you're alone. But then, you catch something odd in your peripheral vision. Or a light gets turned on. Or they step out of the shadows, making themselves known.

And you realize then that you were never alone.

You are happy to know that, because it helps explain things.

I'd always had weird dreams, going back as far as I can remember. The kind other people might be desperate to wake up from, but I was always disappointed when I did. They stopped for a while after I first met Amy, but soon after we started living together, they returned with a vengeance. Now when I'd wake up from them, clenched and sweating, it would be beside her serene, sleeping body, and I'd start playing out scenarios in my head.

But I didn't want to . . .

Look, I was never going to do anything to her. Ever. OK? Not to Amy. She's my wife, my family.

It had to be a stranger, or it wouldn't be *it* at all.

For a while, I had myself convinced that I just needed to get this thing out of my system, that it was merely a curiosity that, once sated, would disappear. I thought maybe I would hire a prostitute—Sorry, sex worker. *Sex worker*. One who was OK with things being a bit rough, who'd let you take it to the very edge before she made you stop. And then I thought about those parties and clubs and whatnot, the places where people who are into that sort of thing tend to go, but to be honest – and, yeah, this *is* embarrassing – I hadn't the faintest idea how to go about finding them and I didn't want to risk asking the internet for help. I even considered travelling, flying far away to a country where monetizing foreigners' dark desires was practically encouraged by the tourist board, but ultimately decided it would be too risky.

Because even though I was telling myself that what I wanted was the *before* bit, the bit that could – hopefully – masquerade as just a certain brand of sex, I worried, deep down, that in the heat of the moment, I might not be able to draw the line there. That thought stopped me doing anything about it for a long, long time.

And then came Niamh's thirtieth birthday.

The worst night of my life and, also, the best one. The start of *this* life.

Niamh is Amy's sister. She was having a party in her house which, thanks to her architect husband – who is a bit of a dickhead, if I'm honest, but we don't have to see them that much – is a collection of windows overlooking the sea in some no-name place on the Wexford coast. Amy had gone down the night before to help with the preparations and now I was driving there, having taken the afternoon off work.

It was mid-January and so dark by five o'clock. On all our previous visits, Amy had been behind the wheel and it had been daytime. I only made it a little ways past Enniscorthy before I somehow got myself lost.

After wandering aimlessly through a network of winding country roads, I pulled in and called my wife, who did her best to give me directions which I scribbled down on the only thing I had to hand: the masthead of a three-day-old copy of the *Irish Independent*. She was annoyed with me because I was already late, and I had our present for her sister – some designer bag Niamh had had her eye on and a big, beautiful bouquet of pinks and greens – and the birthday cake. I'd been entrusted to pick them up from various locations near our home in Dublin and bring them with me to Wexford. They were all on the back seat.

I tried to follow Amy's instructions – I thought I had – but at least fifteen, twenty minutes went by and I was still on what felt like the same network of winding back-roads, but now so deep in the country-side, I didn't even have mobile phone service to call for help a second time. Eventually I found myself on a road with high hedgerows on either side, no lights whatsoever and no other cars—

But then *her*, in my headlights.

A young woman.

Red hair.

Dressed professionally in boots and a long coat.

She was an odd sight; it seemed like there was nowhere near by she could've come from or anywhere close she could be headed to. She was walking towards me on the left-hand side of the road, with a handbag slung over her shoulder and the blue light from the phone she was holding illuminating her face.

When she looked up, I slowed down.

Genuinely, I was stopping to ask for directions. I know we've only just met, you and I, but I promise you I was. I swear.

And I *did*.

I pulled in, embedding the car in the hedgerow she was maybe ten or fifteen feet from at that point. If she wanted to avoid me now, she would have to walk around the car on its driver's side, out into the middle of the road. I put down the passenger window, leaned over so I could see her face – I think it was probably a little dim for her to really be able to see mine – and said, 'I'm sorry – do you live around here, by any chance? I'm a bit lost.'

She asked where I was supposed to be.

I told her the truth: at my sister-in-law's birthday party on the coast. I pointed towards the back seat. I saw her looking in there, clocking the cake box, the bag, the flowers.

'My wife gave me some instructions,' I said, picking up the paper I'd scribbled them on. I read them out to her. She made a noise like *mmm*, and then said, 'I *think* I know where that is. Let me just double-check . . .'

As she started tapping at her phone's screen, I got out of the car.

What were my intentions? I really don't know.

Honestly, I don't.

You see, when I do this, it's not really me. Not in a cop-out way, a not-guilty-by-temporary-insanity way, or a *Sorry, sir, it was my dark passenger* way. (Dexter Morgan. Amy loves that show, it surely won't surprise you to learn. It's like, on some unconscious level, she *does* know.) It's more like I switch gears or modes. Or that I'm kind of drunk. You know the way you do things when you're drunk that you'd never do when you're sober, but you're still absolutely you? It's just a more . . . let's say, *open* version of you. Unfiltered.

The societal shackles are, if not off, then certainly a little looser.

When *he* shows up, everything turns more primal. It's the part of me – the core of me, I'd say – that holds much more ancient desires. That guy remembers what it was like to need to hunt and kill every day just to stay alive. He's much more focused on wants than perhaps he should be. And he doesn't really consider consequences; he just acts.

All I do is let him take the wheel.

That night, though, I had no idea that I was about to do that. And I swear I'm telling the truth when I say I don't know at which point I knew any different. But the moment must have been one of the few between my getting out of the car and my smashing her head into the side of it.

And I do mean *smashing*. I can still hear the crack.

The skin on her forehead parted like the Red Sea, and her eyes went all funny – and then there *was* a red sea, gushing blood, coming out of her hairline and down her face and on to her clothes and on to my clothes and the car and the ground and me and I looked at her and I looked down at me – at my hands, specifically – and all I could think was, *What? What? What?* and *he* chose that precise moment to abandon me.

And *I* panicked.

Like, full-on body shakes. My chest got so tight I thought I was having a heart attack. Asking myself, *What the fuck have you done? What the fuck did you do that for? What the hell were you thinking?* over and over and over, wishing I could just snap my fingers or blink a couple of times or wake up from whatever kind of nightmare this was and it would all just go away.

Maybe I was even doing it out loud, I don't know.

But it was real, and it couldn't be undone.

She slumped to the ground like a bag of broken things, landing across my feet, and while I stood there in a sticky puddle of blood that I could feel more than see – the headlights were on but, because I'd closed the door after me, that was the only illumination in an otherwise black night – a light suddenly appeared in the dark.

A square of amber glow, filtered through curtains.

There was a house directly across the road, behind the trees.

I'd stopped right in front of it.

I didn't think. I didn't consider my options. I just hooked my arms under hers – the blood was warm, sticky, *viscous* – and dragged her to the rear of the car. The woman couldn't have weighed more than eight stone and yet when it came time to get her up off the ground and into the boot, she felt like she weighed at least three times that.

I just didn't have the strength. I couldn't lift her.

In the house, the glass panel above the front door lit up too.

Had she screamed, I wondered? Had *I*? Could that person have heard us? I had to get out of there, and fast. I turned her around so that she was facing the open boot and – somehow – lifted her high enough so that her head and shoulders were over the lip of it and then, before she could slip back down again, I got her arms in there too, and that seemed to tip the balance, so then I was able to pick up her feet and lift her, push her, *fold her* into the boot and get it closed.

I think that's when her arm got broken.

Another light came on, this one outside now, illuminating the house's front door like a single spotlight on the stage of a pitch-black theatre.

I got back into the car. I was freezing but also sweating and shaking and I couldn't manage more than a shallow, panting breath. My body was pure adrenaline; I thought I could actually smell the overflow coming out of my pores. My hands were so tight on the wheel, my fingers burned. I put my foot down and took off, tyres squealing. I drove for . . .

You know what? I really don't know.

I've no idea where that spot actually was. It could've been five minutes, it could've been half an hour that I was driving in a straight line, on what felt like the same, endless ribbon of road.

With blood everywhere and a dead or nearly dead woman in the boot.

I was a murderer, or about to be, and I was definitely going to get caught. Whoever was in the house would've come out, seen the blood and called the Gardaí. They were probably there now, already collecting all the evidence I'd left behind that would point to my identity. Tyre tracks. Boot prints. Hairs, maybe.

Her phone.

It had been in her hand but not afterwards, not when I was getting her into the boot, which meant it was on the ground.

With the *address of Niamh's house* entered into the map app.

Possibly.

Had she actually had a chance to enter it? I couldn't remember.

I was, not to put too fine a point on it, completely and utterly fucked – but the certainty of it, the utter inevitability of that . . . You know something? It focuses the mind. Resigned to my fate, I was suddenly overcome with a frightening calm.

And I knew exactly what to do next.

Why am I telling you all this? Well, because you asked. I know, I know, you probably weren't expecting quite this level of detail, but I haven't had the opportunity to tell anyone any of this before, ever, and, to be honest, it feels good to talk.

And it's safe to tell you, since you won't have the chance to repeat it to anyone else.

# The Trap

The red light above the camera blinked off.

Lucy's blood felt like pure adrenaline, fizzing and electric in her veins, but it was quickly draining away. She was still wired and also completely exhausted; all she wanted to do was crawl into bed in a dark room but she knew that if she did, she'd only lie awake, staring at the ceiling, waiting for her body to calm down.

But it was over.

She'd done what she needed to do.

There were only two other people in the studio: the anchor, Rachel, sitting opposite her, and an older woman who'd introduced herself as the stage manager, still hanging back in the shadowy wings.

They'd explained to Lucy when she'd arrived that this was a brand-new, state-of-the-art set-up. The large cameras she'd expected to see in front of her moved as if by magic, controlled by some unseen operators hidden away in another room. The nearest one pivoted smoothly away from her now.

Rachel was ignoring her. Her head was bowed and she had an index finger pressed to the device in her ear while she nodded furiously. Lucy looked to the stage manager for guidance instead, but the woman just stared blankly back. Then she nodded her head once, twice, before stepping forward into the light and saying, 'And we're out.'

The large TV screen which was showing them the live feed – the one that Lucy had had to concentrate on not looking into while she was on air, because it was showing her own face slightly out of sync with the words she was speaking – was now playing a commercial for breakfast cereal.

Under her breath, Rachel muttered, 'Tell him I'm going to fucking castrate him.' Then she turned to Lucy, flashed a tight smile and said, 'Thanks for coming in.' She threw her iPad on the couch, got up and stalked off. Beyond the carpeted floor of the set, her high heels seemed to clack angrily across the studio's floor.

The stage manager was coming towards her.

'Am I done?' Lucy asked.

'Oh, you're done, love,' she said. 'Yeah, we'll go straight to that VT after the break . . . Yeah. I know. We'll have to switch it out.'

Lucy had no idea what that meant.

Seeing her confusion, the stage manager tapped her headset with her free hand. 'I'm talking to the gallery, love.' The woman was smiling, but her smile was strained. 'They can see and hear everything, like God.' She plucked the little microphone clip off Lucy's lapel and then motioned for her to stand up so she could take the battery pack off her too. 'Reception can help you out with a taxi if you need one.' The woman frowned. 'Yeah, I know. No, I know . . . I'll come up now; we have a couple of minutes.' Then, to Lucy, with another strained smile, 'Thanks again.'

She turned and disappeared behind the lights, leaving Lucy completely alone in the studio – she thought. Because a moment later Jack Keane came storming out of the dark, his face red, his expression furious.

'What the *fuck* was that?' He grabbed her by the elbow, pulled her off the set and started to steer her across the studio floor. 'What the hell were you *thinking*?'

He pushed them both through a heavy swinging door that led them into a dim, curtained passageway, and then another door which dumped them into an overly lit, carpeted corridor.

Lucy squinted at the change in the light.

'I mean, Jesus fucking *Christ*,' Jack spat. He turned to glare at her, his hands on his hips. 'That was *not* what we agreed. This is why you wanted it live, isn't it? You knew exactly what you were going to do. And you wanted to make sure you did it in time for it to be all over the papers tomorrow, and repeated on the later bulletins tonight, and all over fucking social media while everyone is at home on the couch . . .' He shook his head, disbelieving. 'Well, *I* probably just got fired. Thanks a fucking *lot* for that.'

'My sister is missing,' she said, firmly but calmly. 'And you wanted me to come on here and open a vein because you wanted good TV. Well, sorry if I'm not sorry that I took advantage of that. You used me and I used you. We're even. And, honestly, I don't know what you're so upset about. You got what you wanted, your Operation Tide exposé. And I said everything you told me to.'

'Yes,' Jack said. 'Yes, you did. But then, you *spectacularly* failed to shut the fuck up.'

'I did what I had to do.'

'But don't you realize what you've done? You're going to have every crazy in the land lining up to . . . to . . .' Jack's voice changed, became quieter. 'Is there someone at home? Is Chris there? You should ask him to come get you. And maybe go away somewhere for a few nights, stay at a friend's house or in a hotel. Because, trust me, after this, you're going to have no problem getting attention from the media. And after what you said about Jennifer Gold . . .' He shook his head, still disbelieving. 'I think you've got a couple of hours before this is absolutely everywhere. Go get what you need from home and get somewhere else. My advice is, put out some sort of statement saying you've been under enormous amounts of stress and you really shouldn't have gone on live TV in the state you were in, that you didn't know what you were saying, that your sister's disappearance has pushed you into a nervous breakdown, or claim you were on new medication, whatever, but post it online and then turn off your phone. With any luck, this will create a few days of absolute mania and then someone else will do something and everyone will move on to them. I hope so, for your sake.' He exhaled hard. 'And whatever you do, do *not* read the comments.'

Lucy folded her arms, defiant. 'I knew exactly what I was saying.'

'Maybe,' Jack said, quieter now. 'Maybe you did. But I don't think you've any idea what you've just done.' He reached behind and plucked her handbag from a row of hooks mounted on the wall. She hadn't been allowed to bring it into the studio. 'Here,' he said, handing it over. 'Good luck, Lucy. And seriously, stay safe.'

And then he pushed through the door on the right, leaving her alone in the corridor.

With an incessant buzzing noise.

It was coming from her bag.

Her phone.

Lucy pulled it out. She was getting an incoming call from a number she didn't recognize. She rejected it and unlocked the screen.

And saw a flood of new texts, missed-call notifications, voicemails and emails, coming in faster than she could go through them.

Chris had sent a string of messages over the past

hour. They'd started with a benign *I'm at home where are you?* followed by an increasingly panicked reaction to the interview, seemingly in real time. A *Thanks for telling me* followed by a *WTF?* followed by *JFC what are you doing???* Then, five minutes ago, *Stay at the studio. I'm coming to get you. DON'T LEAVE.*

She swiped them away.

Denise. *On my way to the studio call me ASAP.*

Caroline. *All I can say is WOW! Good for you. Proud of you x*

Margaret Gold. *I hope you're happy now that you've put us all in . . .*

Lucy didn't bother reading the rest of the message, which was so long it continued off-screen. Of course Margaret had already found the time to compose, type and send a bloody *essay*.

And then another new message came in.

It was from a number she had stored in her phone only as *Him*, and only so she'd know who it was if he ever tried to contact her.

She'd got his number off Caroline months ago, just in case.

There were only three words, but she stared at them for several seconds to make sure they actually said what she thought they did.

*Can we meet?*

The adrenaline came flooding back. Her plan had worked.

\*

Lucy watched him arrive at the cafe on foot, holding his phone, presumably using a map app to find the address she'd sent him. He stopped outside and looked up at the building, frowning, no doubt wondering if he had the right place. With the lights off and her car parked two streets away, it must look abandoned.

She steeled herself, then went to the door and unlocked it.

The butcher's bell was still hanging over it and it rang loudly as she pulled the door inwards, interrupting the otherwise quiet night.

Roland Kearns looked her up and down as the edges of his mouth began to curl into a smarmy smile.

'Lucy,' he said. 'We meet at last.'

Her name in his mouth made her feel sick. She stuck her free hand in a pocket so he wouldn't see it shaking, then stepped back to let him come inside.

'Thank you.' His body brushed against her as he passed – lightly, but not accidentally. He was dressed in jeans and a T-shirt, both garments stretched tight against his skin, emphasizing the bulging muscles in his arms and legs, the expanse of his chest, the physical power he had to call upon. A big silver watch hung on his wrist, mirrored Ray-Bans from the deep V of his shirt. 'What is this place? Is it yours?'

'It used to be a butcher's and it was going to be a cafe, but I don't know if that'll ever happen.' She turned the bolt in the door, locking them both in. 'And right now, it's mostly the bank's.'

'And is it usually this . . . ?' He was standing in the middle of the dusty floor now, looking around. 'Gloomy?'

'I'm going to keep the lights off,' she said, 'if that's all right with you.'

What was left of the setting sun and the glow of the streetlight outside was going to have to do. While she'd been waiting, she'd taped another layer of newsprint over the floor-to-ceiling window. So long as neither of them lit up their phones, they wouldn't be seen from the outside.

'Fine by me,' he said. 'And probably wise, after your little stunt this evening.'

*My little stunt that worked*, Lucy said silently. Then, out loud, 'It's fine. No one would know to come here. My abject failure to get this place up and running has finally paid off.'

'Then why . . . ?'

'In case Chris comes back,' she said.

He had already been here, half an hour ago, shouting her name and banging furiously on the door, presumably having discovered that she'd ignored his texts and left the studio. She'd sat in the back, lights off, door locked, hoping he wouldn't think to check beyond this immediate area for her parked car and, after about ten minutes, he'd finally given up and left.

This might be Lucy's only shot at getting some answers. She didn't want them to be disturbed.

'He's Nicki's boyfriend,' she started explaining. 'He lives—'

'I know who he is.'

There was a challenge in Roland's tone, an undercurrent of *Who do you think you're dealing with here?*

'Right,' Lucy said. 'Of course.'

She motioned towards the chairs and they both sat down.

She'd purposefully arranged them so they were far apart, but the first thing he did was jerk his a couple of inches nearer to hers. She tried not to wince as the metal legs made a loud, screeching noise against the bare concrete floor. Then Roland leaned forward, settling his elbows on his knees, bringing him closer still.

'It was you, wasn't it?' Lucy said. 'Last night. Outside my window.'

Dive right in. Show him that you're not intimidated.

Or, at least, pretend not to be.

'Busted,' Roland said.

Half his face was in shadow, but she could see a smile.

'What were you doing there?'

'Getting you back,' he said, 'for being outside of mine.'

'What?' She tried to look completely confused. 'What are you talking about?'

'Oh, come on. You hardly thought you were going undetected, did you? I have some news for you, Lucy: you're not exactly MI5. So let me ask you the same thing. What were *you* doing *there*?'

She hadn't planned to start watching Roland Kearns's apartment; it had just happened. A couple of months ago, when it was still bright outside well past ten o'clock, her insomnia had reached new, torturous heights. She'd tried everything to tire herself out, to get even a couple of hours of restorative sleep.

Marathons of *Air Crash Investigation*. Medication, which only left her groggy and increasingly anxious that she might never sleep naturally again. Meditation, which clearly wasn't designed to quiet the minds of relatives of missing people. Walking, for miles and miles, for hours, throughout the night, which, as the weeks wore on and the sun set earlier and earlier, started to feel dangerous – and unnecessarily risky, seeing as that didn't work either.

Having accepted her failure, she concentrated her efforts on trying to find ways to occupy the interminable night.

She drove aimlessly at first, around South Dublin in ever-widening loops. Then sometimes to scenic spots that, at crazy o'clock in the morning, were completely deserted, roofed by a breathtaking blanket of twinkling stars, and felt like places in which she could stop and breathe. And then, on one of her drives one night about three weeks ago, she happened to see a sign for the place where Roland Kearns lived.

It was Caroline who had mentioned it, during a conversation about how Roland had called up Tana's parents soon after she'd disappeared to complain that he'd lost his job and couldn't get another one because everybody thought he'd killed their daughter. He'd had to move out of the half-a-million-euro house they'd shared and swap it for some awful half-finished rental on the outskirts of Dublin. Caroline had had the name and they'd looked it up online together, gleefully flipped through the pictures, satisfied that he was having to suffer in some small way by having to live there.

That first night, when Lucy drove to the complex, she didn't have any plan. She didn't even know what she was doing there, really, other than killing another of the night's endless hours. She'd parked up, turned off her lights, sat and looked out – and, about ten minutes later, watched a taxi drive past her. It stopped outside one of the blocks at the rear, which, even though it was a way away from her position, was close enough for her to identify the man who got out.

It was almost four in the morning. Where was Roland Kearns coming from at that hour? And what had he been doing there?

What if he was just as he seemed: a violent, angry man? What if he *had* killed Tana? What if he'd killed Nicki and Jennifer too?

What if, the next time another woman disappeared, Lucy was able to tell the guards that Roland Kearns hadn't been at home?

What if, if she saw him leave his home in the middle of the night, she followed him?

What if, instead of waiting for someone to answer

her questions about Nicki, she pulled on the only other thread within reach that might possibly lead to the answers?

So Lucy did.

She started returning to Roland's place, not every single night, but most nights, to park outside and watch for him. She never again saw him coming or going – although she had seen him smoke on his balcony a few times, once with a blonde woman at his side, which turned her stomach – but it did make her feel better in some small way.

It was doing *something*.

Until Chris woke up in the middle of the night, found her and the car gone, and freaked the fuck out. She came clean about where she'd been just to stop him shouting at her, and he lost it. She'd had to promise him that she'd never, ever do it again.

But she did.

The last time had been the night before last. On that visit, even though it was closer to dawn than to dusk, all the lights in Roland's apartment were ablaze. Nervous that he might look out and see her car, she'd doubled back and left it parked in the retail park, outside the Aldi, and walked back to his apartment instead.

'I was . . .' She wasn't quite sure how to answer Roland's question; she didn't want to antagonize him until he told her what she needed to know. 'Making myself feel better.'

'So you do think it was me.'

A statement, not a question.

'You know it can't be,' he said then.

'I don't know anything, Roland. That's the point.'

'I have an alibi.'

'But not for Tana.'

Her heart felt like it was going to beat its way out of her chest, but what was the point of this if she didn't say what she needed to say?

'But for the others,' Roland said.

His voice was toneless, eerily calm.

'You were watching my interview,' Lucy said. 'They may not be connected, all three cases. They're probably not. The guards may have made a mistake, intentionally or otherwise—'

'Oh, they definitely *did*.'

'—and actually, the same guy isn't responsible for all three. Or four, if you include Lena.'

'Five, if you include what happened down in Enniscorthy.'

Lucy froze, waiting.

But it soon became obvious that he was going to make her ask.

'What happened in Enniscorthy?'

Roland didn't respond immediately and Lucy got the sickening sense that he was relishing this.

'Denise Pope is your FLO too, isn't she?' he said. 'She stopped by today, and mentioned that she'd been in Wexford, to some place outside Enniscorthy. Made a point of mentioning it. She wanted to know if I'd ever been. After she left, I did a quick bit of googling. Turns out there was a woman who went missing from there back in 2019. Kerry something or other. After what I heard tonight, on your little TV special, I'm thinking that maybe they're realizing there's more women gone, and she's one of them.' He grinned, remembering something. 'Oh, and by the way, I told Denise some woman was hanging around outside my place most nights. But I said I suspected it was Caroline O'Callaghan.'

'*Caroline?* Why?'

'Because I fucking hate that deranged bitch.'

The words dripped with venom, and sent a fresh ripple of fear down Lucy's spine.

She needed to ask him what she needed to ask him, now, before she completely lost her nerve.

'Look, Roland,' she said. 'It's just us here. Just you and me. And so I'm going to be completely honest: I don't care if you killed Tana. Honestly, I don't give a shit. I didn't know the woman, I don't know you, it's nothing to do with me. All I care about is finding out what happened to my sister. To Nicki. That's it. And right now, you're all I have. You're the only suspect in any of these cases. So can you just . . . ?' She stopped, took a deep breath. 'Can you just *please* tell me the truth? If you killed Tana, just tell me. I won't tell anyone. I just need to know. If I know that she isn't part of this, then I can just move—'

'*Stop!*' Roland roared suddenly, rising up out of his

seat at the same time, morphing into a huge, faceless shadow, looming over her.

Now it was her chair legs that screeched as she pushed herself back, tried to move away, but there was a dip in the floor just behind her and the chair caught there, refusing to go any further.

A tense beat passed.

Roland began pacing the floor in front of her. When he turned towards the window, the streetlight's glow lit his face a little but gave him two dark hollows for eyes.

He stopped suddenly. 'Are you recording this?'

'What? No.'

'Prove it. Where's your phone?'

'I said I'm not—'

'*Prove it.*'

Lucy got up so fast she knocked over her chair. She hurried to what remained of the butcher's countertop, reached over and unhooked the strap of her bag from the other side of it. She found her phone and turned to show it to him, tapping its screen to demonstrate its lifelessness. She'd turned it off after she'd received his text saying he was on his way.

'OK,' he said. 'Now empty the bag.'

She didn't argue. She upturned it, letting its entire contents spill out on to the dirty, dusty floor.

Roland bent to pick through it, checking.

'I'm not recording this,' Lucy said. 'Really, Roland. I just need to know.'

He straightened up.

'Listen to me,' he said through clenched teeth, 'because I'm only going to say this once. *I didn't kill Tana*. I had nothing to do with her disappearance. Yes, we fought and, yes, sometimes things got a little . . . But it was both of us. It was her just as much as me. And she fucking knew how to push my buttons, you know? She *provoked* me.'

Lucy bit her lip to keep herself from reacting to this, the go-to, pathetic refrain of people who beat their partners.

'I don't have a time machine,' he went on. 'I can't take it back. But I'm telling you, I didn't kill her. I didn't. I don't know what else I can say to get you to believe me, but whatever this thing is with her and those other women, it's got absolutely *nothing* to do with me, all right?'

But Lucy didn't believe him.

She didn't know if that was because of who he was, of how he acted. Because of what she herself had just seen of his anger, that sudden flare of rage and its promise of violence that had seemingly come out of nowhere.

Or if it was because Roland Kearns was the only thing she had that was even shaped like an answer. In all this time, there hadn't even been a hint of another one, not so much as an indiscernible shape in the mist.

If she believed in his innocence, she'd be left with nothing.

'Why did you come here?' Lucy asked. 'Why did you text me?'

Roland was already moving towards the door.

'Because I know what it's like,' he said. 'The wondering. The questions. When I saw you tonight, pleading, when you looked into the camera and said you wanted to talk . . . I knew you were talking to me. You *thought* you were talking to me. So here I am. We've talked. And now you know that you're actually looking for someone else. And now you can stop hanging around my place at all hours of the night.' The grin returned. 'Unless you're going to come up.' He pulled on the door, discovered it was locked, turned the key in it and tried again. 'And if I were you, I'd go somewhere else. I wouldn't be hanging around here tonight, not after what you did. There's some right fucking creeps out there.'

Then he slipped back out into the night, leaving Lucy alone in the dark.

# Last Seen Alive

Caroline O'Callaghan's home address wasn't far from the bus stop where Tana Meehan had last been seen alive. Less than five miles, in fact; Caroline had been driving home at the time.

After Angela had plugged it into the map app on her phone, a disembodied voice sent her south out of the city to the M7 as far as Kildare town and then out of it, before directing her down a long and winding country road with tall hedgerows rising up on either side. Even with the sun still in the sky – just about – the road felt dark and gloomy.

There were no streetlights and Angela groaned at the thought of navigating it in the opposite direction in the dark. She wasn't used to driving and only did it when she absolutely had to.

Eventually she came to the promised blue dot on her

phone's screen: a small, old, grubby bungalow at the end of a crumbling track, the kind of place you'd see on *Cheap Irish Homes* but before they did any work to it. As she pulled up outside it, her headlights swept across a structural To Do list: missing roof tiles, a pebbledash wall gone green with moss, rotting window frames and a crack going from ground to gutter that looked wide enough to put the post through. Every window seemed to have thick, dirty-grey lacy curtains hanging on its other side.

There were lights on inside and a Nissan Micra parked by the garage door. Despite its abandoned vibes, Caroline O'Callaghan *was* living here, and she was home.

Out of the car, all Angela could see beyond the house were endless rolling fields – and, distant on the horizon, a glow in the dusk that marked the location of Kildare town.

The front door opened and a woman stepped out. She was blonde, twenty-something and dressed in a bright-blue T-shirt and skinny jeans. She was holding a cup of something in her hand. She must have heard Angela drive in.

'Ah, hi,' Angela said, waving. 'Caroline, by any chance?'

The other woman's eyes went to Angela's car, and narrowed.

'Whatever you're selling,' she said. 'I'm not interested.'

'Oh no, I'm not—'

'Get off my property.'

Angela turned and looked at the car too, and realized what had happened.

Back at the MPU, when Denise had learned what Lucy O'Sullivan had done, she'd grabbed her car keys and run. She hadn't stopped to say where she was going, but Don had said he bet he knew: to find Lucy, to make sure she was somewhere safe and then to park herself there, watching her, for the night. Protection on Denise's own time, as he'd put it. He'd told Angela that she should head home.

Deflated, she'd gathered her things and headed for the Luas. But when a tram arrived, she let it pass her by. If Denise was going to spend all night making sure Lucy was OK and tomorrow morning getting a bollocking from Superintendent Hall, she wasn't going to have a chance to call Caroline about the charity-shop appeal, now, was she?

But Angela could. It was really *all* she could do, now, to help. And she felt like she had to do *something*. She wanted to, even if she knew that Denise would tell her off for this, for coming out here before she'd had a chance to call Caroline like she'd said.

But it was easier to ask for forgiveness than permission.

So she'd gone back up to the office, told Don she'd forgotten her water bottle – and she had, but that morning, at home – and retrieved the piece of paper on which she'd written Caroline's details. Dialling the number only resulted in a strange tone; she must have written it down wrong. But the address was less than an hour's drive away.

According to her GoCar app, there was a vehicle available just around the corner, which Angela promptly booked and went to collect. It was a car-sharing service, effectively car rental by the hour, and all the vehicles were covered in the company's white-and-green livery. Caroline must have seen that and assumed, understandably, that Angela was here in some company's car, cold-calling in an attempt to flog their wares.

'No, no,' she said now. 'I'm from the Missing Persons Unit. My name is Angela Fitzgerald. I'm not Gardaí, I'm a civilian – and I don't own a car, so I rented that one, to drive here. And here . . .' She fished her ID out of a pocket and handed it to Caroline, who was still looking unconvinced. 'That's me. You can call Harcourt Square and confirm if you like; I don't mind waiting. But there's something I'd really like to chat to you about, if you have a minute. Detective Denise Pope sent me.'

At that, Caroline's face, finally, softened into something more pleasant than open hostility.

'Denise sent you?' she asked.

'Yes. She couldn't come herself. There's, well . . .'

Where to even start, Angela wondered. But of course Caroline had seen the interview too.

'She'll be trying to track down Lucy, I expect.' She

handed Angela back her ID and nodded at something over her shoulder. 'Shall we sit by the fire pit?'

'Ah . . .' She turned to look. In a corner of the scruffy garden, there was a little stone pit with two plastic Adirondack chairs arranged around it, and no fire in its centre. Angela might not be a guard, and she might never have visited someone's home on the job she *did* have until now, but still, this struck her as an odd suggestion to make. 'Actually, if you don't mind, I've some documents to show you. We're going to need some light.'

'We have our phones,' Caroline said brightly.

'Ah . . . Yes. We do have our phones. But we might need a printer too.'

'I don't have a printer, I'm afraid.'

'Oh.'

Angela was starting to feel an itch she couldn't scratch.

Caroline clearly didn't want her to come inside. But then, Angela pictured her own place: the unmade bed, the dirty dishes in the sink, the smears of various lotions and potions all over the bathroom. And she and her housemates *did* think that people who had the gall to call to other people's homes unannounced deserved to be charged with war crimes, so . . .

Maybe that's all it was.

Or maybe this was the end of Angela's little extracurricular adventure, and from tomorrow she'd be back at her desk in the MPU, trying to bring herself to eat her limp carrot batons, and maybe she was so desperate for something to keep her tethered to this case that she was imagining things.

'Actually,' Caroline said. 'You know something? I didn't realize how dark it had got.' She turned back to the house. 'Come on in. You'll have to excuse the mess . . . We're going to be knocking the place down, you see, so we haven't really done anything with it since we moved in. Waiting for planning permission. You know how it goes.'

So that's all it was, then: a mess.

Angela admonished herself for being so paranoid while, at the same time, trying to remember if she'd seen a planning notice tacked to the gate on her way in.

She was following Caroline inside the house now, over the threshold and into a narrow, dark hall full of muddy browns.

'We can talk in here,' Caroline said, indicating the living room.

Angela went in first. The room was small and cramped and dark – she was beginning to think that was the theme of all the decor – and looked like it'd sat untouched for decades. It also seemed to be home to decades' worth of stuff: framed photos, knick-knacks, fringed upholstery. It reminded Angela of her great-grandmother's house, the place she could only vaguely remember visiting years ago, as a child.

There was one new thing in the room: a huge flatscreen TV, tuned to a soap opera.

'Lots of clearing out yet to do,' Caroline said from behind her. 'It's just trying to find the time, isn't it? We're both so busy with work, and I have my stuff with the families . . . Can I get you anything? Coffee? Tea? Water? Have you eaten? I have some muffins I just baked this morning . . .'

The woman was hyper. Angela definitely wasn't imagining that.

But then, Denise *had* said she was a bit of a busy-body. And some people were inordinately excited by a visit from the Gardaí.

Or, in this case, the Garda-adjacent.

'"We"?' Angela repeated.

'Me and my fiancé,' Caroline said.

Angela's eyes went to the woman's ring finger on her left hand: bare. Caroline's eyes followed Angela's. She put her hands in her jeans pockets.

'What's his name?'

'Why?' Caroline said. But then, perhaps realizing that this was not a normal response to a polite question, said, 'It's David. Dave.'

'Is he here?'

'No, he's working late.' Caroline's expression had darkened a little during this interaction, but now it brightened again. 'Are you *sure* you won't have anything? Not even a glass of water, or . . . ?'

'Actually,' Angela said, 'would you mind if I used your loo?'

'Sure,' Caroline said after a beat. 'Follow me.'

She led Angela out of the living room and further down the dark, dingy hall, to an open door about half-way along it. She reached in and pulled on a string: a light came on, a single bare bulb in the ceiling. It was more than enough to light the space, which couldn't have been more than five feet by five feet.

'Thanks,' Angela said, with a smile. 'Long drive and too much coffee.'

She smiled at Caroline, but Caroline didn't smile back.

Angela flipped down the lid on the toilet bowl and sat on it, and put her head in her hands to think.

On the other side of the door, she heard Caroline's footsteps retreat back towards the living room.

She had no idea what was going on here, only the feeling that something absolutely was. Caroline O'Callaghan was making her itchy. She didn't match this house, and there was something about her demeanour that didn't quite fit, like it was a performance and she was a terrible actress who kept missing her lines.

It was just all so incongruous, off-kilter. A photo that wasn't hanging straight.

It could be nothing, though. Or it could be something that didn't matter. Maybe Caroline was just one of *those* people, the ones who just loved to sidle up to the traumatized, the bereaved, the victimized, and insert themselves into their lives.

Angela had encountered plenty of them through the MPU.

A next-level busybody. They saw tragedy as entertainment, something exciting, a bit of drama in their otherwise boring lives. They elbowed their way into it, offering help and support, supposedly, to people in the worst hours of their lives, in the hope that they'd become indispensable to them.

In itself it wasn't anything criminal but, in this case, Caroline was also playing another role, that of a witness.

She'd reported seeing Tana Meehan at the bus stop in Kildare town that night. But had she really? Or was that just a way to worm her way into this tragedy? How did you prove you had seen a missing person?

As far as Angela knew, a report like that would be taken at face value.

She wondered now: were there other sightings to back Caroline's story up? Did they know that Tana had definitely got the train out of Dublin? Because if Caroline *hadn't* actually seen her, Tana Meehan might never have left Dublin that evening at all. Her last known location might be somewhere else entirely, and that could be hampering the case.

Angela pulled the handle to flush the toilet.

She could see how such a thing would've played out, and why Caroline might think her white lie was a victimless crime. A woman she used to know goes missing. She lives not far from here. Caroline comes up with some story about having seen her at the bus stop in town the night she disappeared.

Maybe she did see someone who looked like Tana, someone who could've been her, but she wasn't sure, and all she did was lie about her certainty. She probably thinks it's harmless. What difference does it make to anyone but her? She gets attention, and some excitement, and access; no harm done.

Angela got up and turned on the tap, let it run for a bit.

Then she took out her phone and composed a text to Denise.

*You can bollock me for this later but I'm at Caroline O'C's house in Kildare and something isn't right. Is she legit? Do we know Tana got the train out of Dublin? Because something is off here. I think maybe she didn't see her. Can't talk but if you can, text back.*

She pressed send and then quietly opened the bathroom door.

Almost directly opposite, another door was ajar, offering a narrow view of what looked like a bedroom decorated in pink-and-blue wallpaper. The light was on in there, which was strange – although maybe this was where Caroline had been when she'd heard Angela's car drive up outside. There was a single bed covered in boxes, and a desk with—

A printer.

A newish one, whose digital display was glowing blue.

That lying little bitch.

Angela checked the hallway: coast clear. She reached out and pushed the door open a little wider, wincing as

240

its hinges creaked. She held her breath, listening for footsteps, but none came. All she could hear was the low murmur of the TV in the living room.

Caroline must still be in there.

She could see nearly the whole room now, which didn't contain much more than she'd already seen: a bed, a desk and a wardrobe.

But now the wall above the desk had revealed itself to her too, and it was adorned with a collection of photos in what she would've guessed were IKEA frames. In their clean, modern, primary-coloured newness, the display looked completely at odds with everything else.

And that was before you looked at the photos themselves.

Angela blinked at them, convinced she was imagining things, and stepped into the room to make sure she wasn't.

No, every single photo – she counted them quickly: thirteen, ranging from the standard 4x6 to something approaching poster size – was of the same person, and that person was, inexplicably, Roland Kearns.

Angela's itch flared up into a third-degree burn.

Why the hell would Caroline have so many pictures of him? Why would she have *any* pictures of him? Were they together? Were they in cahoots?

Was *he* her fiancé?

Had something been going on between them before Tana disappeared – or died? Had Roland killed her to get rid of her so he and Caroline could be together?

But then, earlier, when they'd gone to his apartment, Roland had had only bad things to say about Caroline. She was unhinged. She was obsessed with him. She'd been sitting outside his place at all hours.

Denise had said that was *them*, the Gardaí, that he was being watched.

But had Caroline been there too?

And if so, doing what?

While she'd been mentally asking these questions, Angela had gone all the way into the room.

Now, she was standing within touching distance of the photos. Close enough to see that there was something about them that was much stranger than all of them being of Roland Kearns.

He was alone in every single one of them.

She scanned a second time, just to be sure, but no: there wasn't a single one of him and Caroline together, or of him with anyone else.

And then she saw why that was.

*Every single photo was a crop*. Roland's arm or shoulder or head ended abruptly in every one of them. He had been cut out of larger photos, separated from other people. Several of the shots had disembodied arms or hands belonging to someone else, and in some of them strands of red hair were visible at the edges.

Tana Meehan had had red hair.

Angela knew that from her official photo.

She backed out of the room, back into the hall – still empty – and got out her phone again. With shaking fingers, not from fear but from adrenaline, she sent Denise a second text. *Get here SOS something very wrong.*

Then she held up the phone, zoomed in and took a picture of the world's oddest gallery wall, and sent that to Denise as well.

'Is everything all right?'

Angela turned towards the voice.

Caroline was standing further down the hall, outside the living room.

Watching her.

'Um, yeah,' Angela said, slipping her phone into a pocket. She smiled. 'All good.'

How long had Caroline been standing there? Long enough to see Angela send a text message, or long enough to see her take a photo of the inexplicable room devoted to weird pictures of her missing friend's ex-husband?

'Reception can be a bit patchy here,' Caroline said, her expression unreadable. She waved a hand towards the living room. 'Shall we?'

Angela explained what she needed Caroline to do in as much detail as she could. She took her through each element individually: the letter that she could send to each shop; the list of shops; and the possibility of sharing some sort of appeal on, say, Facebook, aimed at any members of the public who had come across personal items in charity-shop finds that they may not have reported to the Gardaí yet. She talked about a timeline, about the order in which these things should be done. She even told Caroline why they were doing this, although she shouldn't be telling anyone anything about Kerry Long and her personal items surfacing in a donated handbag.

But even so, by the time she'd done all that, Denise *still* hadn't arrived.

And Angela was running out of ideas.

'Would you like to read the letter?' she asked, taking out her phone.

Caroline shrugged. 'You can just email it to me. I'll read it later.'

Angela surreptitiously checked the screen to see if Denise had texted – no – before she put her phone away again. She had to hope that that was because she was too busy driving here really, *really* fast.

'Thanks so much for this.' Angela smiled gratefully – she hoped. 'We're doing everything we can to find out what happened to Tana and the other women. I really appreciate—'

'Didn't sound like it,' Caroline said. 'Tonight, on the news.'

They fell into a silence.

Maybe nothing was actually wrong here. Maybe Angela could quit this excruciating stalling and go. Maybe she *should*.

She made a mental inventory of all the things about Caroline that just weren't adding up. The woman had behaved oddly, initially not wanting to let Angela into her house. She said she was engaged but wore no ring, and Angela hadn't seen any male products in the bathroom, although she hadn't thought to look for them either. Caroline had some weird shrine to Roland Kearns, the ex-husband of her friend who'd gone missing. Who Caroline just happened to be the last person to have seen alive. Kearns had said she was unhinged, obsessed with him. She had infiltrated the families.

What did it all mean? Did it mean anything?

Angela didn't know.

But she knew she couldn't leave just in case it meant *something*.

If there was evidence in this house, the moment she was out the door, Caroline could set about destroying it. Angela at least had a photo of the world's oddest gallery wall, but there could be more here. She couldn't risk leaving Caroline alone with it.

Or, worse again, providing her with an opportunity to flee.

'How did you know Tana?' Angela asked.

'From school,' Caroline said.

'Primary or . . . ?'

'Secondary.'

'And you were still in touch? When she went missing?'

Caroline shifted her weight. 'We'd see each other around.'

'But you must have known her parents, from before?'

'They live close to mine. They wanted to talk to me, after . . . After she disappeared. Since I'd been the last one to see her, I suppose.' A pause. 'At the bus stop.'

'What did you see, that night?'

Caroline's eyes narrowed slightly. 'It's all in my statement.'

'Of course, yes.'

Still no sound of an engine coming up the drive. Still no flashing blue light pulsing through the curtains. Still no authoritative knock on the door, followed by a shouted *Gardaí! Open up!*

What if Denise never arrived? What would Angela do then?

She had a vague memory of something about the power of arrest, about how a non-Garda could effect one if the person was in the process of committing an offence, and they were handed over to a guard as soon as was practical.

But that was designed for security guards and shop-lifters. Angela was a paper-pusher and all Caroline was currently doing was sitting in her own living room, looking at Angela expectantly.

And if Angela was going to fuck this up, there was no point in doing anything.

They'd never get a conviction after an unlawful arrest. If she made one, she might never get to be a guard.

But if she didn't do something, a murder might go unsolved.

'What about Roland Kearns? Did you know him, from before?'

Caroline didn't outwardly react, and maybe it was all in Angela's head, but the air in the room suddenly felt charged with a new tension.

'Just from school,' Caroline said. 'Like Tana.'

'Oh – so you were all in school together?'

A nod. 'Same class.'

Caroline was absently tugging on the thin gold chain around her neck, running her thumb back and forth along it, pulling it away from her skin.

And then, perhaps unintentionally, out from underneath her collar.

Revealing the pendant that was hanging from it.

A small, gold heart, slightly old-fashioned-looking, with ridges across it at an angle and a tiny stone inset, something green. An emerald, maybe.

A piece of jewellery that anyone who followed the news would recognize, because its original owner was wearing it in her official photo.

*Caroline was wearing Tana Meehan's chain.*

Her hand slapped over it now, covering it up, and Angela realized she must have been staring.

Their eyes met.

'Can I see your ID again?' Caroline asked.

Her face was perfectly blank.

'Sure,' Angela said, handing it over.

Caroline studied it intently, even though she already had.

'You're not a guard,' she said then.

'I'm a civilian. Garda staff. In the Missing Persons Unit.'

'So you're not a guard,' Caroline said again.

Angela's phone buzzed.

As she looked down at her device, a new message appeared briefly on screen, offering a preview. It was only enough of the message to see that it was from Denise and it started *Looking for Lucy just leave and ring . . .*

*Fuck.*

'Is there a problem?' Caroline asked, handing back the ID.

'No. Everything's fine.'

'Sometimes you get texts long after they've been sent,' she said casually. 'Like I said, the reception around here is a bit patchy.'

'It's fine,' Angela said.

Even though nothing was now.

Because Denise wasn't coming. She was on her own here.

'I'm very tired,' Caroline said, pushing back her chair. 'It's been a long day. Was there anything else?'

'Ah, well—' Angela started.

'Because if you don't mind, I'd like you to leave.'

Angela stood up too. 'Could we just chat for a minute, before I go?'

'Chat?' Caroline laughed, but the sound was hollow. 'What have we *been* doing?'

'I just have a couple more questions.'

'I *said*, I want you to leave.'

But Angela couldn't.

But by law, now she had to.

But if she left, she was leaving a woman who she was increasingly sure was guilty of something in a house that, potentially, had evidence to prove it.

She needed more time.

She needed to call Denise and get her here. No, there was no time now, not if Denise hadn't even left yet. It would take her an hour to get here from Dublin. Angela could call 999. And tell them what? OK, no, she could call Denise and get *her* to send the locals, and then—

'I want you to *leave*,' Caroline said again.

Angela had to do something.

Anything.

*Time's up*.

'Caroline O'Callaghan,' she said. 'I'm arresting you under the Criminal Law Act of 1997 on suspicion of the murder of Tana Meehan . . .'

But Angela didn't know the rest.

She wasn't even sure she knew that much.

'What the fuck?' Caroline was looking at her like she was certifiably insane. 'Are you having a *stroke*?'

In the beat Angela took trying to come up with a response to that which wouldn't make her look like an even bigger idiot, Caroline bolted for the front door.

*Shit. Shit. Shit.*

Angela ran after her, caught her, gripped her by the

upper arms. She managed to turn her around, swapping their places, so that now it was Angela's back against the front door, blocking Caroline's access to it.

'You can't leave,' Angela said, holding her hands up in a *stop* gesture.

'I'm not going to. *You* are.'

And then—

An engine.

Outside.

Getting louder.

Both their heads turned towards the sound.

While Caroline was distracted by it, Angela flung open the door and ran outside.

Denise was just pulling up, getting out of the car.

'What the . . . ?' she started.

Angela turned to point to Caroline, who turned and ran back down the hall, into the shadows at the rear of the house. 'She's wearing Tana Meehan's chain,' she said breathlessly. 'She's got pictures, a whole load of pictures, of Roland Kearns in the other room. And she's lying. I don't know what's going on but something isn't right. It's not right. I don't—'

'OK, OK,' Denise said, reaching for her gun. No, her radio. Angela watched as she brought it close to her mouth and pressed a finger to the little orange button on top. 'Member in need of assistance. Member in need of assistance.' She called out an Eircode which Angela assumed was Caroline's. Then she threw the device to Angela. 'Go to the gate, watch for them, explain what's going on when they get here. And whatever happens, do *not* come inside the house, OK?'

Angela nodded.

'Go. *Now.*'

Angela did what she was told, turning back only once, to see Denise disappear inside the house with her gun drawn.

# The Knife Ridge

Not long to go now. We're almost there.

There are many stages to an Everest climb; you don't just start up. On the more popular South Col route, after leaving Base Camp, climbers must brave the Khumbu Icefall, a literal river of ice that's in the process of melting, where death by ice boulder, avalanche or sudden crevasse could happen at any moment. If you survive that, you can start making your way up the mountain, stopping at Camp 1 at around 19,500 feet, in a spot known as the Valley of Silence, Camp 2 at 21,500 and Camp 3 at 23,500.

Then the fun *really* begins.

Camp 4, at 26,000 feet, is in what is cheerily known as the Death Zone, a place where the human body is just not supposed to be. It's from here you'll make your summit attempt. You'll leave your tent in darkness, around midnight. You'll ascend in silence, by torchlight, watching the sun rise over the entire world, heading for a piece of rock almost as high as an aeroplane's cruising altitude.

Parts of this last climb have names – the Balcony, the South Summit, the Hillary Step – but only one of them is honest about what it's describing.

The Knife Ridge.

Even if you've never heard of it, I bet you've seen pictures. In fact, I'd be willing to bet you've seen one in particular: a piece of snow-capped, jagged rock that looks like a prehistoric creature's dorsal fin, rising up out of blue sky with a 10,000-foot drop into nothingness on either side of it, topped with a thin but dense line of climbers in their brightly coloured, puffed-up down suits. Underneath that photo was almost certainly a story about the commercialization of Everest, the Nepalese government granting too many climbing permits, and potentially lethal human traffic jams.

Is that ringing any bells? No?

Anyway.

That night, after that first time, I felt like I was stuck on the Knife Ridge. I couldn't move up or down and I was beyond rescue. There was nowhere to go, nothing to do. I had only two options: wait there for death to come, or step off the edge and go meet it.

I was going to kill myself.

That was the plan.

As I drove through the dark, I scanned the road

ahead for something I could drive into, like a large tree or a brick wall. The tank was half full; with any luck, I'd be engulfed in a fireball. I'd die and if *she* hadn't already, she would too.

She was still in the boot then.

That would solve all my problems, and quickly. But there were no suitable trees or walls, at least none that I saw in time, and after driving for a while I emerged on to a coast road. On the other side of a low wall was nothing but beach. I turned right so the sea was to my left, and soon came to a small car park for beachgoers, empty and dark at that time on a cold January evening. I parked at the far end, away from the road and the ramp leading to the sand, with the boot facing the water. I cut the engine and turned off the lights and took a breath for what felt like the first time in hours.

And I thought, *Well, if you're going to kill yourself anyway* . . .

*Why not wait a little while?*

If I did it tomorrow morning, I could go to the party, see Amy and be with her one last time. Enjoy what I now knew was going to be my last night on earth. Say the things that needed saying.

Well, not *all* the things. But something better than whatever my last words to her were as it stood. I couldn't even remember what they were. Probably something like, 'Grand, yeah. See you later.'

I couldn't leave it at that.

So I'd wait until tomorrow when, in the darkness

before dawn, I'd slip out of Niamh's house and come back here. I'd write a note, explaining everything and telling Amy I was sorry and that I really *had* loved her, because I did.

I do.

And then I'd find somewhere I could drive into the water. An open quay or a pier, something like that.

There was just the little issue, then, of the dying woman in the boot and me looking like Carrie after the prom.

Back then, the gym bag I kept in the boot only had gym gear in it. The bag itself was covered in blood – it had been under her head – but bar some socks, the items inside were still dry: a pair of joggers, a creased T-shirt and a pair of running shoes. I garrotted her with her bra, then took myself and the bag down to the shore.

On the beach, the night was freezing with a whipping wind that stung my skin. I did what I could to clean myself up without actually going into the water, partly because I couldn't show up to the party with wet hair and partly because I'd definitely get hypothermia.

Afterwards, everything went back in the bag, the bag went back in the boot with her, and I got back behind the wheel – and then I sat there with the engine running and the heater on full until I could feel my hands and feet again.

That took a while.

Afterwards, I drove until my phone picked up enough

bars of service to call Amy. I told her I was nearly there but had had an absolute nightmare. I said I'd come upon another motorist who'd taken a wrong turn on to a boreen and got themselves well and truly lodged in some mud. I said they'd been standing out on the road, waiting for a passing car, desperate for help. I'd stopped and helped them, and between the two of us we'd managed to get the car out, but I'd got destroyed in the meantime and was now in my gym gear. I joked that Shane, the aforementioned dickhead-in-law, was going to have to lend me something to wear for the evening.

Amy, who sounded like she'd had a couple of glasses of something since last we'd spoken, bought it. She made sure I knew where I was now and where I was supposed to be going, and I told her I'd see her soon.

I remember really wanting to see her, feeling like we'd been apart for months.

Anyway.

Niamh and Shane's house is on a few acres, with a long drive leading from the road up to the house. Cars were parked all along it, the spaces right outside the house long gone: exactly the situation I'd been hoping for. I pulled in behind the first car I came to and got everything out of the back seat. The cake and the flowers and the present. I hadn't been consciously keeping the action out of the back seat that night, but boy was I glad I had. Losing them while assisting another motorist would've been difficult to explain.

Obviously, later, I started putting the women on the

back seat, but by then the stuff their blood destroyed were mere props, disposable.

I don't need to tell you that, though, do I?

I hope you're still listening to me back there.

So, yeah. I went and joined the party. It was, needless to say, a strange night. I was dressed like Shane, for a start. And I was probably a bit hyper, throwing myself into the swing of the enforced fun much more than I would've normally. I hadn't even wanted to go to this thing in the first place, but now it was where I was spending what I thought was going to be the very last night of my life. I acted accordingly. I wasn't worried about the leaking corpse in the boot of my car because I told myself that that was tomorrow's problem, and there wasn't going to be enough tomorrow for it to become one. I'd be gone before it did.

Plus, there was alcohol.

If anyone at the party wondered how someone could've got stuck in the mud on a dry, cold night, or why my helping them out of it resulted in such a mess that I had to change everything down to my socks, they didn't vocalize it.

And they were hardly going to conclude that it was because what I'd really done was kill a woman who was, at that very moment, fifty feet away, locked in the boot of my car, turning blue and stiff, now, were they?

The next morning, I woke to an alarm I'd set for 5:00 a.m. and then woke Amy briefly so I could tell her I was needed back at work, that there was some emergency on a very important project. I kissed her goodbye and told her I loved her and that she was the only good thing that had ever happened to me.

I wanted to say sorry for what I was about to do, for what I had already done, and that she deserved someone good, someone better, and that after all this was over I hoped she'd find him, but I couldn't. Instead, I took some paper and a pen from Shane's study, plus a bottle of whiskey from his bar cart.

The last thing I was going to do was write Amy a note.

I walked down the drive to my car in the pitch-black dark; I had to use my phone's torch app to avoid twisting my ankle. The ground was wet – it had rained overnight. I drove back to the beach . . .

And I drove straight past it.

Because I didn't want to die. Not yet. Not when I hadn't even done the thing I wanted to do. Nearly killing a woman with a blow to the head and then having to finish the job by strangling her, outdoors, with all that blood, all that mess . . .

That wasn't *it*.

That was just me being one of those idiots who trek to Base Camp so they can see a mountain. I hadn't even *started* towards the summit. I'd barely got a glimpse of it through a break in the clouds.

I would do it right and *then* I would end it, I decided. Soon. In the next few days. Before I got that knock on the door.

That particular clock was already ticking, surely.

But I couldn't keep the body in the boot of the car all that time. Obviously. I needed somewhere to stash it.

Somewhere that would be safe, just for a few days.

As it happens, I had just the place.

You see, a few years ago, I'm sitting at my desk in work when, out of the blue, I get a phone call from an heir-hunter. Yes, an *heir hunter*. H-E-I-R. Yes, they're a thing. He was trying to track down the last living relative of some woman in her nineties who had passed away ten months before, who he said was my maternal grandmother's first cousin. I don't have any contact with my family and haven't for years, so this was news to me. I was having visions of having to clear her dusty crap out of some assisted-living facility and getting ready to deny that I was the guy he was looking for when he told me that I stood to inherit the deeds to a cottage in Wicklow.

Now, Amy and I had scraped together everything we had and borrowed more than we could afford to buy a claustrophobic, north-facing three-bed semi in Citywest just the year before. The mortgage payments were killing us financially *and* emotionally, because we didn't even like the place. It certainly wasn't our forever home. Suffice to say that *a cottage in Wicklow* got my attention. In my head, we were already selling both properties to fund the purchase of a site and the building of our dream house when the guy on the phone said something like, 'I'll send you through some pictures via email but, trust me, the reality is worse.'

He wasn't wrong. The 'cottage' was actually four crumbling stone walls and a rotting roof, already derelict and well on its way to being condemned, with no electricity, heating system or phone line. It sat on a tiny plot of level land on what was otherwise a steep incline, just about accessible in good weather via a dirt track and not at all in bad, miles from anywhere else, in the foothills of the Wicklow Mountains, within touching distance of the Dublin county line.

Once the paperwork went through I put it straight on the market as a *development opportunity*, but it didn't even get many views on the property website, let alone any enquiries. The agent said it would take a miracle to sell it. And even if Amy and I changed everything about our lives, future plans and personalities and decided that we could live in a place like that, we didn't have the money to make it liveable while also paying for an actual place to live, so all we could do was wait and hope that someone would, eventually, want it. But that morning, I was glad we'd never got as much as a sniff.

Because that's where I went.

With her.

And my bloody clothes.

And to wash the car once they were all out of it. The only thing still working in that hellhole was the plumbing, luckily.

That was the day I discovered the cellar.

I went there the next time too. And the time after that.

It's where we're going now, but you probably figured that out already, didn't you?

Why didn't I stop? Well, it's simple really. That first woman . . . No one seemed to care that she was gone, let alone where to or who with. I saw one little article online about her being a missing person and then nothing at all after that.

No one came for me.

And that was despite me leaving her phone at the scene with God knows what on it, although maybe she hadn't had a chance to plug any address in yet at all, and when it rained that night perhaps it had washed away the blood or whatever, but there was still my massive fuck-up.

You see, the strap of her bag was still around her shoulder when I buried her up at the cottage, and stupid me assumed that everything that had been *inside* the bag still was. Then, one morning, Amy's had a big clear-out and we're taking bags of stuff off to the clothing bank, and I'm folding down the back seats to make more room in the boot, which involves lifting up a flooring panel, and what do I see?

Stuck down the side, right in the corner: keys and a purse and a card and a bra.

*Her* keys and purse and card and bra, the one I bloody killed her with, *bloody* being the operative word.

261

Honestly, I nearly shit myself.

Amy had come out of the house. She was only a few steps away. I had one second, maybe two, to decide what to do. I reached in, opened one of the handbags Amy was donating and swept all the items inside it. Later, after we'd arrived at the clothing bank, I found a second to hide the most troublesome item inside one of the bag's zippered pockets. Then I shoved the bag down the chute myself, pushing until it disappeared into the darkness, making sure there was no way anyone else could come along and pull it back out.

The signs said that all donations went to a central location to be sorted into recycling, charity, resellers and whatever else. I just had to hope that bag would end up in a recycling plant somewhere, lost for ever.

Whatever happened to it, no one came for me.

So I did it again.

That next one *was* missed, from the get-go. The attention was insane. I didn't know what the difference was, but it was nothing like the first one. I had been far more careful, but this one's face was all over the news. I figured I'd do it one more time, soon, because surely now time *was* running out.

And she turned out to be a right pain in the arse. Not even worth it, to be honest with you. Eventually she became so unmanageable that I took her out of the cottage, threw her back in my boot and drove off, higher into the mountains. I was going to take her out in the most desolate place I could find to show her there was no point in resisting, that there was nowhere else for her to go and no one had any idea where she was, and the only other option was death so, you know, thank your lucky stars and all that.

But then the stupid bitch only went and escaped.

Yeah, I did not know there was a fucking *glow-in-the-dark* emergency release button in my boot that opened it from the inside. We have idiotic children and their litigious parents to blame for that. It's been a safety feature for something like twenty years, it turns out.

So now I'm thinking, *Well, that's it. It's over. My time has come.* I tell myself one night to clean up everything at the house and one more night with Amy, and then I'll finally do the deed, but then I turn on the radio and what do I hear? The bitch has been run over. She got out of my car and ran right into the path of another. And she *died*, taking care of the problem she'd caused me all by herself.

I mean, you couldn't make it up.

But I was a little freaked out by the whole thing. It was all headline news now, all the time, impossible to ignore.

I was, as the mob guys say on TV, starting to feel the heat.

So I packed up my gear, turned my back on the mountain and started the long trek out of Base Camp. My mountaineering days were over. The memories of what it felt like to stand on the summit would have to sustain me.

And then came you.

Just when I thought I couldn't get any luckier.

Because I've been absolutely haunted, haven't I? In the Cork sense. When we say that, we mean exceptionally lucky. As in, *I was haunted the flight was delayed by two hours because the second I got to the airport, I realized I'd left my passport at home.* I used to think everyone in Ireland said it until I went to college and got the complete piss taken out of me.

Anyway.

I hope you've enjoyed our conversation, because we're here.

Welcome, finally, to the Pink House.

The trees were hiding the moon and its light from her, but the stretch of sky she could see was a blanket of twinkly stars. There was no breeze, but the air was gloriously cooler and a little damp. She held her breath and listened but couldn't hear anything that didn't belong to the night.

Cautiously, she picked her way along the path to the lake, moving slowly but steadily, barefoot and practically naked and not caring about either of those things.

Sometimes she feared she was turning truly feral.

Other times she had to acknowledge that she already was that.

The forest fell away behind her and she felt rather than saw a big open space ahead. Then she heard it: the lazy lapping of the water. When her eyes adjusted, she could see the starry sky reflected on its surface and then, gradually, the rocks dotted around its shoreline coming into view too.

She was at the lake, finally.

She lowered herself on to one of the rocks and

slipped her legs under the now rippling stars, into the cold, liquid black beyond—

She exhaled sharply, loudly, and then regretted it.

But it felt *divine*.

And so then she thought, *Fuck it*.

If she was going to break the rules, she might as well smash them to pieces. Make it worth the punishment. She pushed herself off and plunged her whole body into the lake, sinking until every last part of her was beneath its surface, the water a cooling balm on her skin.

She let herself sink a little lower, into the dark.

Down into the depths of its icy cold.

And then she started to think that the easiest thing to do would be to stay there.

Because she couldn't live like this and yet, she couldn't leave. She might find a way to *physically* leave – maybe – but even then, where was there to go? They were miles from everywhere and a lifetime removed from the Before, the Outside, her Previous. But things were deteriorating here, and she wasn't sure how much more she could take. Resignation reached out to her like the arms of water nymphs, pulling on her limbs, tugging on her hair . . .

How easy it would be to let go, to sink, to end this.

But when her lungs began to burn, her body overrode her mind and she started kicking. By the time she broke the surface, gasping, the feeling was gone, the nymphs having retreated to the lake's depths.

She was swimming, and she was cool, and she was

alone. In this place, living like this, they were all things to be grateful for. For the next hour or so she swam and floated and swam some more, feeling languid and loose. Peaceful. Free. She tried not to think of what had led her to this moment or what might come after it, tomorrow. Instead, she clung desperately to the Now, as though it was a lifeguard and she was drowning.

Afterwards, she stood with her feet planted in the shifting silt of the shallows before the shore and watched the sky welcome the sun. She should go back, she knew, before her absence was discovered. She should go get water for the others, like they'd asked.

But instead she made her way to a patch of yellow grass on the bank and sat there, cross-legged and dripping, the skin on her fingers pale and wrinkled, mesmerized by the shards of sunlight dancing on the surface of the lake.

A tiredness overtook her, descending like a heavy curtain, a warm weight on her limbs and eyelids demanding the sleep she hadn't been able to get during the night. She lay down and gave in to it, turning on her side to rest her cheek on her praying hands.

That's where he found her.

# Spoiler Alert

After Roland left, Lucy collected the contents of her bag and set about locking up the place. She was going to head home and face the music. Or face Chris, at least. She was outside the door, still holding the keys in her hand, when she heard a voice say, 'Lucy.'

She turned to find a car parked lengthways across the parking spaces, and a man leaning against the side of it, facing her. There was a streetlight just yards away but it was behind him, and the sky was dark enough now for the amber glow to paint him entirely in shadow.

It occurred to her that he could see her face perfectly well.

'Lucy,' he said again.

She hadn't seen anyone arrive – but then, she'd gone into the back to set the alarm – and she thought for a second it might be Roland, returned, or not even left yet.

But she didn't recognize his shape or his voice.

It wasn't him.

'Can I . . . ?' She squinted into the darkness. 'Can I help you?'

'No. No, actually . . .' The man straightened up. 'I'm here to help *you*.'

'Sorry – do I know you?'

Her tone was artificially light, forced casual. She knew that she definitely didn't know this man but she did know that something was wrong. At the first sight of him, she'd felt a prickle of fear at the back of her neck, but now, even though nothing had actually happened, she was drenched in a cold, electric terror. It was as if her instincts were a few steps ahead, a little further into the future, and they already knew that things were about to go very, very wrong. The keys were still in her hand and she listened to the primal signal deep down inside of her that said, *Put your hand in your pocket, hide the keys in there, and manipulate them so one is pointing upwards, out of your fist, ready to scratch or poke or maim if it comes to it.*

'No,' he said. 'You don't know me. But you know who I am.'

His voice had an odd quality to it, somehow warm and friendly but cold and aloof all at once.

'I don't think I do,' Lucy said, stalling.

She was running through her options. She was at

the door to the cafe, her back almost touching the glass. She could turn around, put the keys back in, open it and lock herself inside. But he'd be on her before she managed that, and even if she did, everything was made of glass. He could smash it if he was intent on getting inside. She might have run by then, through the shop and out the back . . . But there was a heavy lock on the rear door, and it was sticky, and even if she got to it before he caught her, would she get it open before he did? She could say someone was waiting for her. Make like Chris was in his car, just out on the street, and try to leave. But for all she knew, this shadowman had done some reconnaissance before he'd parked here, and he might know that was a lie. And what then? There were houses out there, dozens of them. They were on a residential street. She could just run. *Should* run, to one of them. If he grabbed her, she'd scrape him with the keys, down the side of the face or maybe even right across the eyes, and then—

'You wanted to see me,' he said. 'You asked for my help.'

'I asked for your . . . ?'

Her voice trailed off as the pieces fell into place: the interview. He was here because of the TV interview. This was exactly what Jack had warned about. He'd said it would bring out every crazy in the land, and here was the first guy in the queue, showing up mere hours later.

Lucy's left leg began to shake uncontrollably. Inside that pocket, she gripped the keys until she felt the edges and angles of them digging into her flesh, lest they start to jangle. If they did, her fear would give away the location of what might be her only weapon.

She was terrified. She wanted to run. But she couldn't run because she was terrified that that would be the wrong decision.

'Look,' he said then, 'let's do this.' He straightened up and she braced herself, thinking he was about to come at her. But instead, he walked *away* from her – around the bonnet of his car, to its other side, to the driver's door.

She could run now, she thought. Bolt. Off to the right, around the boot of his car and out on to the street. She was sure she'd get to the kerb before he could get to her, and she could run down the road to the bigger, busier one it intersected with, or into one of the houses, or—

He pulled the driver's door open, filling the car's interior with a bright white light, which confused her.

What confused her more was his getting in and turning towards her, so she had a clear view of his face. He looked to be in his thirties, with short, reddish hair, and she didn't recognize him.

He was smiling.

'Is this better?' he said, holding up his hands. 'I want this to happen on your terms, Lucy.' Then he reached out and pushed open the passenger door. 'Hop in, if you want.'

Lucy's brain supplied a series of ever more ridiculous explanations for this man's presence, for who he could be, for what this confusing exchange was actually supposed to mean.

Because, she reasoned, she'd said lots of things in that interview, not just that she wanted to meet the man who'd taken Nicki. He could be a therapist who thought he might be able to help her get over her obsession with knowing what had happened. Or a psychic who thought he had information from another realm that could help. Or maybe he was someone high up in the guards, some commissioner or something, and he was here to clean up the shitty mess Operation Tide had made and finally solve this goddamn case.

But that wasn't what was important.

What was important was that whoever or whatever he was, he was now twenty feet away from her, inside a car with his nearest door closed.

Lucy pulled her handbag from her shoulder and started rifling through its depths, desperately searching for—

Her fingers closed around the smooth, hard surface of her phone.

'I wouldn't do that if I were you,' he said.

She froze, and then pulled her eyes from the phone to look at him in question.

'Look,' he said, getting out of the car again. 'Here's the deal, Lucy. I'm going to be completely straight with you, OK? You can ring the guards right now. You can even use my phone to do it if you like.' He was coming back around the car's bonnet; she stepped back against the cafe door. 'You can take a photo of my face. Or my licence plate. Hell, I'll even give you my ID to take a photo of, if you like. Fuck it, have the original. If you want, you can tie me up in your car and drive me to the local station.' He stopped at the open passenger door, putting a hand on top of its frame. 'But you won't need to do any of those things, because I won't run away. I'll wait here for them to come and get me. Or for you to go inside, grab the biggest knife you can find and then come back out and slit my throat with it. I'll let you do it. I promise I will.' He paused. 'If that's what you want, Lucy. But take a second to think about it. *Is* that what you want?'

Lucy was completely lost now, staring at him blankly, waiting for him to say the thing that would thread a line of logic through everything else he'd said.

'Because the thing is,' he said, 'if you *do* do any of those things, you will never, ever know what happened to your sister. To Nicki.'

*Nicki* sent a rush of blood into Lucy's ears.

'Or the other girls,' he said. 'Sorry – *women*. Because I'm the only person who can tell you what happened to them. I'm the only person who knows where they are. And you know why that is, don't you?'

'Who are you?' she asked in a whisper.

But he was right.

She did know.

It was *him*.

'And if you're thinking,' he went on, '"Well, we don't need him; now that we know who he is, we can find them," you'd be wrong. Dead wrong. No one will ever find them. I mean, nobody has so far, have they? And if you think I'm being overconfident, or delusional or whatever, well, fine. But do you really want to take that risk?'

'Who *are* you?' she asked again, louder now.

'What do you want, Lucy? A name? An address? A family history? You *know* who I am. I just told you. But you knew who I was the moment you saw me here.'

Had she? Is that why she'd instantly felt so afraid? Was it about something more than a man hidden in the shadows, waiting for her out here in the dark?

'I don't believe you,' she said, unsure if that was even true.

He sighed. 'I do understand your predicament, Lucy. I do. You did just go on national television and invite every lunatic in the land to come and say hi to you. And I'm sure the nation's utterly unhinged will be here soon. The creeps. The psychics. Maybe I'm one of them. Maybe I just got here first. Or maybe your plan worked. Maybe I've done exactly what you asked me to do.'

'So tell me where she is. Where they all are.'

'I want to do better than that,' he said, pointing to the passenger seat again. 'I want to take you to them.'

Lucy shook her head. 'I'm not going anywhere with you.'

Now, he looked bemused. 'Is that your final answer?'

Her grip was so tight around her phone that her fingers ached and the screen was slick with her sweat. She was afraid she was about to drop it. She let go of the keys and pulled her other hand out of her pocket, so she could hold the phone with two.

'Don't you want it all to be over, Lucy?' he said. 'To finally know every last detail? Get all those answers you so desperately seek? What happened that night. If it was that night, or the next day, or later. How our paths crossed. Why I chose her.' He paused. 'Where she is now. Because, you know, you *said* you did. In that interview. I was watching. And I know it's the truth. Obsession must be a terrible thing. Has it happened yet, Lucy? Have you started caring more about finding out *what happened* to your sister than you do *about* her?'

'Fuck off,' Lucy said through clenched teeth, hot with a sudden flare of rage.

'I will if you want me to. But we both know that that's not what you want at all.'

What she wanted was not to be here. What she wished for was that a morning would come when she would wake up and none of this would ever have happened. What she needed was to *know*, so she could start digging her way out of this hole and make her way back to the life she had been living before all of this, so she could at least start pretending that none of it had happened.

But she couldn't do this. No.

It didn't matter what she'd said in the interview.

She couldn't get in this random guy's car just because he said he'd take her to Nicki.

*Could* she?

'You want me to get in your car,' she said, taking a step away from the door, 'so, what? You can take me to where you killed her and dumped her so that you can kill me and dump *me* there too? Do you seriously think I'm going to do that? Do you think I'm stupid? Do you think I'm *crazy*?'

'No,' he said softly. 'But I do think you're desperate. I think you've hung on for as long as you possibly could, but you can't do it any more. You can't spend another night lying awake wondering where your sister is. If she's alive. If she's dead. If she suffered. If she called out for you in the last moment. If she's buried, or dumped, or cut up into pieces. Or if she's locked away somewhere, in the dark, waiting for you to come and save her. And I'm telling you, Lucy, you don't need to spend one more night like that. It can all be over. You can find out. Right now.'

'Is she OK?'

He smiled briefly. 'So you believe me?'

'Is she OK?'

He looked at the ground for a long moment, considering something, then exhaled hard. 'Spoiler alert, Lucy: I didn't kill your sister. But her time is running out.'

# Debrief

Angela had been sitting in the passenger seat of a Garda car parked on the road outside Caroline O'Callaghan's house for over an hour. No matter where she looked, pulsing blue lights lit up the night. When she closed her eyes, they continued to flash on the back of her eyelids. She was getting a headache.

Finally, she saw Denise walking down the drive, lifting the blue-and-white Garda tape and ducking underneath it. Angela studied her for clues as to what had happened inside the house, but there were none; Denise looked exactly the same as she had when she'd arrived. She wasn't even flushed.

The driver's door opened and Denise got in. There was a beat of silence before she turned to Angela and said, 'So. How do I put this . . . ? How about . . . What the actual fucking *fuck*?'

Angela felt her cheeks colouring, but there was no point doing anything except telling the whole truth now. She took Denise through everything that had happened since Denise had left her in the MPU: her deciding to come to Caroline's house, what she saw when she got there, what she'd said, what she'd done.

'Well,' Denise said when she was finished. 'The good news is that the car you rented by the hour is now part of a scene, so God only knows when you'll get it back.'

She'd been barely able to afford renting it for the few hours she'd thought this errand would take. The prospect of an eye-watering charge should've made her feel sick to her stomach but, tonight, that felt like the least of her problems.

'I'm sorry,' Angela said.

'Aren't we all,' Denise muttered.

'What made you decide to come?'

'What do you mean?'

'You sent a text,' Angela said, 'telling me to leave and ring you.'

'That was in response to your first one. But then I got the SOS and the picture, so things changed.'

'Oh.'

Angela had got Denise's first text *after* she'd sent her the SOS and picture. Caroline had been telling the truth about one thing: reception around here was indeed patchy.

'Where is she now?' Angela asked. 'Caroline?'

'Still in there.' Denise cocked her head to indicate

the house. 'They're going to bring her to Naas any minute.'

'Has she said anything?'

'Only that she wants to contact her solicitor.'

'What happened in there?'

'I caught her trying to get over her garden wall,' Denise said.

'What's happening now?'

'Well . . .' Denise hesitated. 'Let's just say there's a patch in the garden that doesn't match up with the rest.'

'Shit. So she . . . Are you saying that Caroline killed—?'

'We don't know anything yet,' Denise said firmly. 'And we never assume. But it turns out we *don't* have any evidence that Tana Meehan was on that train, even though Heuston has cameras everywhere, including inside the trains, and she would've probably got the Luas to the station, which also has cameras, which nobody thought to check either. The local boys just took Caroline's word for it that Tana had arrived back in Kildare. By the time Tide got going, all the data that could've proved otherwise was long gone.' Denise shook her head. 'Bloody morons.'

'But what do you *think*?' Angela pressed.

Denise turned to her. 'What do *you* think?'

Angela tried to push aside her headache and organize her thoughts.

'I think she has some sort of weird obsession with

Roland,' she said. 'Maybe going back to when they were all in school together. Maybe she did see Tana Meehan at that bus stop that night, but she picked her up and brought her here, and something happened – maybe Tana saw her little gallery wall – and Tana ended up dead. Or maybe it was all pre-planned, so Tana would be out of the way and Caroline could have Roland for herself. Either way, afterwards, Tana's parents make contact with Caroline and . . . Well, maybe she gets close to the families because that keeps her close to us, the Gardaí, via the FLOs, and keeps her abreast of the investigation, of what's been found, of what they know. Or maybe she's just a fantasist in all areas of her life, and she just liked being a part of this.' She stopped and looked to Denise, eyebrows raised, waiting for confirmation.

But Denise just shrugged and said, 'Maybe.' She sighed, long and loud. 'We won't get any answers unless Caroline starts talking and, anyway, who cares? It doesn't matter why. That's not going to help anyone. What matters is getting a conviction. I don't need it to come wrapped up in a neat little bow. And if there is something out in the garden, well . . . We can give Tana's parents their daughter back. That's what's important, don't you think?'

Angela nodded.

'Caroline fucking O'Callaghan,' Denise said. 'Who'd have thought?'

'Well . . . Roland Kearns did.'

'What?'

'When we were at his apartment,' Angela said, 'he said she was unhinged. Obsessed with him. He thought it was because she thought he was guilty, but maybe it wasn't. Clearly it wasn't.'

'So we live in a world where my suspect knew more about this case than me?' Denise shook her head. 'How reassuring.'

'Maybe it just takes one to know one. A sociopath, I mean.'

'Maybe.'

'What about Lucy O'Sullivan?' Angela asked. 'Did you find her?'

Denise shook her head. 'She left the studio, she didn't go home and she isn't at her place of business. Chris is still out driving around, but if she wants to be alone . . . I have the lads in Dundrum keeping an eye on the house. They'll call me if they see her.' She settled back into her seat, stretching her legs a little, leaning her head against the headrest. 'So, tell me. What happened with the PCT?'

Tonight, Angela had disobeyed her superior's instructions. She had attempted to arrest a civilian even though she had no authority to do such a thing and didn't even know what people who *had* authority were supposed to say when *they* did it. She had breached Caroline's civil rights by not only attempting to detain her, but failing to leave her private property after she'd asked, twice. And because of all this, Angela had single-handedly destroyed any chance of securing a conviction in what was becoming a murder inquiry.

*What happened with the PCT?* wasn't the next question she was expecting.

'I blame the video,' Angela said.

There was an official video, available online, that had been produced by the Gardaí themselves, which claimed to outline what was involved in the Physical Competency Test. A bleep test; push-ups and pull-ups; an obstacle course, which had been set up indoors in a space that reminded Angela of primary-school PE; and, finally, the push-and-pull test.

And on the video, it looked fine.

*Entirely* doable.

Angela had seen much worse on problematic reality TV.

'And,' she said, 'working where I work.'

How bad could it be if the point of it was to ensure that applicants possessed *the operational fitness required to undertake the actual job* (as the guy on the video said)? The uniformed men and women she saw every day seemed to come in all shapes, sizes and athletic capabilities. There were a few bloated gym-bros in there, sure, biceps straining under the T-shirts they evidently couldn't find in their size, but they tended to be in the ERU or other specialized response units. Most Gardaí didn't even carry *their own hands*, for God's sake. Every one of them walked around with their thumbs hooked into the sides of their stab vest.

'*And*,' Angela said, 'I didn't do enough preparation. I didn't do any at all, actually.'

On the day of the test, she had known immediately that she was in trouble. Perfectly fit and healthy twenty-somethings were fainting, throwing up, crying or, in one poor guy's case, getting so puce in the face that the medical officer had forbidden him from continuing. She'd done her best, and she'd got through the course, but her times just hadn't been good enough.

'Look,' Denise said. 'Don't beat yourself up about it. The PCT isn't fair. And I mean literally. They say they set different passing thresholds based on age and gender, but did you know that across all ages, a disproportion-ate percentage of women fail the test?'

Angela shook her head. 'No.'

'We have to work harder than the lads to pass it,' Denise said. 'Which in a way is fitting, considering it's supposed to prep you for being on the job, and that's what you'll have to do the entire time you're here: work much, much harder than they ever do, just to be treated as something approaching their equal. If you're lucky.'

A lump was forming in the back of Angela's throat because, after tonight, the PCT was a moot point.

She wasn't going to get anywhere near the guards now, unless one of them was arresting her. She probably wouldn't even be allowed to keep her job in the MPU. She had fucked up so majorly, there could be no coming back from this.

'You'll pass it the second time,' Denise said.

Angela looked at her, confused.

'I'm going to take your statement now, OK?' Denise took out her notebook. 'We're going to go through exactly what happened here tonight, when you realized that Caroline O'Callaghan wasn't telling the truth about her witness statement and you remained in the house under the pretence of the very real reason I had sent you there in the first place until I had a chance to arrive, evaluate the evidence for myself and perform a legal and just arrest.' She looked at Angela. 'Are you ready to do that?'

Angela opened her mouth, but no words came out.

'Are you *ready*?' Denise asked again.

'I . . . But what about—?'

'You'll be a great guard, Angela. I'm just making sure of it.'

Denise's phone started to ring then.

Angela, on the verge of tears, turned and looked out of the window at the white overalls and flak jackets milling around Caroline O'Callaghan's property and took what she hoped would be calming deep breaths, trying to compose herself.

'Chris,' she heard Denise say. Angela couldn't make out the words that came down the line then, but she knew this: there was a very panicked man on the other end. 'Hang on, hang on, slow down. She's *what*?'

She was sent to the caravan to await her punishment. It was a four-berth tourer from the seventies whose exterior might have once been a vibrant tangerine but which was now a faded peach colour, tinged green from tree sap and rusted with age. The interior felt damp and smelled terrible, and everything was either fake beech-effect or upholstery printed in a swirling pattern of browns and oranges with a fringed edge.

But the top half of the door was open, the curtains were drawn and the caravan sat in the shade of an enormous oak tree, so it was much cooler in here than it had been in the cabin. She'd even been furnished with a large jug of cold water and something to wear.

It felt less like punishment and more like a reprieve. For now.

The caravan was parked at what they all referred to as the 'top' of the property even though, geographically, it was the lowest point: just after the stone pillars that marked the entrance, about halfway along the

only road in. In the early days, Bastian had told her –
back when Bastian still told her things – it had served
as a sort of security office, a makeshift gatekeeper's
lodge. But during the lockdowns, the rest of the world
seemed to forget they were here, and nowadays no one
ever came wandering up the road.

She herself had been the last person to do it, over a
year ago.

The caravan had been empty that day and pretty
much abandoned since – until Bastian started imple-
menting his *rules* and everything changed. Now, it was
used as a place to separate troublemakers from the rest
of the community until they agreed to stop making
trouble, or leave.

Her stomach flipped at the idea that she might be
forced to go, might be expelled back out into the world,
banished back to her Before life, the one she'd blown
up into a million little pieces when she'd left. (Well,
she'd set a fuse and lit its end. She hadn't stayed to witness the explosion.) She couldn't do that, and she had
nowhere else to go.

And despite everything, she didn't *want* to leave.

She just wanted things to change, to go back to how
they'd been when she'd first got here.

When she'd thought she could stay in this place for
ever.

When she would've been happy to.

Footsteps, on the gravel path outside. She stood and
saw through the half-open door the person they belonged

to: Jamie, already dressed for the day in a T-shirt, shorts and muddy boots, his long limbs tanned and sinewy. He was wearing his trademark baseball cap, the one that was seemingly glued to his head; she wasn't sure she'd ever seen his hair, or even if he had any.

He was carrying a plate of fruit in one hand and a battered tin mug of what smelled like coffee in the other.

'I brought you some breakfast,' he said.

Jamie was from Northern Ireland, somewhere in Fermanagh she'd never heard of, and she loved the sing-song lilt of his accent. He'd been the last arrival before her, and on her first night here had stood and made a speech about the relinquishing and transfer of his newbie status. She'd laughed so much. Everyone had.

Things had been so different then.

'Are you allowed?' She made a face. 'I thought I'd have to make do with gruel. Or starve.'

'Ah, now, don't be like that.'

She opened the door and stepped back to allow him to come inside. He set down her meal on the little table at the caravan's far end, the one with a window that offered a view, underneath the oak's branches, of the stone pillars at the entrance.

Then he took a seat there.

'You're staying?' she said, surprised.

'Well, you can't leave, and I wanted to talk to you.'

'About what?'

She sat down opposite him and pulled the mug of coffee towards her.

'Seed yields,' he said, grinning. 'What do you think?'

'I'd happily talk about seed yields.'

'Are you going to tell me what happened last night?'

She took a sip of the coffee. It was strong and bitter and instantly made her feel a little better.

'I had the audacity to go for a swim in the lake after dark,' she said. 'Because the temperature in that bloody cottage was about a billion degrees, and we were all in danger of dying from heatstroke. We need somewhere else, Jamie. We can't stay in there any more. I won't.'

'And he saw you? At the lake?'

'I fell asleep on the grass afterwards. He found me there and lost his goddamn shite. For no reason.' Her voice was rising. 'He seems to forget we're all *adults*. This is supposed to be a community we're building together, not a fucking dictatorship. I mean, what am I doing in here?' She waved a hand, indicating the caravan. 'Am I being *held* here? Is this some kind of jail cell? Under what law, exactly? Under whose authority?'

Jamie sighed. 'You know what I'm going to say. *He'd* say—'

'—that this is his land and he makes the rules and we can fuck off if we want,' she finished. 'Yeah, I know. But that doesn't sound very *community-spirited* to me.' She plucked a strawberry off the plate, took a bite of it. 'You know, I'm beginning to think all he's interested in doing here is getting free labour. That once everything is built, he'll kick us all out anyway. Make us suffer now, *convince* us to suffer now, by dangling the promise of getting to live in utopia for the rest of our lives, but actually his plan is to evict us all off his land once we've helped him build it.'

Jamie sighed again.

'Try and think about it from his perspective,' he said gently. 'Nothing is more important to Bastian than building this place. But the bigger his ambitions, the more people he needs to help him realize them, and the more people come and stay here, the harder it is to let them live free. Things happened. There was the fire that completely destroyed the main house. Then that couple show up, become best friends with everyone, and run off in the night with everything worth taking that wasn't nailed down. And then poor Tom—'

'—got drunk and drowned in the lake,' she interrupted, impatient. 'I know, I *know*. I've heard all this before. But none of it gives Bastian the right to be an absolute prick. I should be able to sleep where I want and do what I want. Otherwise, what's the point? And things happen. He can't stop them. If someone accidentally cuts themselves while chopping the veg for dinner, what will he do? Ban all knives?'

'He hasn't banned knives, though.'

'Yet,' she muttered.

'He's banned fires in the sleeping quarters and swimming in the lake unaccompanied, especially at night. I don't think any of those things are especially unreasonable, given what's happened.'

'What about forcing us to sleep in what feels like an oven?'

'I think that's more to do with showing your commitment to the community than anything else.'

'Oh, fuck off.' She took another sip of coffee and slammed the cup down a little too hard on the table, spilling some of it over the lip. 'He can't prevent every bad thing. And he'll be living in his little sustainable paradise alone if he doesn't stop this. We came here to live a better life, not suffer through an even more uncomfortable version of the ones we had out there. I came here to get *away* from rules.'

'Speaking of rules,' Jamie said then. He glanced towards the open door. 'I came here to tell you . . . Bastian loves making them, but he doesn't always follow them himself.'

She scoffed. 'We know that. I've seen him swim in the lake by himself numerous times. That's what really irks me about—'

'No,' Jamie said. 'I'm talking about the bigger rules. The biggest one.'

But she didn't know what he meant.

'When he goes into town,' he continued, 'Bastian reads all the papers. Sometimes he even goes into the pub and watches the television. Football matches, mostly. From what I hear. But sometimes . . . Well, sometimes he watches the news bulletins.'

This, technically, wasn't a rule-break. The community was supposed to be free of news from the outside world, because it was just *noise*, and that was also why phones and computers were banned. They were here because they'd all agreed to live simply and peacefully, but they weren't disconnected from the outside world entirely. They couldn't be. People had to leave to fetch supplies, and the funds for materials and the utilities and such came from selling produce at local farmers' markets, and sometimes people had to visit a doctor or leave for a family funeral or whatever. You just weren't supposed to bring anything you heard out there back in here, although there had been exceptions: dire weather warnings, a global pandemic, a good deal going on some material or tool they needed. Consumption alone wasn't a contravention.

It *was* surprising, however, that their great leader, the founder of this place, would *want* to consume it.

'How do you know this?' she asked.

'I hear things,' Jamie said. 'From our regular customers.'

'What else did you hear? Has he been' – she gasped theatrically, pressing a palm to her chest – 'consuming single-use plastics as well?'

But Jamie didn't laugh.

'He saw you,' he said.

'What do you mean? Saw me where?'

Jamie couldn't mean in town, because she hadn't stepped foot beyond the boundaries of the property since the day she'd first stepped inside them.

At first it was because she was hiding, trying to

disappear. Then it was because there was never any real need to, and the longer she stayed hidden, the better chance she had of staying disappeared. Now, lately, it was because she was terrified that, having been here for so long, she wouldn't be able to cope with the world out there.

If Bastian actually did kick her out, she didn't know what she'd do.

'On the news,' Jamie said, and for a beat she didn't know what he was talking about now, didn't connect those words with the question she'd asked him.

'Television and papers,' he added. 'More than once.'

'But why . . . ?' She laughed now, because the only logical explanation for this conversation was that this was all some kind of joke. 'Why would *I* be on the news?'

'Because people are looking for you.' Jamie cleared his throat, evidently uncomfortable with having to deliver whatever news was coming next. 'And I think . . . I think Bastian's told them where you are. He was so pissed off with you, after last night. And your complaining about the cottage, and the rules in general . . . He thinks you have a bad attitude and that it's best that you go. But he doesn't think you'll leave quietly, or willingly, and he probably knows no one else will back him up, so he, ah . . . He called them. He called them and told them you were here.'

'Called who?'

Noise then, outside.

A car horn. The roar of engines. A distant shout.

'I'm so sorry,' Jamie said.

'What are you . . . ? Who did he call?'

She got up and looked out of the open door, and got the answer to her question.

A vehicle was coming through the stone pillars, towards them, wheels crunching on the gravel. There was a woman at the wheel and another one beside her, in the passenger seat.

It was a Garda car, and there were two more behind it.

# Phantom

And then there was that feeling again, that vertigo, like the entire world had tilted up sharply at one end, taking Lucy's insides with it, but her outer body hadn't moved at all. Her stomach swam and pushed bile up into her throat and she swayed a little; she had to put all her weight back against the glass to keep herself from falling over.

'I didn't kill any of them,' he said. 'Well, no. I tell a lie. I did kill one of them, but I didn't plan to. The first one. But her name was never even in the papers. No one even missed her. And then there was the last one, the idiot, who ran off and into the middle of the road and got herself killed.'

Lucy tried to think of things that only the killer would know.

'Tana Meehan,' she said. 'The woman who

disappeared from Kildare town. The first one, according to the Gardaí. Did you kill her?'

'I told you, I didn't kill—'

'Did you *take her*, then? Is she one of them? One of . . . ?' She had to swallow back a mouthful of acrid bile to get the rest out. 'One of yours?'

Because she was still sure that was Roland Kearns. More than ever, after tonight.

The man met her eye, shook his head.

'No,' he said. 'I don't know who she is, or why they've included her with the other disappearances. But that one wasn't me.'

If there had been a wall between Lucy and believing this man, that revelation made a crack in it.

'The one who wasn't in the papers,' she said. 'Where was she from?'

'I've no idea,' he said. 'But it happened in Wexford. Just outside of Enniscorthy.'

The crack split off in multiple directions, weakening the entire wall. It was hard not to push against it, to knock away the stone, to fling herself through.

'Is Nicki alive?' she asked.

'I told you, I didn't kill her.'

'But is she OK?'

'You can see for yourself,' he said, 'if you come with me.'

'Why do I need to go with you?'

'Because this will be over soon,' he said. 'And they'll put me away for a long, long time. So, in these final hours, I think I should get to do things the way *I* want, don't you?'

'Where are we going?'

Another smirk. 'You hardly think I'm going to—'

'How long is the drive?'

'At this time . . .' A glance at his wristwatch. 'We'll be there within the hour, depending on traffic. Long enough for me to answer all your questions on the way. And I will, Lucy. I promise you that much. I'll tell you everything, right from the start.'

*An hour's drive.*

Nicki was alive and had been within an hour of her home all this time.

But Lucy caught herself before that thought could grow roots and take hold. She didn't know anything for sure. Nicki could equally be dead in a ditch somewhere and this guy could just be off his meds.

But if he was, why not claim Tana Meehan too?

'Is it an actual place?' she asked.

'We really should get going, Lucy.'

'Like a house or a barn or well?'

'A *well*?'

'Or is it just some stretch of beach or forest or something, where you go to rape the women who tell you no?'

A hard look fell over his face like a guillotine. It changed his features, turning his eyes glassy and black. It made him look, just for a heartbeat, like an entirely different person. A person who, underneath, wasn't really a person at all.

Then Lucy blinked, and the look was gone.

His face had softened again. He was back to the pleasant, open, almost friendly expression that he'd been wearing before.

'Maybe,' he said evenly, 'you shouldn't antagonize the only person in the entire world who can give you what you want.'

'Sorry,' she said, feeling sick.

'I accept your apology. And as a show of good faith, I will tell you something about it, OK? I'll tell you its name. We call it the Pink House.'

*The Pink House.*

The blood in her veins turned to ice.

That's what Jack Keane had told her Lena Paczkowski had said before she'd succumbed to her injuries. That's where she'd been.

And he'd said *we*.

*We call it the Pink House.*

'Who else is there?' she asked.

He moved away from the car, taking a step closer to her.

'Just imagine, knowing.' His voice was gentle, quiet. 'All the mystery, all the unanswered questions, the torment, the torture of the last . . . how long has it been? A year? A little more? All that gone. Dispelled. Banished, for ever. And in its place, peace.' He paused. 'And in your arms, your sister.'

He took another step closer, then another, and by then he was close enough to reach out and touch her arm.

Lucy didn't recoil.

She was too transfixed by the idea of the moment he'd just described, too drunk on the promise of it to react to anything that was happening in the here and now.

'That's what you want, isn't it?' he whispered. 'You can stop trying. Stop searching. Stop hurting. Come with me and I'll make all of that go away.'

She looked up at him, into the shadows of his face.

'All you have to do,' he said, 'is get in the car.'

And, in that moment, she knew she would.

She was always going to. This was the inevitable end of the inexorable path she'd set herself on.

An overwhelming tiredness settled on Lucy's shoulders like a heavy blanket, enveloping her. She was empty, drained, depleted to the point where she had nothing left. She had lived this life as many days as she could manage. She had been eaten away by guilt. She had done everything she could to try to get the answers. To stop wanting them in the first place. To pretend she could work around the gaping hole her questions had left in the middle of her life.

If this was the only way . . .

'OK,' she said. 'OK.'

He raised his eyebrows, apparently surprised, but recovered quickly.

'There are some conditions,' he said. 'You can't bring your phone and you have to give me your bag.'

She slipped the bag off her shoulder and handed it to him. 'What are you going to do with it?'

Instead of answering her, he held out a hand, flat, for her phone.

Her gut screamed that she should do something before she relinquished it. If this really was him, it was going to get left behind. He must take them off the women and throw them away. So she should throw it herself, now, so that it didn't completely break – into the hedges off to the side, so he wouldn't waste time looking for it, he'd just take her and go and the phone would be there for someone to find. Before she did, she should do something that would help the guards find her. Could she start a voice recording? Initiate a call? Ring Denise and throw the phone and let her figure out what had happened? She could shout out details as they walked to the car. What it was like. What he looked like. The reg. Maybe Denise would hear, if she picked up immediately. Or maybe she could send a text, to Chris.

But then she remembered that it was off. Still off. There wouldn't be time to turn it back on.

There was a rushing sound and then the phone was gone, flung into the night.

He'd hit it out of her hand.

The smash it made when it landed left no doubt that it was in pieces now.

'We really need to go,' he said. 'Come on.'

She followed him to the car, going for the passenger door, but he slammed it closed in front of her, almost catching her fingers, and directed her to the back seat instead.

'Lie down,' he said. 'On your side. Bend your knees.'

'Why?'

'The Q&A portion of the evening is over, Lucy. Just get in. This is how it has to be.'

'Was this how it was for her?'

'This is different,' he said. 'You're coming willingly.'

She saw a flash of Nicki then, screaming and struggling, eyes wide with terror—

Lucy started to cry.

She got into the back seat and lay on her side, as instructed. The voice in her head was screaming, *Are you actually doing this? Is this really happening? Have you seriously put yourself in this position? Wake up! Look around! You aren't just being taken; you're giving yourself away. This man could be lying. And don't you realize it's worse if he's not?*

But there was a comfort in having made this decision, in relinquishing all control, in knowing that she was being taken to Nicki instead of having to search the whole world for her. She let him tie her ankles together with a seatbelt, and then do the same with her wrists. The bindings were tight, already uncomfortable, the material cutting into her flesh.

He tugged on them to make sure she was secure, slammed the door closed and got behind the wheel himself.

The engine revved to life.

There were several jerking movements as he got

himself out of the cafe's little car park, and then a swerve as he turned out on to the road.

'So,' he said then. 'Where did it all start? That's always what people want to know, isn't it? Where it began. I have to say, I never really understood this obsession with the beginning until I inadvertently developed it myself, watching true-crime documentaries. Surreptitiously watching them, mind you. I never do it openly. Not because it would, you know, arouse suspicion or anything. *Please*. I just don't want to be known as someone who does that. Because let's be clear . . .'

The keys were still in her pocket. He hadn't noticed them. Lucy couldn't reach them now, of course, but whatever was going to happen was going to happen when they stopped.

When they got to the Pink House. When he released her.

When she was reunited with Nicki.

As soon as she was, she was going to find a way to use them.

She was going to save them both.

# Safe and Well

The address the local boys had given Denise was actually for the station in Bandon, because, they warned her, the only way to find this place was to meet them there and follow them to it.

Now that they were here, Angela could see why.

There was no sign, no letterbox, no gates or fencing. There was nothing at all visible from the road. There wasn't even a *road* really, just a gap in the treeline through which, if you knew what you were looking for, you might spot two parallel tracks in the dirt leading you into the forest.

'How is anyone supposed to find this place?' she asked.

Beside her, in the driver's seat, Denise shrugged. 'I think that's the point, isn't it?'

A pale arm in a short blue sleeve shot out of the

driver's window of the marked car in front of them, waving to get their attention and then pointing down at the ground.

*Stop here.*

All three vehicles took this literally, stopping where they were, lined up one behind the other in the dead centre of the track.

Everyone got out, wiping glistening foreheads and gulping back warmed bottled water, revealing dark patches under their arms. A couple of them untucked their polo shirts from the back of their waistbands and flapped them a little, presumably trying to get some air to – if they were anything like Angela – the pools of sweat in the small of their backs. The Irish weather could always be relied upon to improve in the first week in September just as all the schools went back, but this year it had excelled itself, following an official late-summer heatwave with another week of above-average temperatures. In a country famous for rain and pale skin, where homes were built to hold the heat and air conditioning was only something you worried about when you were booking your Spanish sun-holiday, it only took a few degrees to get everyone melting.

They gathered in a group on one side of the track, drawn to the one whose trees offered some shade. There were nine of them in total: Angela, Denise and seven uniforms.

Everyone listened intently as the man who'd introduced himself to them as a sergeant told them what to expect when they reached the property. He described the layout – there was a lake, he said, gardens and at least seven small buildings dotted throughout – and warned that its owner was unlikely to welcome them.

No one except Denise was armed, and that was only because, as a detective, she always was; there was zero expectation that anyone on the property would have any weapons, least of all firearms.

Everyone assembled was wearing their stab vest anyway, because they had to.

Even Angela had been given one. The others were complaining that it was *way too warm for this shit*, but she liked hers, liked the feel of it. It made her feel taller, somehow. She walked with a straighter spine with this thing on her. And she couldn't help but hook her thumbs under the straps at her chest, like all the guards did.

'They've always been a friendly bunch,' the sarge said, diverting a rivulet of sweat that was running down the side of his face into his hairline with the back of his hand. 'But we haven't seen much of them for the last two years – understandably – and what I've heard around the town suggests the atmosphere here has changed considerably in that time. So let's be friendly but firm. We don't have any beef with them, but we are not leaving until we speak to her. No lights, no sirens, no attitude. OK?'

Heads nodded.

'Detective Pope will take the lead and, when we locate her, do all the talking. Everyone else hangs back and ideally keeps anyone we meet in there well back too. Understood?' There was more nodding and a few affirmative sounds. 'Good. Let's go.'

As they all started back to the cars, Angela felt a grip on her arm, stopping her.

When she turned back, she found herself caught in Denise's intense glare.

'You don't need to tell me,' Angela said immediately. 'I know. I won't say a word.'

Denise nodded and let her go.

They both got back in the car. In just the few minutes it had been sitting still, the air inside it had thickened into a dead, suffocating heat.

Denise put up the windows and turned the cold air on full blast.

As the convoy set off again, Angela took a deep breath.

'Um, look,' she said. 'I just want to say . . . Thank you. For everything. And for bringing me along to this. I know I don't deserve it.'

Denise's eyes stayed on the road.

'Well,' she said, 'you've come this far. You may as well see it to the end. And fuck knows, we both need the closure.'

This was true, but Angela couldn't help but note that Denise hadn't corrected her.

They drove on in silence.

The road – the track – appeared to be interminable, looping and winding through the trees in a nonsensical shape that the trees must have dictated. Angela felt like she was in a mediocre fairground maze, designed to make the trek from entrance to centre feel much longer than it actually was, to give the *impression* of distance. More than once, the track curved so much it seemed to double back on itself, and the position of the sun's glare backed up Angela's theory that the track wasn't taking them from A to B so much as it was supposed to deter anyone who might find it from making the journey.

If she hadn't been being led down it in a convoy of Garda cars in broad daylight, she might have worried she was being led to her death.

'Maybe this is where they all go,' Denise muttered.

'Who?'

But now the expression on the other woman's face made it clear she hadn't intended to say that out loud and for a moment it seemed like she might tell Angela to forget it.

'All the missing women,' Denise said then. 'When they leave the face of the earth. Because that's what people always say, isn't it? About unexplained disappearances. The ones where it's all dead ends and no leads. *It was as if she'd disappeared off the face of the earth.* Well, maybe where they went is here. Or a place like here. That isn't on any maps, out in the middle of nowhere. A place no one even thought to look. A nice place.'

Angela said, 'Hmmm,' like she agreed there was merit to this theory, but she didn't – and she was surprised to hear such total shite come out of Detective Pope's mouth.

She didn't need to be on the other side of Garda training to know that most missing women were not off enjoying another life of nature and open sky and peace.

They were broken bones caught in scraps of ripped, rotting clothes, or bloated, decaying, fluid-leaking bodies that would be bones soon enough.

They were hastily buried in shallow, unmarked graves in forgotten places, or hiding under new foundations in busy ones, or trapped leagues under the surface of whatever body of water their killer had dumped them in.

They were fierce family secrets or suspicions too vague ever to act upon or the dark heart beating beside some other woman in a marital bed, who was still pretending she didn't feel it.

They were the premature ends of dreams and plans and generations.

They were unfinished bridges jutting off the edges of cliffs, ending in mid-air, no further on for the love to go.

They were faces frozen in time, in their official photos.

They were dead.

The woman who was here *wasn't* missing. That was the only reason *they* were here.

'I've put in for a transfer,' Denise said. 'Fraud Squad. I can't look for stolen women any more. Give me phishing texts and fake Nigerian princes and a Mr Right who can't wait to come visit but just needs you to loan him the money for his plane ticket first.'

And Angela knew then that Denise didn't actually believe what she'd said about the fate of missing women.

She just desperately, for the sake of her own sanity, needed to think that she could.

The trees overhead suddenly burst open into a stretch of bright-blue sky just as two stone pillars appeared, one on either side of the car. The track continued beyond them, but there was still no signage, no visible buildings and no people. The pillars themselves seemed to be the only evidence of civilization.

Until a caravan, tucked beneath an enormous oak tree, came into view.

And then, a moment later, a woman stepped out of it.

'Shit,' Denise said, slowing the car.

Angela undid her belt and leaned forward, getting as close as she could to the windscreen without actually leaving her seat.

The whole way here, she hadn't really believed that they were going to find what they'd been promised would be waiting for them, a missing piece of the puzzle that had never been missing at all, but had just been here, waiting to be discovered, all this time.

But they had found it.

'It's her,' Angela said, incredulous. 'It's actually *her*.'

# Summit

The irony was that he actually had been reading *We Don't Know Ourselves: A Personal History of Ireland Since 1958*. Properly reading it, not just pretending. He'd been totally engrossed when Amy suddenly said, 'You are fucking *kidding* me,' from the other end of the couch. When he turned to her for some context, he saw that she was staring open-mouthed at her phone. He didn't ask, 'What? What is it?' because he knew he need only wait.

'Lucy O'Sullivan,' she said, pronouncing each syllable distinctly and, in his opinion, with an excessive amount of glee, 'is live on TV right now talking about her sister.' As Amy spoke, she continued scrolling through a busy WhatsApp chat that, from what he could see, was mostly just GIFs of people eating popcorn. 'And apparently she isn't holding back.'

He understood the words, but not the sentences. He had never heard the name before – if he had, it hadn't stuck with him – and he had no idea why he should care about this woman *or* her sister.

Amy clearly cared, but that didn't mean much. Based on his wife's broad range of interests, the likelihood of this woman being NASA's first female astronaut was about on a par with her being famous for sticking needles into her lips.

His wife was hopping up off the couch now to grab the remote and flip impatiently through the channels until she found what she was looking for.

Which turned out to be a slightly chubby, pale, unremarkable woman.

'Who's she?' he asked.

'Shit, I've missed ten minutes,' Amy muttered, furiously jabbing at the buttons on the remote until the scenes on screen began to move backwards at high speed. 'Oh – that's the sister of one of the missing women. The one from Dundrum.'

The one from *Dundrum*?

He saw his own quizzical expression reflected in the TV screen and instantly let it fall from his face.

When the backwards-moving people on screen changed to ads, Amy pressed play and plopped back into her seat on the couch.

He looked down at his book. He'd just turned to the start of a new chapter. '1984–1985: Dead Babies and Living Statues'. He felt its pull, but . . .

'Yvonne says she's absolutely *hanging* the sister,' Amy said, reading a message on her phone as if it were an item on a restaurant menu that was making her mouth water.

He gave up. He closed the book.

And then he watched the pale, chubby woman look directly into the camera and ask him to help her.

Of course, the woman on TV didn't know that she was talking to *him* specifically. And she didn't know that he couldn't possibly help her. But he was sitting inches from Amy, who was staring at this woman on screen, entranced by her and what she was saying, and this woman staring directly into the camera, talking to *him* . . .

Christ, it was thrilling!

He felt as if the air in the room was crackling with the electricity of the moment, *sizzling* with it. It took everything he had not to react. To hold himself perfectly still, to steady his breathing, to keep his expression somewhere between mildly curious and totally neutral.

And it got him thinking.

The hardest part, by far, was getting them in the car. The second hardest part was finding someone suitable at the right place and time, and under the right conditions. That was also the stretch of proceedings that carried the most risks.

But what if there was a woman who'd just get in the car? One who was willing?

'I just want to talk,' she was saying on screen, voice

cracking, eyes glistening. 'I just need to know . . . Tell me what you did . . . Show me. Please. Come get me. I will go with you if you take me there.'

She was so fucking desperate. And desperation made people do very silly things. Stupid things. Like push for the summit even though they knew they didn't have enough left in the tank to get down the mountain, literally and figuratively. Or get into a car with a man who, for all they knew, was a goddamn serial killer, just because they had to know what had happened to their sister even if the only way to find out was to have the same thing happen to them.

Because she couldn't possibly think she was going to survive it, could she?

Unless . . .

This could be a trap. A ruse. A set-up. Some harebrained scheme courtesy of the guards running that three-ring circus – what did they call it again? Operation Tide? What the hell did any of this have to do with *tides*? – that was designed to force him out of the shadows, so they could pop out swinging their gundicks around and arrest his arse.

He'd be rightly done for then.

He felt fairly confident that he'd made himself extremely difficult to find if you worked backwards from the scenes, but if they were *starting* with him, if they had a name and an address and a registration number and property records, they'd have no trouble making their case.

It'd be all over. No more climbing.

He wouldn't even be able to trek to bloody Base Camp then.

And yeah, OK, he had never been trying to get away with all this indefinitely, but that didn't mean he wanted to serve himself up on a platter like a right fucking idiot either.

When her interview finished, there was this whole other segment, something the voiceover referred to as 'our special investigation' several times that, in summary, made it clear the guards were far too lazy and stupid to come up with something as elaborate as that, let alone carry it out.

It even suggested that the reason the guards hadn't found the missing women was because they hadn't even managed to identify the right ones.

A fact which he knew to be true.

So he decided that he would take one last risk and approach this sniffling, desperate girl. To call her bluff. To see if she'd get into his car.

If she refused, he'd just revert to his usual methods.

But it had been even easier than he'd hoped. She was in the back now, behind him, and he was telling her everything.

He was going to tell her the whole story, from beginning to end, and in chronological order so there'd be a little twist in the tale.

It felt good to talk.

What was even more surprising to him than her

getting in was how docile she'd been since they'd driven away. How calm. Not resigned exactly, but accepting of what was going to happen.

Unless she didn't quite realize what was in store.

Or maybe she thought that pathetic little bunch of keys in her pocket was going to save her.

Surely, he thought, at some point, she'd realize what she'd done, what was happening to her, and the penny would drop. She'd have second thoughts. Start thinking clearly. Panic.

And that's exactly what happened. After they left the amber glow and car horns of suburbia, and the intermittent bright lights of increasingly infrequent villages and crossroads. When they finally plunged into the deepest dark of the countryside – that was when she came to her senses.

It could've also been because, beneath the car, the ground was rising and had been for some time.

It must have occurred to her that they were heading into the mountains.

She started screaming.

*Really* screaming, like she was being attacked by an animal or something.

Actually, it reminded him of that Werner Herzog documentary, the one about the guy and his girl who got eaten by a bear. A video camera had captured audio of the entire attack – only audio, the lens cap had remained on – and that footage had ended up in the hands of one of the dead guy's ex-girlfriends. The documentary hadn't included the audio, but there'd been a really odd, silent scene where Herzog listened to it via headphones and then told the woman that she should never, ever listen to it and basically if she'd any sense, she'd destroy it.

The viewer had had to imagine what the attack must have sounded like and, in *his* head, it had sounded like this.

Screams.

Some high-pitched, out of pain.

Others guttural and raw.

And, just like if you're getting eaten by a bear out in the middle of nowhere, completely and utterly pointless.

'Look,' he said, 'if you can't stop screaming, I'm going to have to make you.'

And he did.

# Answers

The Nicki O'Sullivan that Angela knew was the woman captured in her official picture, the one that had been given to the guards and distributed to the press. In it, she was sporting bright-purple hair that had been inexpertly dyed and haphazardly cut. The torn collar of a green T-shirt was visible, her eyes were ringed with smudged black make-up, and she was making a face. Brows raised, face turned slightly to the side, as if asking, *Well, what do you think?*

And that's exactly what she had been doing. The photo the nation was so familiar with was a selfie Nicki had snapped on the bus home after getting a friend to dye her hair. She'd sent it to her sister to show her her new look. That was why, whenever it appeared in the press or on television, the image seemed a little blurry:

Lucy only had the low-resolution version of it she'd saved to her phone from WhatsApp.

When the guards asked families for photos of their missing loved ones, the advice was always the same: if possible, provide a recent photo, and one in which the person looks the way they did when they disappeared. If you have a guard who's particularly empathetic, or who knows something you, the family member, haven't yet been told, he or she might lower their voice and add that you should perhaps choose a photo that isn't a favourite, of an occasion that wasn't important or which there were plenty other photos of, because there might come a time when you never want to see that picture ever again.

Now, as the real-life, 3D version of Nicki O'Sullivan walked towards them, Angela saw the fallacy in relying on a single photo to accurately capture anyone.

The short, purple hair was gone, replaced by shoulder-length dark locks that were flowing freely. Her skin had the kind of colour you get from being outside a lot – a deep, even tan – and she looked thinner, maybe even underweight. She was barefoot, in shorts that looked like they'd been designed for men and a plain white T-shirt that hadn't been white for quite some time.

Even her face looked different, now that there were other angles to it.

Denise had pulled over and she cut the engine just as a man came out of the caravan too.

He was of a similar age with a similar tan, wearing

a faded baseball cap. He stopped just outside the caravan and frowned at them.

Nicki, meanwhile, looked furious.

She greeted Angela and Denise with, 'What the fuck is *this*?' when the three of them met at the edge of the track.

'I'm Detective Garda Denise Pope' – Denise showed Nicki her ID; Nicki folded her arms and refused to look at it – 'and this is my colleague Angela Fitzgerald from the Missing Persons Unit. Can you confirm that you're Nicola O'Sullivan, known as Nicki, with an address on Ballinteer Road in Dundrum, Dublin 16?'

'What's this about?'

Angela glanced towards the pillars, where the other two marked cars had stopped. The uniforms were getting out but staying there, hanging back, watching.

Even though they had located one of the state's most high-profile missing persons, everyone's expressions were grave.

If only they'd found her earlier.

If only, at some point in the last year, she'd called them.

Baseball Cap Man came and stood next to Nicki and touched her arm gently, as if to calm her down.

'We're here,' Denise said to her, 'because your sister, Lucy, filed a missing person report in June of last year. You're not in any trouble and you don't have to leave with us, but we would like to have a quick chat before *we* leave. Is there somewhere we can talk?'

Angela hoped no one would suggest the caravan.

Not in this heat.

'How about over there?' Baseball Cap said, pointing. One of those all-in-one picnic-table-and-chairs was just visible on the other side of the oak's trunk.

In the shade, Angela noted. Thank God.

Nicki shot Baseball Cap a murderous look.

'Great,' Denise said. 'Thank you.' Then, to Nicki, 'Shall we?'

Baseball Cap whispered something to her that sounded like *just talk to them* and she rolled her eyes and started stalking away, towards the table, exhaling loudly, like a sulking teenager who's heading upstairs to slam their bedroom door and blast early Metallica albums.

'She'll be fine,' he said to them, apologetic. 'She's just . . . It's already been a bit of a day here, you know?'

Angela nodded, even though she knew that whatever had happened before they'd arrived would be completely forgotten by the time they left. It wouldn't matter a damn. And Nicki O'Sullivan was never going to be fine again. She didn't know it yet, but she was in the final moments of the last truly good time in her entire life. However she felt now, whatever mood she was in, whatever life was like for her here, in this place – it was a peak. A high point. The crest of a great wave. All that was waiting on the other side was a descent into hell.

And they were the ones who were going to have to push her into it.

Denise and Angela set off across the grass, which was littered with parched leaves and rotting acorns, and joined Nicki at the table, taking seats side by side, opposite her.

'Obviously,' Nicki said, folding her arms, 'I'm not missing. And I'm not leaving here, OK? You can tell her that.'

'This won't take long.' Denise had taken out her notebook and began to read from it now. 'Nicki, your sister, Lucy, filed a missing person report on the four-teenth of June last year. She told Gardaí she hadn't seen you or had any contact with you since you'd left your home two nights before, on Saturday the twelfth, to meet friends in town. She said you were living at the same address with her and your boyfriend, Chris, who also was concerned he had had no contact with you. When Lucy contacted the friends you'd been with in the – it was the Duke, wasn't it? – they told her you'd left without saying goodbye and that they hadn't seen or heard from you either.'

Nicki looked surprised. 'Luce contacted my *friends*?'

'Your phone was found discarded in a laneway,' Denise continued, 'near the Duke, having suffered sig-nificant damage. You were captured on CCTV moving along Duke Street towards Grafton Street, but after that, cameras were unable to pick you up again. You left your passport at home and you never touched your bank account.' She stopped to flip the notebook to a fresh page. 'Nicki, can you tell us what happened between you leaving the pub that night and you arriving here?'

Silence.

Then Nicki said, 'CCTV?'

Denise nodded. 'Yes.'

'And you . . . Someone looked at my *bank account*?'

'We investigated your disappearance, Nicki. The Gardaí did. There was concern that you may have come to harm.'

'*What?* Why?'

'Because your sister didn't know where you were,' Denise said evenly, 'and she had no way of contacting you.'

At this, Nicki rolled her eyes.

'Let's go back to that night,' Denise said. 'To your phone. Is there anything you can tell us about that?'

'What do you mean?'

'Did you put the phone there, or . . . ?'

Now Nicki looked genuinely confused. 'How else would it have got there?'

'So you did?'

'*Yes,*' she said impatiently.

'Can you tell us why you discarded your phone?'

'Because I didn't want anyone to be able to contact me, obviously.'

'Why not?'

Nicki threw up her hands. 'Because *I didn't want anyone to be able to contact me*!'

The end of that sentence had come with another

eye-roll, and now Nicki was regarding them like they were a pair of absolute idiots.

'So,' Denise said, 'you didn't tell your sister you were planning to come here?'

'No.'

'Can I ask why not?'

'It's not a crime, is it?'

And that wasn't answering the question, Angela thought.

'When you left the pub that night,' Denise said, 'and discarded your phone, had you already decided at that point to permanently leave your home?'

'Well, I was going to have to permanently leave it anyway, wasn't I?' Nicki said. 'Lucy had decided to sell it.' A new thought seemed to occur to Nicki then; her face changed into something less confrontational, more curious. 'Did she? Has it been sold?'

'No,' Denise said. 'It hasn't.'

'Well . . . *Good*.'

Denise looked around. 'Nicki, what is this place? Does it have a name?'

'We just call it the Farm.'

'*Is* it a farm?'

'Sort of,' Nicki said. Her features softened; this change in topic had relaxed her a little. 'It's a community. For living simply and sustainably. If you want the same things that the people who are already here want, you can join. In exchange for food and board, you contribute. We have chickens, we have a polytunnel, some people bake . . . We live off the land and we sell what we can at local farmers' markets to buy what we need but can't grow. And Bastian – he owns the place – I think he leases a few acres to a local farmer too. An organic one. That money is used for building materials, hiring machinery, getting people in when there's something we can't do ourselves. Things like that.'

'What are you building?'

'Well, *everything*,' Nicki said, waving a hand. 'We only have outbuildings, really, at the moment. A few tents, a couple of caravans. A mobile home – we use that as an office. Bastian works in there and it's where we have group meetings. There is a house, the original farmhouse, but there's only, like, two bedrooms in there, and the place is falling apart. Well, everything that's already here is falling apart, which is why we have so much work to do. The idea is for there to be an entire village here, eventually.' She exhaled. 'Bastian's been at it in some form or another for, like, ten years.'

'How many people are here?' Denise asked.

'Thirteen, at the moment. Including the children.'

Denise looked surprised. 'There's children?'

'Three,' Nicki said. 'Bastian's two. They're toddlers. And Marissa just had a baby, like . . . He's, what? Four months old now, I think?'

'Where is everyone?'

'Where they always are,' Nicki said, pointing over

her own shoulder. 'We're a mile away from it. This is just, like, the security cabin.'

'Did you come here voluntarily?'

Nicki's face hardened again. 'Of *course* I did.'

'You came here straight from Dublin?'

'Basically, yeah,' she said to the tabletop.

'How did you know it was here?' Denise asked. 'We couldn't find anything about it online and only the farmhouse is on the map. And it's there as a private residence.'

Nicki glanced towards the caravan, and when Angela did the same, she saw Baseball Cap sitting in its open door with his elbows on his knees, watching them.

'I spent a summer working in the Algarve,' she said then. 'As a holiday rep. One of the guys there – he worked in the local Irish bar – he'd been here, the summer before. That was, like, four years ago now, so I didn't know whether or not it was still here, or exactly where it was, but he had said if I was ever looking for it, I could just ask around in town and they'd know where to send me. You're not allowed to put anything about it online, you see. While you're here or after, if you leave. Bastian doesn't want it. He doesn't want glampers and Airbnbers and people who only want to live off the land long enough to make a fucking *reel* about it.'

'Right,' Denise said. 'So you . . . ?'

'I met some people. That night. After I left the

Duke. A gang of Dutch students, travelling around Ireland for a couple of weeks. Just, like, randomly. On Grafton Street. They asked me to take a picture of them, and we got talking, and they said come for a drink, and they seemed so cool . . . My friends had been . . . well, pissing me off, frankly. I crashed on their couch that night, in the place they'd rented in Temple Bar. They'd rented a car and were heading south with it, and I just, you know, asked if I could tag along.'

'Was this the following day?'

Nicki chewed on her lip for a moment, as if weighing up whether to answer yet another of Denise's questions or tell her where she could stick it.

'I spent, like, five nights with them,' she said then. 'Got as far as Cork. And then with what cash I had left I got a bus to Bandon, and then another one to Dunmanway, and there I walked into a cafe on the square and asked if they'd heard of this place. The guy behind the counter took me back outside and said, "Bastian, she's looking for you." He was right there, across the road, on a market stall. We got talking and I convinced him to bring me back here with him.'

Denise and Angela exchanged a glance. That was probably why the CCTV had lost her: because in the middle of a crowded street, she'd slipped into a group of other women. Their rental car explained why Nicki had never been picked up on cameras at bus or train stations, and their being visitors here on holiday explained why they'd never reported having met her. The people who might have seen her on the buses she took to West Cork would only have had a slim chance of seeing anything in the news about her being a missing person, because, like all other low-risk adults who disappear, she'd only got a couple of virtual column inches to begin with.

'And you like it here?' Denise asked.

'It's fine,' Nicki said.

*But you've stayed here all this time*, Angela thought.

'But you've stayed here all this time,' Denise said.

'Yeah, well.' Another shrug. 'I liked it more in the beginning. When there weren't as many bloody *rules*.'

'Is there internet here? Do people have phones?'

'That's one of them,' Nicki said. 'That we don't bring noise from out there in here.' She paused. 'That's one of the rules I *like*, actually.'

'But when you leave here,' Denise pushed. 'For the farmers' markets and what have you. You never see newspapers or—?'

'I've never left here.'

'Never?'

Nicki shook her head. 'Not once.'

'In more than a year?'

'I haven't been off the property since the day I arrived.'

'How come?'

Nicki threw up her hands, exasperated. 'Because I came here to get *away* from everything out there, OK?'

The man who had called the Garda Confidential Line to say that he knew where Nicki O'Sullivan was hadn't left a name or any contact details, but he *had* said that she had no idea what had been playing out in the headlines since Jennifer Gold disappeared and Operation Tide commenced.

Which seemed impossible, and also convenient.

But maybe it *was* true.

'Why did you feel like you couldn't let Lucy know where you were?' Denise asked. 'Or even just that you were OK? At any point, in all this time?'

Angela noted the careful phrasing of the question. What Denise was really asking, of course, was: *How on earth could you let your sister, your only blood relative, think that you were lying dead in a ditch somewhere when you were actually here, in the beautiful West Cork countryside, living the good life, enjoying unprecedented peace?*

Nicki frowned, genuinely confused. 'But why wouldn't I be OK?'

'Well,' Denise started, 'it's just that—'

'Look, I know what you're thinking: that I'm a selfish bitch.' Nicki said this to Angela, who immediately tried to rearrange her face to that of someone who was definitely *not* thinking that. 'But I'm an adult. And you don't know my life. And I have every right to do whatever I want with it. Nothing I ever did, or was ever going to do, was going to make my sister happy. Because she doesn't want to be happy. She wants to be sensible. And responsible. And boring. And she wants me to be all those things too because ... Well, honestly, I think she sees my life and the things I've done and the places I've been and she's jealous. She wishes she could be like me, but she can't, so she doesn't want me to be like me either. All that's happened here is that one day, I got some sense and I stopped trying to please her. And Chris. And everyone else. I came here because I can't live out there, with them, and all their expectations and their little comments and their potent, never-ending, bottomless fucking disappointment in me, which, incredibly, all stems from the simple fact that *I* don't want what *they* want.'

'Did you ever talk to Lucy or Chris about this?' Denise asked gently.

Nicki shook her head. 'They wouldn't have listened. Or understood.'

'But you could've—'

'*Yes!*' Nicki shouted suddenly, throwing up her hands. 'Fuck. Yes. I *know*. I could've called, or sent a text or a fucking telegram or a carrier pigeon or whatever. But why should I? She was doing what she wanted and she didn't ask me for permission, did she? She was opening that fucking cafe – because that's what the world needs, *another* hipster joint with a stupid misspelled name judging you for putting sugar in the coffee that they've overcharged you for and served to you in a plastic cup. She wanted to sell the house, and I knew she wasn't going to leave me alone until I agreed to it.

As for Chris . . . You know we met working abroad? On Crete? Well, let's just say it turns out the guy I met there was just pretending to want the same things as me. When we got back here, he started acting the same as everybody else.' Nicki paused. 'Look, I nearly did, OK? Contact Lucy, I mean. A few times. Not because I wanted to, not because she deserved it, but because I knew it was the' – another eye-roll – '*right thing to do* or whatever. But every time . . . It was just easier not to. I didn't want to think about that life, out there. So I kept thinking, *I'll just enjoy a few more days of this.* And then . . . Well, then I just didn't.'

She sat back and exhaled deeply, as if deflated.

Angela felt deflated too. There was no mystery here. No dark secret. No unfathomable puzzle. Nicki had left her life because she'd wanted to, and hadn't contacted her sister because she *hadn't* wanted to. She had come to this place simply because this was where she wanted to be.

And in doing so had set a series of events in motion that she couldn't possibly have foreseen.

'So,' Nicki said, 'what happens now?' She folded her arms. 'I told you, I'm not leaving here. She can't make me.'

The only sounds were birdsong, the breeze gently rustling the branches of the oak tree overhead and the low murmur of voices drifting towards them from where the cars were parked.

*Enjoy this*, Angela said silently. *Savour it.*

*The last truly good moment of your life.*

Denise leaned forward, put her palms flat on the table.

'I'm really sorry,' she said gently. 'But I have some bad news. Lucy is missing. She has been for three weeks now.'

# The Face of the Earth

Lucy wakes with a start.

She enjoys one glorious heartbeat of not remembering, of just *being*, before, in the next, the questions come rushing in.

*Where am I? How long have I been here? Is he going to kill me?*

And then, hot on their heels, comes the pain.

The pulsating hammer-blows at the wet swelling on the side of her head. The throbbing in her left arm that she thinks might be a broken bone. What feels like a row of tiny knives in her stomach that rub against her insides every time she takes a breath.

The burning between her legs that she refuses to think about.

She's taken *that* pain and locked it in a box and pushed it far, far away.

There are other feelings too, not quite bad enough to count as pain on their own, more like discomforts that have been mixed in with it: hunger, thirst, the hard floor beneath her body getting more and more uncomfortable with every passing hour, the cold because he took away her clothes.

Too many to make any sort of definite inventory.

And then there's the smell too. She's never experienced anything like it. It's so bad, so thick, so pungent, it feels like a presence in its own right.

It's so bad she fears there could only be one possible source of it.

Or, worse again, *three*.

*Don't panic. Stay calm. It's OK. It's OK. It's OK.*

This isn't the first time she's woken up here. Her guess is that it's her third, but she can't be sure. She has tried to keep track, but she thinks she might have been unconscious for a while, and when she woke up the second time she felt woozy and heavy, like he'd given her something to make her sleep.

But this is the first time she's woken up to see light.

Daylight, weak and watery, is forcing its way through the dirty lace curtain hanging from the room's only window: a small, rectangular pane close to the ceiling. It's so high up it gives her the sense that she is low down, that this space is perhaps in a basement or a cellar or something like that.

That's an important detail, she thinks. Something she needs to remember for when she gets out. She will find a way to escape, like Lena did, and when she does it's vital she's able to lead the guards back to the spot she ran from.

She looks around, moving her eyes but not her head, because when she does the pain gets worse, and the way he has her tied only permits a little movement.

The room is small and bare, the walls sprayed with spots of black mould. Rings of brown – spreading water stains – cling to all four corners of the ceiling, and a particularly dark one in the middle, above a bulb-less ceiling light, sags a little, as if whatever's above it is threatening to fall through. Branches of some root have sprung up in a far corner. The floorboards are bare. A large, industrial-looking pipe covered in rusty scales is jutting up from the floorboards by her right side; the other end of the chain that binds her is tied to it.

She can't see a door. It's either behind her or there isn't one.

There is, however, a square hatch in the ceiling with a series of fingertips marked out around its edges, in the dust. Perhaps he's been coming and going through there.

Lucy has never seen him arrive or leave her. Whenever she wakes up, he's either failed to appear before she falls back asleep, or he's already there when she opens her eyes.

Like now.

He's standing in the corner, arms folded, back against the wall. Watching her silently, impassively, expression-less. He's very tall and she's lying on the floor, so he looms over her like some supernatural monster, even though she knows he's just a man.

She *hopes* that he is, in there somewhere, still.

Despite all evidence to the contrary.

'Where is she?' she asks with what's left of her voice, which isn't much. The words burn her throat and she feels her lips crack and split, protesting against her moving them. A trickle of warmth as blood bursts from a rip in the middle of her bottom one. Her tongue feels swollen and unwieldy in her mouth. 'Where's Nicki?'

'*Where's Nicki?*' he repeats, mocking her.

'Please.'

She'd done everything he asked. She'd got into his car. She'd paid the toll.

Now, she needs to know.

Not like she'd needed to know before, out there, for the last year. That, she's come to understand over these last few . . . however long she's been here. Hours. Days. Weeks. That, she knows now, had been a *want*. She'd *wanted* to know where Nicki was, what had happened to her, whether she was alive or dead.

To silence the questions.

Banish the mystery.

But things are different now. Now she's here, with him. Now she actually does *need* to know what happened to Nicki, because that is the last thing standing between her and a blind, primal panic.

The only thought still tethering her to her sanity.

The only hope she has left.

Because Lucy knows it's over.

Even as she was telling herself to remember the detail of the cellar, she knew she'd never be able to tell anyone about it. She'd never get the chance. He was going to kill her soon.

He nearly had already.

But that was OK, that would be OK, everything would be OK if, before he did that, she could feel it, just for a moment.

*Knowing.*

'Where is she?' she asks. 'Where's Nicki?'

And that's when he frowns and says, 'Who?'

The pain on the side of her head seems to dislodge itself and float over her vision, making it difficult to see, so she mostly hears him cross the floor and hunch down beside her, and then feels him trace a single finger down the side of her face.

Across her bare chest.

In a straight line down her stomach.

Between her legs.

'Oh *yes*,' he says. 'Nicki. Your sister. Of course ... Sorry, I probably should've mentioned this sooner, but I don't know any Nicki. I never met your sister. I don't know where she is. My sympathies if she's gone missing but, if someone took her ... Well, I'm afraid it wasn't me.'

'It was,' Lucy says, her voice a dry and rough and raspy thing. 'It was you.'

He shakes his head. ''Fraid not, no.'

She doesn't believe him. This is just more torture, another type of pain he's delighting in inflicting on her.

Of *course* he's going to say that. Of course he is.

But back in the car . . .

The first girl had been on the side of the road somewhere in Wexford. He said the second got lots of attention, a crazy amount – and that one of them was very young, too young, and she'd had a dog. That was Jennifer Gold. The third, he'd told her, had escaped from his car and run out in front of another one. That had to be Lena.

She'd assumed he was just holding back about Nicki, taunting her, making her wait. Making her suffer. But what if . . . ?

*No. No, no, no. Not possible. Of course it was him. Of course it was.*

His finger is moving in the opposite direction now, retracing the line he drew on her trembling body.

But when he reaches the point at which he started, he doesn't stop. He moves off her face and into her hair, pulling a strand of it back, away from her ear.

Puts his lips to it.

Whispers.

'And when I said I didn't kill them, I wasn't lying. Because there's a difference, isn't there? Between actually killing someone and just, you know . . . letting them die.'

*Don't panic. Stay calm. It's OK. It's OK. It's OK.*

The Trap

Lucy is only vaguely aware of him getting up and moving away from her. She's thinking of all the information there is to go on, out there, in the world. Someone must have seen him parked outside the cafe. One of those houses, they could have one of those video doorbells or private security systems that captured his number plate. His fingerprints might be on her phone and a man like this doesn't just start with the worst crime you can commit, he works his way up to it. He must have some minor convictions already; his prints will be on file. They can set up some kind of stake-out operation, follow him here. And even if he suspects, even if he spots the unmarked cars on his tail and doesn't come here, they'll surely have some sense of the general area, and they'll start searching here. And when they see a pink house, they'll connect it to what Lena said before she died, and they'll storm in here and rescue her.

And she will let all this go.

She *will*.

She already has. She doesn't need to know what happened to Nicki. It's over. No more searching. She's accepted that she'll never have the answers – and that's OK.

Being alive will be enough.

'I promise,' she whispers.

And that's when she sees it, on the walls.

The first time she looked, all she saw was mould. But now she sees what's under it.

Pink.

Every square inch of wall in this place has been painted pink. It's faded and chipping, but there's no mistaking it, and it's everywhere. A sickly, medicinal pink: the kind that makes her think of stomach remedies and E-numbers and the accessories that come with baby dolls.

*We call it the Pink House.*

She thought that meant a house whose exterior was painted pink, a house whose nickname would give it away, a flashing beacon in the countryside that would lead the guards straight to its door, to its captives, to this horror.

To her.

But it gets its name from its interior.

The Pink House is pink on the *inside*.

*Don't panic. Stay calm. It's OK. It's OK. It's OK.*

But she can't and nothing is and she doesn't.

All the moments of the rest of Lucy's life are rushing at her at once, looking like this, feeling like this, happening here, in this broken place. There will be no other life after this one. Its ending has already begun.

No one will ever find her.

And she screams and she screams and she screams.

# One Year Later

*She'd been* out-out, *and town had been busy. Stumbled out of the club to discover that there wasn't a taxi to be had. Spent an hour trying to flag one down with one hand while trying to hail one via an app with the other until, resigned, she'd pushed her way on to a packed night bus headed not far enough in sort of the right direction. Her plan was to call someone at its terminus, apologize for waking them and ask them to come get her, but by the time she got there – to a tiny country village that was sleepy by day and empty by night – her phone had died. She'd been the last passenger and the bus had driven off before she could think to ask the driver if she could perhaps borrow* his *phone. It was four in the morning and beginning to drizzle, so she'd started walking. Because, really, what other choice did she have?*

This is the story Nicki recites in her head as she leaves the edges of the village and enters the thick, solid night beyond. If someone stops for her and starts asking questions, she'll be ready.

She has her lies all prepared.

What she's actually done is drive Lucy's car out here, park up and wait for the last bus from town to amble its way into the main square and then out of it again. Count five minutes off the clock, just to make doubly sure that anyone who actually took the bus to this glorified cross-roads at this ungodly hour is long gone before she makes her move. Change her shoes into something much more unsuitable. Hang an impractically tiny, glittery bag from a strap on one shoulder and lock the jacket a sane person would wear in these conditions into the boot. Shove the key fob down between her breasts until it's lodged behind the point in the band of her bra where the two cups meet, secure but completely hidden. Turn off her phone. Set out to walk a lonely country road like she's done on so many other nights before this, hoping to bait the man who took her sister.

Thirteen other nights, so far, in seven other villages.

The drizzling ramps up into a hard, stinging rain and this pleases her, because she *should* be wet and cold and shivering. After the footpath runs out and she starts to stumble in her high heels, she fantasizes about hearing the crack of a bone in her own ankle and the searing pain that would follow, the kind so bad it takes your breath away. The balls of her feet burn and the strap on one of the shoes is working to rub away the top layers of her skin, exposing red and raw flesh, and Nicki welcomes the distant stinging that she knows will turn to burning soon.

She deserves it all and more, after what she did.

At the time, it didn't feel like a bad thing. It didn't even feel wrong. It felt *miraculous*, as if she'd been slowly suffocating for days in a tiny, airless space and had just managed to kick a door open, to the outside, and gulp down lungfuls of fresh air.

It had become obvious to her that she and Chris weren't going to last. Lucy was hell-bent on selling the house, the only fixed compass point Nicki had. And then she'd gone out that night, to meet her so-called friends in the Duke, and when they weren't talking about the kinds of lives that sounded to Nicki like slow, torturous deaths, they were telling her that Luce was right, and that Chris was great, and that all *she* needed to do was stop being the problem, basically.

So she'd left them without saying goodbye, slipped out, into the warm night. She'd seen a new message from Luce about there being a viewing at the house the following morning and thrown the phone away in a flash of fury. Hours later, she'd woken up on an unfamiliar couch and realized that absolutely nobody who knew *who* she was knew *where* she was, and no one had any way to contact her.

And thought, *What if I just left?* There and then. With only the clothes on her back and the cash in her wallet, and without anyone's permission or blessing.

Nicki didn't want to hear all the reasons why she couldn't do the thing she knew she absolutely *could* do. She didn't want to have to justify wanting it. She didn't want to talk about it at all, actually, especially not with people who'd never understand.

It didn't feel selfish, it felt empowering. Doing what you wanted with your own adult life wasn't a crime. As for telling Luce and Chris, her priority wasn't the concerns of people who didn't seem to care one bit about what *she* wanted. And anyway, wasn't this what you were *supposed* to do? Make space for you. Speak your truth. Live authentically.

She was going to tell them. Of course she was.

At some point.

But before she could, three Garda cars had come up the track.

So now Nicki must pay for all the pain she's caused.

This is part of her penance. And anyway, she'd rather be out here than at home. Ironically, she hates the house now, hates the neighbours who whisper behind her back every time she comes or goes, hates that every journalist in the land knows exactly where to find her, hates that every crazy idiot in the country knows it too.

The hate mail isn't arriving by the literal sack-load like it was a year ago – that had been news to her, that if you got enough post, they'd deliver it in actual hessian sacks – but it still comes dribbling in, and someone with a shaky hand sends her envelopes stuffed with faintly photocopied prayers at least once a week without fail.

Last Friday night someone put a brick through Chris's car window, presumably mistaking it for hers.

But she can't leave. She won't move.

Starting again somewhere else, where nobody knows her face or her story or her crime, isn't an option. Not yet, anyway. She needs to earn that second chance.

Atone for what she did.

Find her sister.

Or, failing that, the man who took her.

Chris has stayed because those rooms are the only part of the world that still echo with the life of the one O'Sullivan sister he still cares about. That's her theory, anyway. These days, they barely speak and he can hardly stand to look at her. When they do have to talk, he looks over her shoulder, or away.

He knows all about these, her little night-time excursions. She's made no effort to conceal them. The first few times, she even left him a note. She told herself that it was so, should she disappear (again), he'd know what had happened. But deep down, she knew it was because she wanted him to know that she was doing *something*, that she was at least trying to atone.

But he didn't care, about that or her safety.

Which she thinks says it all, really.

Nicki hears a mechanical whine, somewhere behind her in the wet night.

Getting louder.

She thinks, *Engine*. And then, *Out here? In this weather?* Her pulse quickens at the prospect that maybe – maybe, possibly, finally – tonight will be the night.

She turns just in time to be blinded by a pair of

sweeping high-beams. Twin orbs are still floating across her vision when the car jerks to a stop alongside her.

She stops too.

It's silver, some make of saloon.

The passenger window descends in a smooth, electronic motion and a voice says, 'You all right there?'

At first, he's not entirely sure it *is* her.

The dark, the rain, the angle – him sitting in the driver's seat, her standing by the passenger side – combine to make identification difficult. She says something about a night bus and he pretends he didn't quite catch it, that his hearing isn't great, and she helpfully bends to align her face with his open window and then, better yet, leans her head and shoulders over the frame, into the opening, into his car.

He could grab her right now. She's already done half the work for him. She's only a slight, willowy thing. If he suddenly reached out and yanked on her upper arms, the rest of her would be inside the car before she even knew what was happening.

But he won't, because it *is* her.

The sister.

The *other* one.

The woman they all thought was missing, but she wasn't. The one who's responsible for her sister actually being missing now.

The rumours are true. He can't believe it, especially considering the source.

But no, here she is, out here in the middle of nowhere in the middle of the night, trying to get herself abducted.

It was Amy who told him about it, funnily enough. It's been a difficult pregnancy, although they've no frame of reference, with longer and longer bouts of prescribed bed-rest. His wife is bored out of her mind and, having worked her way through every true-crime documentary available, has moved on to books and podcasts and even message boards, poring over all manner of horrors with her laptop perched on the dome of her belly that houses their unborn child.

A girl.

They found that out last week.

It was on one of the message boards that she'd come across what he'd presumed must just be some silly, made-up rumour: that Nicki O'Sullivan, sister to Lucy, once thought to be missing woman two of three, regularly went walking by herself late at night on country roads, trying to get taken by the man who had taken her sister.

He'd rolled his eyes and grinned and said something about people having too much time on their hands and then, as casually as he could, he'd asked Amy, 'Where are they claiming she goes?'

'"The foothills of the Wicklow Mountains",' she'd told him, reading from the screen. 'And apparently she's been spotted a couple of times near where that Polish girl got knocked down.'

If she'd been spotted there a couple of times already, she was sure to go back.

And better yet, that was nowhere near the Pink House.

He hadn't been planning a return to Base Camp. He hadn't been there since. Yeah, *OK*, he'd boarded a couple of creaky flights to Kathmandu and got himself a hostel room, fair enough. And once he'd started to trek out of it in the general direction of Everest, but not because he was going to make a summit attempt. His climbing days were behind him. He'd hung up his crampons, put away his ropes.

Things were different now.

There was a baby on the way.

Although this, tonight, was the baby's fault, actually. Technically. Amy had moved into a separate room because she was more comfortable with a bed to herself, and she'd chosen the one in the attic conversion because her sleep was so precarious, she needed to be as far away from potential disturbances as she could possibly get. Up there, she couldn't hear him if he stayed up later than her, or got up out of bed to use the loo, or snuck out in the middle of the night to look for this idiot woman with the new baby seat out of the boot and in the back seat a little earlier than planned.

Nicki O'Sullivan looks different to the photo they printed in the papers, but it's definitely her. She says something about a bus and shows him her supposedly dead phone, and he's happy to play along. He sees her clock the baby seat in the back, the mess on the floor in the front. He pretends to look for a charger, says he came out without his phone too. And then he suggests that he give her a lift to a garage not far down the road, one of the twenty-four-hour ones, and, after barely a moment's hesitation, she gets in the car.

Just like her sister.

Stupidity must run in the family.

Not like Kerry Long, his first, whose skull he'd smashed the night of Niamh's birthday party. Whose bloody bra had been found in a charity shop, for fuck's sake. He had worried a little about the fact that it had been inside *Amy's* handbag, before remembering that, first, she'd have emptied everything out of it before donating it and, second, fingerprints don't mean shit unless you've a set to match them against. Unless his wife was secretly some kind of criminal mastermind, he very much doubted her prints were on file and he knew his weren't. They didn't have DNA either, so the bloody bra was just as moot.

Jennifer Gold had been the easiest. The best mannered. The most helpful. By far the stupidest. He'd opened the passenger door and Jennifer had *sat in the car* to look at what he was claiming was a map to his friend's house. Getting the dog's lead out of her hand before he drove off had been the only challenge there, really. It was just a shame she turned out to be so young.

Lena Paczkowski had been an absolute pain in his

arse until she helpfully ran into the path of an oncoming car and solved that problem for him.

And Lucy O'Sullivan had come willingly, but shouldn't have.

There were no others, and he's stopped now. Stopped taking them *and* stopped visiting the Pink House.

But that doesn't mean he can't have a little fun.

He presses the button that locks all the doors simultaneously and, out of the corner of his eye, watches as the loud *click* makes her flinch.

'So,' he says then. 'Was it a good night, at least?'


Denise had been surprised to hear from Chris Noonan after all this time, and after everything that had happened.

In the wake of Lucy O'Sullivan's disappearance – and the reappearance of her sister, his former girlfriend – he'd been extremely vocal in his criticism of the Gardaí, complaining about their failures to everyone from the Minister for Justice to the ringmasters of misery who hosted phone-in radio shows around the country. When Denise saw his name come up on her phone, she'd presumed he was calling to complain to her too.

And she'd let him.

After all, he had a point.

She hadn't seen him in person since she'd arrived on his doorstep three weeks after Lucy's disappearance with a healthy, suntanned Nicki in tow, promoting his waking nightmare to a living hell. She was no longer his FLO or anyone else's. Someone new had been assigned that job, and she'd heard that when they'd gone round to the house to introduce themselves, he'd told them to fuck off and then slammed the door in their face.

But no, Chris was calling her for another reason.

He was worried that Nicki O'Sullivan was doing something even more dangerous than her sister had, which was saying something, and he was hoping that Denise could help save her from herself. That's why she's sitting in her car, parked on the main street – the only street – of some tiny speck of a village somewhere in the Wicklow Mountains, watching Nicki get out of what was her sister's car.

And ditch her jacket.

Swap her trainers for strappy heels.

Lock up the car, tuck the keys into her cleavage and walk off into the night, stumbling a little, hands swinging loose by her sides, looking like the twilight hours between the Night Before and the Morning After.

But it's all an act.

The girl is stone-cold sober. She wasn't out on the town this evening; Denise has followed her here from her home. And if Nicki had been driving even a little like she's walking, Denise would have arrested her long before now.

She's baiting him, the man who took her sister.

Just like Chris said she was.

Nicki's sister didn't have the patience to let the guards do their job and now she, evidently, doesn't either. Like Lucy, she thinks she'll do better if she takes matters into her own hands. It's so stupid, so reckless, so dangerous, so pointless.

What on earth does she think she's going to achieve? What *is* it with this family?

Denise lets the girl walk off into the dark, waits five minutes and then drives after her slowly, with her headlights dipped. She wants to catch Nicki in the act before she reprimands her, having walked away from her car and down the road a bit, so she can't pretend she was parking up to go visit a friend.

But Nicki has disappeared.

'Shit,' Denise mutters.

Even at running speed, there's no way Nicki would've got this far down this road in the time it's taken Denise to get here. She must have turned off somewhere, or gone back. Denise circles the village a few times, taking various routes in and out of it, but there's no one around at all. There isn't a single other pedestrian. There aren't even any other cars. The night is silent except for the hum of Denise's vehicle, rumbling slowly through it.

Where the hell did Nicki go?

Denise pulls up a map on her phone and looks for something, anything, near by – and finds that there's a service station, a Circle K, not that far away. It's the only thing that's even feasibly within walking distance that might be open at this hour, even though the map says it would take a half-hour to get there on foot, and probably double that in the shoes Nicki has on her.

She decides to go there and wait for a little while, see if Nicki shows up. If she doesn't, she'll go back and wait by the car, catch her there. They're going to have words. As Denise drives, she rehearses her speech in her mind.

*Your sister disappeared because she couldn't stay at home and wait for us to find you, and now you're out here putting yourself in danger because you can't wait for us to find* her. *This stops right now or I'm going to charge you with impeding an investigation.*

The Circle K is surprisingly busy for this time of the night, especially since there seem to be so few vehicles on the roads around here. There are three in the forecourt, despite the fact that it's now gone 4:00 a.m. But then, the station *is* on the one main road that cuts through the spaghetti mess of local ones, boreens and dirt tracks around these parts. If people are going to be anywhere, Denise supposes, they'll be here.

She parks on the far side of the forecourt, away from the pumps and the shop, in a spot the station's lights don't quite reach, and surveys the scene.

One car is filling up at the pumps.

Another is parked right outside the shop. The woman coming out of its doors at this very moment is waving at the man behind its wheel.

A third is parked directly across from Denise, directly under a bright light, and—

Nicki O'Sullivan is getting out of it.

At first she worries that something has happened while she was in the car, because now Nicki seems genuinely worse for wear, the stumbling no longer an act, looking sweaty and grey in the face as she heads around the side of the shop, apparently following a sign for the toilets. Denise has one hand on the door and one on her gun, checking it's there even though she knows it is, even though she can feel its weight against her hip, ready to run, to catch the man – she's assuming – behind the wheel before his tyres squeal and he drives off.

But he doesn't drive off.

And it *is* a man, getting out of the car while its lights are on and the engine is still running.

He looks to be in his mid-thirties, six foot or just over it, average build, with strawberry-red hair cut close to his scalp. His T-shirt is on inside out and he looks generally dishevelled, and that makes Denise push open her door, switching the courtesy light on, illuminating her.

But something tells her to wait, that if the obvious explanation was the right one, he wouldn't still be here, that he'd have hightailed it out of here as soon as his victim was out of the car.

The man does a quick scan of the forecourt and she manages to pull the door closed again, extinguishing the light, just before his head turns towards her.

She pulls down the visor and starts tracing a finger

across her lips, waits a beat, and then lets her gaze travel back to him.

He's opened one of the rear doors, and she watches as he reaches in and lifts out a baby seat. An empty baby seat. He transfers it to the boot, looks around the forecourt one more time, and gets back in his car.

That's when Denise gets the feeling.

It's like a tug, deep in her stomach, sounding a silent alarm. Signalling that there's something very wrong with what she's seeing.

Telling her to look harder.

Denise takes out her phone, zooms in with the camera app and gets a clear snap of the man's licence plate before he drives off.

Why would a man go to the trouble of removing an empty baby seat from his car in a service-station forecourt just after four in the morning and then immediately drive away in it, moments after a young woman who presumably isn't known to him got out of the same car? What was the urgency of getting the baby seat into the boot? Why did he have to do it now, here? Why couldn't it wait until he got home?

Denise taps a number in her favourites list and puts the device to her ear, watching the corner of the building for Nicki O'Sullivan to reappear.

'Yo,' a female voice says after one ring.

'"Yo"?' Denise repeats. 'Is that how we're teaching new recruits to answer the phone these days?'

On the other end of the line, Angela laughs.

'Sorry, I thought it was Johnny ringing me back. He's gone to Mickey D's to get us some breakfast. Or late dinner. Or midnight lunch. I don't know which, I've lost track.'

'Apart from thicker arteries, how's it going?'

'To be honest,' Angela says, lowering her voice, 'it's kinda boring. When I get a day shift, all I seem to be doing is signing passport forms. And at night, it's mostly staring into space and waiting for the phone to ring.'

'And getting McDonald's.'

'And getting McDonald's, yeah.'

'Well, of course it's boring,' Denise says. 'Most recruits don't report for duty with a high-profile abduction case and the arrest of a murder suspect already under their belt, now, do they? Hang in there. You'll get back to the exciting stuff.'

'I know,' Angela says, sighing. 'Yeah.'

'In the meantime, I need you to look up a reg for me.'

'Thank God. Something to do, at last. Go ahead.'

Denise calls out the registration number of Mr Empty Baby Seat's car and listens to the clacking of computer keys as Angela plugs it into the PULSE system.

'What do you want me to say it's for?'

'I don't even know where exactly . . . Hang on.' Denise puts the call on speaker and brings up the map app on her phone. 'Say the R755, near Roundwood. Suspicion of driving while intoxicated.' She pauses. 'I don't want to be too specific.'

'Gotcha.' More key clacking. 'Lots of fraud going on out there in the Wicklow Mountains at four in the morning, is there?'

'Like you wouldn't believe.'

'Hmm.'

'Did you find him?' Denise asks.

'Yeah, I have him here. So that's a one-five-one Ford Mondeo, grey, registered to a Darren Turner of 251 The Park, Citywest, Dublin 24.'

'Anything coming up for him?'

'No. Nothing at all. Clean as a whistle.' Angela pauses. 'Is this about—?'

'Weren't you already in enough trouble?'

'But you could've called anyone,' Angela points out. Denise smiles.

This one is going to make a great detective.

'I don't know anything yet,' she says. 'I just have . . .'

But she trails off as she sees Nicki O'Sullivan reappear. She's coming around the side of the building, holding her phone, face bathed in its blue glow.

Walking steady now, but it looks as though she's been crying.

'A feeling?' Angela finishes.

'Yeah,' Denise says, getting out of the car. 'Something like that.'

# A Note from the Author

In 1981, my parents purchased a JVC HR-3660, one of the first VHS-based VCR machines commercially available in Ireland. It was top-loading, weighed over thirteen kilograms and had a row of gleaming silver levers that reminded my mother of piano keys. It cost 795 Irish pounds, or almost a quarter of my father's annual salary at the time, and it wouldn't technically be theirs until they paid the final monthly instalment three years later. By that point, they'd also have me.

My earliest memories of this metal monstrosity involve scratchy tapes of family-friendly things recorded off the telly: *Annie*, *Mary Poppins*, *The Sound of Music*. Later, the purchase of a new release on VHS, one we owned and could keep, was a major occasion; I think the very first was *The Little Mermaid*. But the machine really came into its own for me when I started getting pocket money, and so was able to rent videos. Our local video-rental shop was small and independent, with a limited selection, and I quickly exhausted all my options on the 'Children's' shelves. It was then that I, for reasons lost to me now, moved on to the 'True Life' section and started working my way through the titles there.

These were all low-budget, melodramatic, made-for-TV movies about infamous American crimes. In *Small Sacrifices*, Farrah Fawcett played Diane Downs, who claimed a car-jacker had murdered her seven-year-old child and attempted to murder her other two children, aged eight and three, when actually she had. *Menendez: A Killing in Beverly Hills* told the story of the Menendez brothers, Lyle and Erik, who shot their parents dead so they could either escape their father's abuse, as they claimed, or start spending their inheritance, as the prosecution did. In *Victim of Beauty: The Dawn Smith Story*, pageant queen Dawn's younger sister Shari is kidnapped and killed by a man named Larry Gene Bell, who starts calling Dawn on the phone, taunting her about it. (If you've read my novel *The Nothing Man*, some of this might ring a bell. As it happens, a young Eve Black had very similar viewing habits . . . )

I watched them all, and more besides, long before my thirteenth birthday.

I must have watched some of them *very* long before it, because Shari was what I always called my 'main' doll when we played Barbies.

When I tell people this now, in the age of trigger

warnings and parents' guides and OFCOM complaints about *Love Island*, mouths fall open in shock, especially if those mouths have young children. But these films were produced for broadcast on American network television more than thirty years ago; visually, they were about as graphic as an episode of *Murder, She Wrote*. And their subject matter was hardly new ground for me. At the same time as watching the likes of *The Amy Fisher Story*, *I Know My First Name Is Steven* and *Ambush in Waco*, I was utterly devoted to *Unsolved Mysteries* and getting to know Patricia Cornwell's fictional medical examiner, Kay Scarpetta, who seemed to spend most of her time cutting dead people open and describing in graphic detail what she found inside.

I think my parents would probably like me to state for the record at this point that they are very responsible people, the eldest always gets away with murder – pun absolutely intended – and hey, it all worked out OK.

But I often wonder: why wasn't I scared?

I can really only think of three pieces of nightmare-fodder from around that time: the raptor scene at the beginning of *Jurassic Park*, the Wheelers in *Return to Oz*, and – for some reason, perhaps a traumatic art class? – the papier-mâché heads the escapees left in their beds in the Alcatraz episode of *Unsolved Mysteries*. (When I saw them in real life and *in situ* twenty-odd years later, trust me: they were just as terrifying.) But charming serial killers? A cult whose followers end up being burned alive? A mother calmly and deliberately shooting dead her own child at point-blank range because the guy she liked wasn't all that into having kids? None of that had any effect on me and, looking back now, I think I know why that was.

I was in Ireland.

At that time, news flowed into our house four times a day: two papers, the then *Cork Examiner* and the *Evening Echo*, and two TV news bulletins, one at a minute past six, after the bells of the Angelus, and another at nine. And yet there never seemed to be anything worthy of one of my made-for-TV movies among them. There were murders here, yes – 23 of them in 1993, out of a population of 3.5 million – but if they had a random, there-but-for-the-grace-of-God element, it was far more likely to be a terrorist's bomb than a serial killer's dark compulsion. And none of them ever happened in Cork, the county in which we lived.

Ireland was a place where doors were still left unlocked, hitchhiking was prevalent, and there were no guns, on us or on the people who policed us. True crime was about as relevant to my reality as science fiction. (Oh – speaking of, I just thought of another thing that gave me nightmares: when the visitors reveal their true selves in *V*. If you're unfamiliar, let me point you to a YouTube video descriptively entitled 'V Final Battle – Unmasking John – Julie rips his face off'. You're welcome.) All the horrors I was watching on screen felt securely confined to the other side of it. I was safe. I lived in a country where we could confidently tell ourselves, *Things like that don't happen here.*

But then, they started to.

The first woman to go missing was a twenty-seven-year-old American named Annie McCarrick. She had moved to Sandymount, Dublin, from Long Island, New York. On 26 March 1993, she told a friend she intended to go walking in the Wicklow Mountains. The last sighting of her was thought to be on the Enniskerry bus that afternoon, heading in that direction. Over the next five years, seven Irish women would follow Annie off the face of the earth. They ranged in age from seventeen to thirty-nine and were last seen in locations that, if you plotted them on a map, formed a loose triangle centred on the province of Leinster in the east of the country, in which the capital city of Dublin and the Wicklow Mountains lie.

The media dubbed it the Vanishing Triangle.

The front pages filled up with images of these gone girls, the official ones their families had supplied to the Gardaí. We watched eerie re-enactments on television, designed to jog memories and stir guilty consciences. We listened to heart-breaking interviews with the loved ones left behind, wondering how much suffering a person could take. In 1998, after Gardaí established Operation Trace, we held our collective breath, convinced that now, *surely*, there'd be some news.

But none ever came.

Ask any Irish woman over a certain age and I bet

they'll be able to name at least one of the missing women, even now. Most of the women I know can name more than that. When I first moved to Dublin in 2014, I made the mistake of telling my mother I was taking the bus to Enniskerry for a walk around Powerscourt House, and she immediately cited Annie McCarrick's disappearance twenty-one years earlier as a reason why going on my own was a bad idea. In a truly horrific coincidence, in January 2022, twenty-three-year-old Ashling Murphy was murdered while jogging on a stretch of towpath alongside the Grand Canal just outside of Tullamore, Co. Offaly, named for one of the missing women, Fiona Pender, who'd lived near by: Fiona's Way.

I'm sure the so-called Vanishing Triangle is a huge part of why I write the kind of fiction I do and why I always set it at home, in my small, relatively safe country. Because just when I got old enough to start paying attention to the news, the news was that a faceless phantom was snatching women. I was ten years old when the vanishings started and I turned seventeen the year they stopped, the same age as the youngest woman to disappear, Ciara Breen. While I'd been growing up, the horrors of my age-inappropriate childhood video-shop rentals had, somehow, escaped from the screen.

But the real horror was something we couldn't have known back then, and would have struggled to believe: that three decades later, we wouldn't know a single thing more about what had happened to these women. There are eight in the unofficial tally – Annie McCarrick, Eva

Brennan, Imelda Keenan, Josephine 'JoJo' Dullard, Fiona Pender, Ciara Breen, Fiona Sinnott and Deirdre Jacob – and to this day, no one has ever been charged in connection with any of their disappearances, and no trace of them has ever been found.

(In the midst of all this, on the day before Christmas Eve 1996, Frenchwoman Sophie Toscan du Plantier was brutally murdered outside her holiday home in West Cork. Readers outside of Ireland may already be familiar with this case thanks to Netflix's *Sophie: A Murder in West Cork*, Jim Sheridan's documentary *Murder at the Cottage*, and the hugely popular *West Cork* podcast hosted by Sam Bungey and Jennifer Forde. Her killer too remains at large.)

*The Trap* is, obviously, not about the Vanishing Triangle or the women it seemingly swallowed whole. It's a story I made up, set in the present day, about entirely fictional people. But I was certainly thinking about those women as I wrote it. Even though the internet has never been able to prove this, I'm convinced I once heard the great Irish writer Edna O'Brien tell an interviewer that she wrote as a way to grieve for what she read in the headlines. I think I write as a way to solve the mysteries I find in them. Sometimes – tragically, infuriatingly, inexplicably – fiction is the only place we have to go for answers.

Catherine Ryan Howard
Dublin, 17 January 2023

# Acknowledgements

My agent, Sara O'Keeffe, has now changed my life twice: first, in March 2015 when, as an editor at Corvus, she pre-empted my debut, *Distress Signals*, and then again, in February of last year, when she became my agent. We truly are the dream team and we are only just getting started. Thank you for everything.

Thanks also to Vanessa Kerr and the entire Aevitas Creative Management UK team; to Frankie Gray, Imogen Nelson and everyone at Transworld and Penguin Random House Ireland; and to Josh Stanton, Josie Woodbridge, Michael Signorelli and everyone at Blackstone Publishing. For the most exciting emails ever, thanks to Allison Warren and Kayleigh Choi at ACM, and to Hilary Zaitz Michael and Carolina Beltran at WME. Because of all of you, I get to do my dream job, and I never take that for granted.

I doubt Niamh O'Connor even remembers the random coffee we had in the glitz and glamour of the M&S Café on Grafton Street after that podcast recording that time, but it was when you told me about x and the hunting lodge, and I think that unlocked something in my brain and brought me all the way to the Pink House, so thank you for that. Casey King is, as ever, my Garda-procedure consultant extraordinaire, and more importantly provided the DFS joke. Any mistakes in official procedure, geography, etc. are my own, except they're not mistakes because this is fiction, and making stuff up is the whole point.

To my fellow crime-writers: I don't want to risk naming any names in case I accidentally omit someone, but you know who you are. Thanks for the advice, the gossip, the inspiration, the gossip and the hangovers. Oh, and the gossip. Meet you in the festival bar.

To the booksellers and librarians, the Bookstagrammers and Book Tok-ers (did I say that right? I don't know, I'm forty) and to everyone who has ever read one of my books and then told someone else that they should too: thank you, thank you, thank you.

To Hazel Gaynor and Carmel Harrington – I'm going to plagiarize myself from an earlier book just because I can't say it better than she did: I *could* do this without you, but I wouldn't want to.

Thanks to Mum, Dad, John and Claire, because they'd be annoyed if I left them out, and to Rob because he's part of the family now too, and to Dexter, because even though he's a dog, my mum joked that I should include him and actually I don't think she was joking at all, you know, it was really rather pointed ... So, thanks, Dexter – I guess? (And yes, we did name him after a fictional serial killer.)

And finally to you, the reader, unless you haven't read the book yet but come straight here to read the acknowledgements because you're nosey – it's OK, I do the same thing – but do come back after you're done to collect *your* thanks, because you truly are the most important person of all.

Read on for an extract from

# BURN AFTER READING

*by*

*Catherine Ryan Howard*

'Catherine Ryan Howard is the
Queen of the Unguessable Twist!'

C. L. Taylor

Coming 2024 and available to pre-order now!

Muffled, furtive footsteps. The creak of a floorboard. A gentle tinkling, metal on metal.

These sounds first reached Emily in her dream, which so far wasn't making any sense. She was at home in Dublin with Mark, but it wasn't their apartment and Mark didn't look like Mark. In the middle of the night, Not Mark had woken her up to show her the first finished copy of his new book which he'd said had just arrived. But when she'd turned on the bedside lamp, she'd seen that its pages were covered in handwriting – her handwriting – because actually it was a diary – *her* diary – but she didn't understand because she'd never kept one and she was about to ask Not Mark what was going on when she heard it.

Footsteps. Floorboards. Tinkling of metal on metal—

Emily opened her eyes.

—and the unmistakable *clink* of a key in a lock.

It took her brain a beat to slip the bonds of sleep and piece together where she was and what was happening. Lying, fully dressed, on a couch that wasn't hers. The couch was in a house in the town of Sanctuary, Florida, where she'd been staying. Working. Helping a man to protest his innocence, to write a book about why he wasn't the murderer of his wife and her friend. She'd had half a bottle of wine for dinner and that's why she had a dull headache now. The noises were real.

*The noises were real.*

Had someone broken in? Was someone else in here with her right now?

Emily jerked upright, into a sitting position. She was in the lock-off, a small studio apartment over a two-car garage attached to the main house, so called because it had a set of connecting doors enabling it to be 'locked off', forming a self-contained guest house. From the couch, almost all of the space was within her eyeline and there was just enough light – Moonlight? Street light? Security light? – filtering through the thin window blinds to see it.

The light had an odd quality to it, like a sunrise over snow.

Someone could, theoretically, be hiding in the bathroom or behind the breakfast bar, but Emily didn't think anyone could've got in. Over the last forty-eight hours, she'd become paranoid about safety chains and deadbolts and window latches, and developed a routine that involved checking and double-checking all of them before she went to sleep. It was possible that she'd forgotten to do it earlier this evening, especially after what had happened, but that was a moot point, because Emily could see now what was making the noise.

She was the only one in the lock-off, but she wasn't alone: there was a shadow on the other side of the glass front door.

A tall figure, bent a little at the waist, head level with the lock.

Her heart began to hammer beneath her breastbone.

*A burglar*, she thought. *Someone is trying to break in.*

They must think the place was empty, vacant for the winter months. An easy mistake to make, seeing as practically every other house in this ghost town *was* empty.

Emily jumped up and smacked the light switch on the wall behind her to alert the thief to their mistake, but nothing happened.

She flicked it again, and again, but no light came on to banish the dark.

She lurched at the lamp on the end table, knocking it over, catching it just before it fell. Feeling its ceramic neck for its switch, but it clicked uselessly too. She jumped up and ran the five steps to the bathroom, hitting the switch on the wall there.

Still nothing.

The power was out.

She looked back at the front door and saw that the shadow was gone. She took a few tentative steps forward to get closer, to get a better view, to double-check.

There was no one out there now.

They must have heard her moving around and run off. Or maybe there'd been no one out there to begin with. Maybe she'd imagined it, confused the twilight zone of her dreams with reality.

That's when she smelled the smoke.

She *saw* the smoke now, too: a thin, lazy haze, hanging in the air. It was what had made the light look odd to her, she realized in hindsight.

Where was it coming from?

Maybe some kids had built a bonfire on the beach. Maybe the dry, wiry brush that sat between the house and the sand had caught and now smoke and the smell of it burning was wafting inside. This was her first thought, despite the fact that all the windows were closed and she couldn't see anything like a bonfire through the windows on the balcony side. In fact, the beach looked pitch-black.

She picked her phone up off the end table. Only 11.20 p.m. She'd been asleep for, at most, a couple of hours. When she activated the phone's flashlight, the smoke became a grey, ghostly mist in its beam.

Emily turned slowly, sweeping the light across the room, until it landed on the door that connected the lock-off to the main house.

Smoke was drifting lazily in underneath it.

The door had a mate on its other side, like doors in

adjoining hotel rooms. All week, she'd been making sure that the one on her side was securely locked, its bolt slid into place. Now she ran to it to reverse the action and pulled back her door, revealing the other connecting door closed behind it.

She rapped a fist against it, once, twice.

'Hey?' she called out. 'Hey, is anybody in there? Hello?'

When there was no response, she pressed both palms flat on the door.

The wood was warm.

A snippet from some health and safety training from a temp job she'd had a few months ago came back to her: *Don't open a door if it's warm or hot to the touch.*

And then she thought, *Get out get out get out get out get out.*

That same health and safety seminar had said to leave all valuables behind, but now she ran to the breakfast bar, where her backpack was hanging from one of the chairs. She unzipped it and thrust a hand inside to confirm what the weight of it suggested, that her laptop and notebook and a sheaf of loose pages were still inside. She slung the backpack over one shoulder and shoved her phone into the pocket of her jeans.

She should call 911. She should call the others, try their phones. She should go next door, around to the front door of the house and bang on it, in case anyone was still sleeping in there.

And she would, but she had to get out of here first.

It couldn't have been much more than a minute since Emily had woken up, but the situation had already rapidly deteriorated. The smoke was getting thicker by the second, feeling gritty in her eyes and hot in her mouth. It had a solidness now, a physical presence. Its tendrils were reaching into the back of her throat to snatch at her breath.

She started coughing, which only drew more smoke down deeper into her chest.

But it was OK, everything was going to be OK, because she was at the front door now, sliding the dead-bolt back, and in a second she'd be outside, in the fresh air, safe. Emily pulled on the handle, braced to run—

The door didn't budge.

Confused, she pulled harder. Checked the deadbolt. Depressed the handle more.

Pulled even harder on it again.

Placed both hands on the handle and leaned back, putting all her body weight behind her, pulling until her arms burned with the strain.

The door rocked a little on its hinges, but didn't open. It was jammed shut.

Emily didn't know why this was happening but she knew there wasn't time to figure it out. Her chest felt like there was a large weight settling on it and she was starting to feel funny, as if her head was too heavy for her shoulders.

She needed to find another way out, quick.

She thought, *Balcony*.

It must be twelve, maybe even fifteen feet off the ground, but she'd probably survive a fall. She wouldn't survive suffocating or being burned alive. It was sand she'd land on, and there were cushions on the chairs out there on the balcony. Big, thick ones. She could throw them over first, make herself a landing spot.

She just had to make it to the other side of the room first.

The distance may as well have been an ocean. She feared she'd drown before she made it to the other shore.

*Wet a rag and hold it over your nose and mouth.*

She felt her way along the kitchen counter to the sink, and to the neatly folded towel she knew she'd left there this morning. She soaked it in cold water from the tap and pressed it to her face. The cold water was glorious against her hot skin, on her parched lips. She wanted to drink some of it, too, but there wasn't time.

*Stay low – crawl beneath the smoke.*

She dropped to her hands and knees.

It had been eerily silent but now noises were coming from the other side of the connecting door. An occasional *whooshing* sound. Popping and crackling.

A dull, loud *boom* as something heavy fell over.

Emily found the balcony door by touch, and then, when she reached up, its handle. It only had one lock, a simple knob that turned easily through ninety degrees. She flipped it clockwise, hoisted herself to her feet, pulled open the door and went to run—

Blooms of white, hot pain exploded across her vision as her forehead instantly met something solid and hard.

Emily fell over backwards, landing on her left side, on the backpack. The corner of the laptop jabbed painfully between her ribs. When she opened her eyes, she saw yellow-red flames flickering around the edges of the connecting door.

She remembered something else from that health and safety seminar, something one of her colleagues, a twenty-something with a head of thickly gelled hair and a spotty chin, had whispered to her during the video part.

*Burning alive only hurts at the start.*

After the flames burn away your nerve endings, you don't feel the pain.

Emily was tired, her eyelids heavy. Every breath was

a battle. She'd lost the wet towel. She had an over-whelming urge to stay where she was and succumb to sleep. But . . . no. She was *at the balcony door*, inches from being outside, from being almost safe. From being able to breathe again.

All she had to do was go through it.

*Move. Come on. Get up.*

Slowly, she hoisted herself back up on to her knees. When she reached out her right hand, it closed around the edge of the balcony door. So she *had* opened it. But when she reached out her left, into what should now be a portal to the outside, she felt something hard and smooth and . . . Metal? Plastic?

She dragged her hand down the length of it, feeling evenly spaced horizontal ridges, and, with a sickening feeling, she realized what it was.

The hurricane shutters.

She'd found the switch hidden behind one of the curtains on the day she'd arrived and pressed it just to see what it did. There'd been a mechanical *whirr* and then off-white PVC shutters had started to descend over the windows and door at the back of the lock-off, covering up the glass. She'd retracted them again and gone out on to the balcony, looking up at the large, ugly white boxes fixed over each window and the door. Sore thumbs in an otherwise cohesive seaside-style aesthetic, but absolutely necessary when you were on the beach in an area frequently at risk of hurricanes.

Now the shutters were down and, with the power out, she couldn't get them back up again.

And the front door wouldn't open.

She was trapped.

Emily felt for her phone, but her jeans pocket was empty. It must have fallen out as she crossed the room, or when she'd fallen. It didn't matter now, anyway. Unless help was already right outside, she was out of time.

She felt strangely detached from the situation. She didn't feel fear or panic; she just wanted to sleep. She was so tired. Emily lay on the floor and thought about how quickly everything can change. A few minutes ago she'd been asleep on a couch in a house by a beach, and now she was going to die in a fire.

But then, this *hadn't* happened quickly, had it? This was an ending to a story that had been years in the writing.

She'd for ever be a character in it now, too. Someone had made sure of that.

The shutters must have made a loud, grinding noise as they descended. She wouldn't have slept through it, not in any kind of normal sleep, anyway. And since when had half a bottle of wine knocked her out? No. There must have been something in it, something to keep her asleep while someone else came in and brought the shutters down.

The shadow hadn't been trying to get inside; they'd been locking the door behind them as they left.

Locking *her* in.

Making sure that, when the fire took hold, she wouldn't be able to get out of here.

And that everything that held the truth, the only things that did – her laptop, her notes, the torn pages – would be completely and utterly destroyed.

Emily thought, *Well, at least now the book will have an ending*.

As she closed her eyes, she wondered who they'd get to write it.

**AVAILABLE TO PRE-ORDER NOW!**